PAPER DOLL

Janet Woods

This first world edition published 2010
in Great Britain and in 2011 in the USA by
SEVERN HOUSE PUBLISHERS LTD of
9–15 High Street, Sutton, Surrey, England, SM1 1DF.
Trade paperback edition first published
in Great Britain and the USA 2011 by
SEVERN HOUSE PUBLISHERS LTD.

British Library Cataloguing in Publication Data

Woods, Janet, 1939–
    Paper doll.
    1. Fathers and daughters – Fiction. 2. Adultery – Fiction.
    3. Nineteen twenties – Fiction. 4. Love stories.
    I. Title
    823.9'2-dc22

ISBN-13: 978-0-7278-6970-8   (cased)
ISBN-13: 978-1-84751-300-7   (trade paper)

All Severn House titles are printed on acid-free paper.

Severn House Publishers support The Forest Stewardship Council [FSC],
the leading international forest certification organisation. All our titles that
are printed on Greenpeace-approved FSC-certified paper carry the FSC logo.

Mixed Sources
Product group from well-managed
forests and other controlled sources
www.fsc.org Cert no. SA-COC-1565
© 1996 Forest Stewardship Council
FSC

Typeset by Palimpsest Book Production Ltd.,
Falkirk, Stirlingshire, Scotland.
Printed and bound in Great Britain by the
MPG Books Group, Bodmin, Cornwall.

Congratulations to the Romantic Novelists' Association
on their 50th birthday

One

1921 London.

Rosie the paper doll had been one of the Howard Toy Factory's best sellers for the past eleven years. The doll had been a gift for Julia Howard's tenth birthday. Her father had created the doll in his daughter's image and she'd been given the task of naming her, a task which had afforded her many hours of thought and pleasure before she'd decided on her maternal grandmother's name of Rosie – something that had pleased the old lady before she'd passed on.

The latest and final doll had been released on to the market four months previously, when Julia had turned twenty-one. They'd had a party in the factory, with sherry and sandwiches for the employees, which had been rather jolly. After that was a dinner party at home, with a mixture of her father's friends and her own in attendance. Her best friend, Irene Curruthers, had rather shocked people by playing the vamp. Posing on the piano in a pair of silk lounging pyjamas, she'd held a gasper in a long black holder and had made eyes at all the men, including the hired pianist.

Irene could be an absolute scream at times, Julia thought with a grin.

Irene had taken an interest in the Rolls belonging to Latham Miller, who was a friend of Julia's father – a rather odd friend she'd always thought because her father was almost ready to retire whilst Latham was in his forties, and considerably younger.

Julia had to admit that Latham was attractive in a saturnine sort of way, with the grey edging into his dark hair at the temples. There was something rather deliberate and forbidding about him. He'd always been polite when they met, and, unexpectedly, he'd given her a brooch for her birthday. Although it had been sweet of him, she'd been obliged to protest at the expense and had tried to return it.

'Good grief, you silly girl! The trinket cost next to nothing,' he'd said, and had laughed it off, which had made her feel like a fool and left her thinking that the stones, though mounted in silver and gold, were reasonably small and were probably paste.

Latham had taken Irene outside to show her how to drive his Rolls, and they'd gone off together with her at the wheel. Irene had looked a little self-conscious and crumpled when they'd returned.

'Latham gave me a driving lesson,' she'd said loudly, and Julia didn't understand why she'd sounded so embarrassed about it until one or two people had sniggered.

The Rosie doll was now thoroughly modern. Like Julia, she was slim-hipped and small-breasted, and her boyish cardboard form was dressed daringly in feminine peach-coloured combinations edged with lace.

Rosie's hair had also changed along with that of Julia's. From dark ringlets with ribbons the pair had progressed to the latest hennaed bob, a colour that suited the clear green of her eyes. Sales of the doll were slow though, even through the lead-up to Christmas.

'The economy hasn't recovered from the slowdown during the war and exports are still down,' her father had said, and he'd looked so worn out that she couldn't bear it, and had hugged him.

'But we'll be all right won't we, Daddy darling? I mean . . . we have money in the bank and property, and there are the jewels my mother left me. If need be I can sell those.' The thought of her mother, who'd died in the first wave of the flu epidemic when Julia was eighteen, saddened her. 'I don't think I could tolerate being poor, especially when I remember Mrs Brewster, who has a husband who was gassed in the trenches to look after, as well as two children. She looks so old and worn out, though she's not much older than me.'

'Yes, she does. But she's a good woman who never complains about her lot in life; I'll say that for her.'

'I could look for work, too. Perhaps I could train to be a secretary or a nurse, so you wouldn't have to pay me an allowance. That would help, wouldn't it?'

Her father had smiled at that. 'My darling girl, I need you to run my household. Besides, you practically faint at the sight of blood, so what sort of nurse would you make?'

'Not a very good one, I imagine. I could learn to use one of those typewriting machines I expect, though. My spelling is good and it doesn't look too hard. All you have to do is press the key with a letter on it, like playing the piano.'

'Of course you can learn how to use one, dear. A girl should always have a skill to fall back on. I'll buy you a typewriter and you can enrol on a course. However, we're better off than most people, and things will improve before too long, so I don't think you need to sacrifice your allowance.'

'Oh, good,' she said with some relief, because she'd heard that wages for women were low.

The typewriter had arrived in due course, along with a box of ribbons. Her hands had got covered in ink putting the ribbon in position, but then she'd been too busy to try it and had put the machine in a cupboard, telling herself that she'd start the course.

Her intentions had come to nought though. When the time came the course had been full and the woman in charge of it had gazed with disapproval at her for some reason. 'It's not a hobby. The course is designed for girls and widows who need to support themselves, and who are training for a career. There's a waiting list. You may register and I'll notify you when, or if, there's a vacancy.' She gazed at the application form. 'You've never worked, it says here.'

'Well, not for money, of course. I'm good at organizing though; everyone says so. I've sat on committees, helped to arrange dinners and balls to raise money for various charities . . . and I run the house for my father.'

The woman had looked so stern that Julia felt guilty and had shelved the idea of becoming a typist for the time being. When notification of a place on the course had arrived the timing turned out to be inconvenient and she couldn't take advantage of it, for she'd have had to cancel several long-standing engagements.

Right now though, she hoped sales of the Rosie doll would pick up. Julia had designed the fashions for the paper doll's coming of age. Rosie would go through the final year of production in tubular dresses with real beads, a coat with fur collars and muffs to match and the latest cloche hats. To finish her wardrobe off was a beautiful calf-length wedding gown made of paper lace.

It had a sweet little veil of real chiffon attached to a beaded band that fitted around her forehead.

Julia gazed at her father and smiled. 'Rosie's a bride without a groom. We shall have to design a hero husband for her . . . a returned soldier perhaps.'

Benjamin Howard shrugged at the thought. 'I'm in no hurry for you to wed, my dear. Besides, people want to forget the war. I had high hopes for you and Dickie Henderson. He was a fine lad with prospects. Damned shame, really. What an appalling loss of life the war was.'

'Poor Dickie, they never found his body.' She shuddered at the thought that he might be ground into the Flanders mud. Her late fiancé seemed remote from her now, unless she wore the diamond ring he'd given her. She avoided thinking about him if she could. As Dickie would have said, Life goes on, old thing, it's no good moping. 'Dickie was such a good sport, and such fun to be with, and the same with Nigel Devison and Willie Carpenter, though I never thought Willie would be a hero, not with his stammer. He was awfully shy, you know.'

'Only around you. I think the fellow was in love with you.'

She laughed. 'You think everyone is in love with me. Men are in short supply now, and if you want grandchildren to inherit the factory and your estate I shall have to find someone to marry me and father them before it's too late. Goodness, all the eligible men are being snared as swiftly as possible, and there are a suspicious number of babies being born, supposedly premature.'

'You won't do that, will you, my dear?'

'Do what?'

'Get yourself into a spot of bother. Men don't respect fast women, especially if they're tricked into marriage by them.' A look of embarrassment stole over his face. 'I'm only saying this because you haven't got a mother to tell you these things.'

Julia felt her face grow pink. 'Good gracious, how can you think such a thing? Mummy and I had a good chat about the birds and the bees when I was sixteen. And before she died, Grandmother Howard gave me a lecture on becoming a woman.' Her grandmother, sweet old thing, had been frightfully stern and prudish. She'd said the marital union was something women had to put up with if they wanted children, and that they didn't actually enjoy it, even though men frequently indulged the wicked side of themselves with their wives.

'Tosh, and more tosh!' Irene Curruthers had said to that idea. 'What do you think all those sensations churning inside you are for? It's lust, pure and natural, my dear. People like your grandmother secretly enjoyed the attention, they just wouldn't admit to it because they were told that they shouldn't.'

'You think so?'

'Of course. It's best to lose your virginity as soon as possible. It's fashionable to have a lover, you know. A wicked man is just the thing, since he knows how to make a woman feel too wicked to want to stop him, and he has enough sense to protect her.'

Julia remembered with shame the little damp rush of pleasure Irene's words had brought. 'Protect her?'

'From getting herself knocked up . . . by using a French letter for protection, you ninny. You do know what that is, don't you?'

'Of course,' she lied, her mind scrambling to her schoolgirl French. 'It's a billet-doux.'

Irene had shrieked with laughter. 'How gloriously droll of you, darling. I can't wait until I tell Charles. Never let a man near you without a frenchie. They are so careless about such things, so it's up to the woman.'

Julia managed to hide her mystification. 'Oh . . . perhaps I'll just wait until I wed.'

'What if you never marry, you don't want to go through life being a virgin, do you? How absolutely dreary that would be. I could probably fix you up with my brother, Charles, if you like. He's just oozing with lust and experience, but I warn you, don't fall in love with him because he's rather louche, and definitely not the marrying kind.'

'As if I would. Actually, I have no intention of marrying until I'm at least thirty.'

'Then I'll have to invite you to the country for New Year, when Charles is home from Oxford. You should trot over to the Marie Stopes clinic in Marlborough Road; she give lectures about birth control, which scandalizes certain people no end, of course.'

Julia grinned at the thought of changing her image, and of having Charles Curruthers as a male friend. There would be a certain glamour attached to it because, as Irene had pointed out, her brother was quite a prize. If she were to lose her virginity for the sake of fashion, why not to Charles? He was as lithe and lean as a leopard and had a laconic sort of charm. He'd also had other leopard attributes the last time she'd set eyes on him. 'Does Charles still have spots on his face?'

'Good God, no! Charles is the cat's whiskers now. He's doing well with his studies . . . and he's learned to fly. Women adore him. I first did it when I was eighteen with one of Charlie's friends.'

'Which one?'

Irene had slanted her head to one side and her eyes had narrowed. 'That would be telling.'

Which didn't seem quite fair to Julia and she pointed out, 'But you would know who I'd lost my virginity to.'

'It's not exactly the same, my dear. I was only offering you my advice, since you're not actually fast by nature, and are really quite naïve for your age. One doesn't usually discuss intimate affairs, one just gets on with them and enjoys them for what they're worth. Take my word for it, everyone, but *everyone*, is doing it now, even the most unlikely people.'

Julia had gazed upon her father with some fondness and thought, not everyone, since her father was too old, and anyway, he didn't have a lady friend.

This morning Julia and her father, already dressed in his business clothes, breakfasted together in the dining room of their serviced mansion flat in Earls Court. The flat looked out over the road. Not that the traffic could be seen today and the sound was partly smothered by an overnight, but thinning, pea-souper of a fog.

Dear daddy, he was so old-fashioned. Julia felt a rush of love for him. 'I do wish I'd been born a boy, then I wouldn't have to bother about tiresome things such as marriage and producing children. I could just run the factory for you. As it is, I'm absolutely hopeless with figures.'

'You don't have to worry. I'm interviewing a new manager today.'

'Oh, I see. What's his name? I might know him.'

'I doubt it, dear. His name is Martin Lee-Trafford, and he's a doctor of medicine. His family hails from Hampshire . . . Bournemouth I recall.'

'He's a doctor. How odd. Why would a doctor want to manage a factory?'

'He practised his profession during the war. He saw too much and it affected him badly. He's been recovering, and as yet doesn't feel able to return to his former profession.'

Her eyes widened. 'You mean that he's mentally ill? Good Lord, Daddy, be careful; some people can be quite violent. I saw a man begging outside a chemist shop the other day who had eyes staring out of his head, and he was shaking fit to bust. The poor thing; I dropped a shilling or two into his cap, of course.'

'Oh, good for you, my dear. Those men had a terrible time of it.'

'The chemist came rushing out and shooed him away. He told him he was frightening the customers off. The man swore horribly, and the chemist told me he was shell-shocked, which was a sort of madness brought on from being at the front. He was terribly unkempt and had a notice around his neck saying he was looking for work. But I doubt if anyone would employ him acting like that. The way he acted was quite frightening.'

'I would have. He could have worked on the packing bench.'

'Well, I suppose.' Julia hoped she didn't sound as doubtful as she felt. Her father was too soft-hearted for words and she hoped he wasn't going to allow himself to be taken advantage of. 'Surely you can find someone better to manage the factory. What would a doctor know about toys . . . or management come to that?'

'Can you think of anyone with a better character than a man who cared for fallen soldiers in their time of need. Lee-Trafford won a DCM with bar.'

When she raised an enquiring eyebrow her father sighed. 'Didn't they teach you anything at that expensive school you went to?'

'Not manly things, but I can cook a soufflé and talk about nothing.'

This time he laughed. 'One of your strong points, I might add. The DCM is short for the Distinguished Conduct Medal. Besides which, Martin is the son of an old friend of mine. I went through school with David Lee-Trafford. He manufactured domestic goods before his retirement. David is gone now. Spanish flu took him, the same as your mother. Lee-Trafford practically grew up on the factory floor. He has solid ideas, and what could be better than that?'

Janet Woods

'You mean he's a fuddy-duddy like you.'

'I mean nothing of the sort. If I take him on, which is likely, he can start work on the Tuesday after New Year.'

'But a doctor in charge of a toy factory . . .' She gazed dubiously at him. 'Wouldn't he consider it beneath him?'

'Having a job and feeling useful – no matter how humble that job – gives a man back his pride. So if you come across that poor damaged man again, you send him round to see me and I'll try and fit him in somewhere.'

'Actually he was rather churlish; he didn't even thank me, or look me in the eye come to that.'

'Having to beg wouldn't sit well with most men, especially one who had served his country well. Can you blame him?'

'I see, well, you know best, I suppose. Now . . . could I bother you for a small advance? Please say yes.'

Her father smiled indulgently at her. 'My past experience of that statement suggests that you've spent your allowance for this month.'

'Most of it, but you know how expensive the Christmas season is. I saw a darling little beaded evening bag in the window of La Belle Moderne the other day, and with a matching headband. I'll just die if I can't have it. It was wildly expensive. But there . . . If we're hard up then I must learn to go without these things. It will do me good.'

'You know very well that a little evening bag for my favourite girl won't make much of a dent in my overdraft,' he said, and chuckled. 'Take some money from my safe; you know the combination.'

'More tea, Daddy?'

'Yes please. You haven't any plans to go away for Christmas, have you?'

'And leave you moping here all alone with only thoughts of Mummy for company? Good Lord, what do you take me for? We'll go to the midnight service together, as usual, and we'll visit Mother's grave. I've been invited to a weekend party at the Curruthers' country house in Kent for New Year though.' She didn't tell him that Irene and Charles' parents would be staying in the city.

'I see.' He gave a bit of a worried frown. 'I can't say I approve of the Curruthers girl. She's a bit scatty. What does her father do?'

'Oh, investments, I think. And he's met King George and Queen Mary at a reception so is perfectly respectable. He's a Baron or something. Irene is tremendous fun, you know. She said that Charles has invited Edward, Prince of Wales, to the party. It will be thrilling if he turns up.'

'I should imagine it would be, but don't count on it,' and he smiled. 'I understood the Prince was on an overseas tour. India comes to mind.'

Julia hid her disappointment with a shrug. 'Yes, well . . . Irene is disposed towards exaggeration, I suppose.'

'And her brother, what's he like?'

'I've only met him a couple of times and Irene says he's doing frightfully well up at Oxford. He has a motorcycle and a sidecar, and will pick me up on Friday evening. I'll be home on Tuesday, the following year.'

He smiled at her. 'You're chattering, Julia.'

Gently, she said, 'I don't want to hurt your feelings, but I'm old enough to take care of myself, you know.'

'Of course you are.' He smiled at her. 'I keep forgetting that you're grown-up. Just make sure that girl doesn't lead you astray. Your mother would have wanted you to keep yourself tidy for marriage.'

She blushed, hoping he didn't suspect what her intentions were for New Year's Eve. 'Daddy, stop it at once, you're embarrassing me! What's in the paper, anything interesting?'

He made a show of opening the *Telegraph*, which the maid had brought in. 'The Anglo-Irish treaty has been signed.'

'Oh . . . that's wonderful. I didn't know we had a treaty with the Irish. How jolly. Does that mean there won't be any more trouble?'

'On the contrary, it will more than likely be the cause of more trouble in the long run,' he predicted rather gloomily.

'Oh, that really is too bad.' Picking up his toast she scraped some of the butter off and scolded, 'You shouldn't eat all this greasy food; it's bad for the heart, and you're getting quite paunchy.'

'And you were complaining about me telling you what to do.'

They had breakfast sent up from the kitchens that serviced the apartment block, though Julia preferred to cook the evening meal herself in the well-fitted apartment kitchen. 'I must tell the kitchen not to send so much up.'

'You'll do no such thing. The fact is, my dear, you resemble a starving greyhound. There's nothing like a good English breakfast to start off the day. I enjoy it, and I'm not going to deprive myself of it because of a stupid fashion that directs we all must look as though we're suffering from intestinal worms and malnutrition.'

Julia nearly choked on a sip of her black coffee. 'Good Lord, what a perfectly vile thing to say at breakfast! I shan't stay here and listen to another word of it. I'm going to take my bath; after that I'm doing some last-minute Christmas shopping before meeting some of the girls for lunch at the Popular Café in Piccadilly. They usually have an orchestra.'

'I took your mother to lunch there shortly after it opened. It's a very well-patronized venue.'

'It's handy for the shops in Regent Street, too. She slanted her head to one side and gazed at him. I do miss Mummy, you know, but she wouldn't want us to be sad. If you're good I might buy you your favourite cigar as a treat, though you should really give up smoking. You were coughing in your sleep last night.'

He chuckled. 'May I remind you again that I happen to be the parent, and you're the child.'

'Hardly that any more.' She rose, and pulling her robe around her she kissed her father's balding forehead. 'Good luck with the new manager. I'll come to the factory to say hello later on. You can introduce us. What time is your appointment with Martin Lee-Trafford, did you say?'

'I didn't, but it's two p.m. Before that I have an appointment with Latham Miller.'

'Oh, what for?'

'Nothing that would interest you, dear, just business,' he said vaguely.

'Latham Miller is a strange man, quite active in society. I often see him, usually as part of a crowd and at the centre of attention.'

'He's very wealthy.'

She laughed. 'That's a rather mercenary thing to say. I do hope you don't put me in that basket . . . but then, I don't have to marry for money. Besides, Mr Miller is quite handsome in his own way. I'm sure he could attract a woman without having to flash his wallet at her.'

Her father made a quiet humming sound in his throat. 'Tell me what you think is odd about him.'

'Oh, I don't know. I think it's because you expect a man of his age to be settled down and married, not hanging around younger people at parties. He must be in his early forties. Irene describes him as filthy rich, and she thinks the sun shines out of his, um . . . *eyes.*'

'He was married once . . . before the war, to an American woman. She was a very nice woman, who lost her life when the Titanic went down.'

'Oh, the poor man, how dreadful for him . . . and for her, of course. She must have been terrified.'

'One can only hope for a more peaceful end.'

Talking of death was unsettling. She kissed him. 'I'll drop in at the factory later with your favourite cake for afternoon tea, about three I expect. It will give me an excuse to look Martin Lee-Trafford over. Then I'm coming back home to decorate the Christmas tree. I've booked one with the doorman, just a small one for the two of us to enjoy. His brother sells them. He's a former soldier, so it's all for the cause . . . and I'm going to cook us a proper Christmas dinner with a turkey.'

'A small turkey, I hope.'

'Well . . . it's larger than the doorman led me to expect. He said there's no such thing as a small turkey unless we wanted a chicken. Anyway, the poor creature is hanging in the larder. We'll manage, I expect.'

And at least she could cook well, so she wasn't entirely useless, Julia thought as she headed towards her bedroom. She turned on the tap in the adjoining bathroom, added some bath salts, then going back to the bedroom threw the wardrobe doors wide open.

Her glance travelled along the rack of clothing while she waited for the bath to fill. She selected a classic calf-length dress in olive green. Over it she'd wear her fawn coat with the raglan sleeves and fur collar. She'd also wear the brooch that Latham Miller had given her, a pretty twinkling star set in a crescent moon. Brown court shoes with Louis heels and pointed toes matched her handbag, and completed her outfit – even though they were crippling.

After a while, her father shouted goodbye from somewhere near the outside door to the hall.

'I'll see you later, darling. Don't forget to wear your scarf,' she called out.

An hour later she blotted her lipstick on a piece of toilet tissue, picked up her bag and went downstairs to raid her father's safe. Taking six crisp, white, five-pound notes from the safe she folded them into her purse. It was better to take too much than too little, she thought, and if she didn't need it all she could always put it back.

If Latham Miller was annoyed he didn't show it. Benjamin Howard had demanded far too much for his factory. The building was in good repair and fairly central, but as a toy factory it was no longer profitable, mainly because of overstaffing. If Latham bought it as a business, he'd need to cut staffing by a third. The wily old owner knew that and had made it part of the requirement that the staff be kept on.

'I'm a businessman not a benevolent society,' Latham pointed out. 'I'd be manufacturing domestic ware, and I'm negotiating for some government contracts. I'll be installing machines if my tender is successful. Some of your workers are well past retirement age. They should be put out to grass.'

Benjamin had got on his high horse at that. 'The staff are loyal and dedicated. The toy factory was started by my grandfather. It's a tradition and I want it to stay that way. If I sell it, it will be as a going concern.'

More fool him, Latham thought. Nobody would buy a failing toy factory that had outlived its usefulness and had been running at a loss for the past three years. It would have to be sold in the end, and for less than Latham would pay for it now.

'I've seen the books, Benjamin. If you hang on to it much longer you'll be bankrupt, and forced to sell it below market value to cover your debts. I'm interested in buying the building so my other interests have room to expand, not in buying the toy business itself. You'll have to negotiate. No businessman worth his salt would buy this place with so many conditions attached to it.'

'Things will look up in the New Year, and I'll have a new manager to run the place. Martin Lee-Trafford. Do you know him?'

'We've never met.'

'He's sound. I was at school with his father.'

And that was the only factor Benjamin would consider; he'd put his faith in the old school tie. Latham didn't want to wait, but he would. In the end he'd get the place for the price he was willing to pay. He'd give the old man six months to come to his senses.

As he was leaving a young man was coming in, probably Martin Lee-Trafford. He had a haunted look in his eyes that stated he'd seen too much.

Poor sod, Latham thought, and nodded to him as they passed each other.

Two

The interview was over, the appointment his. Martin was surprised that he'd been offered the position, when the man he'd passed coming in looked like a manager should in a tailored grey, single-breasted suit and navy-blue tie, his coat folded over his arm. He looked sure of himself, with briefcase in hand.

For the past three years Martin had been unemployed and unemployable, living off a legacy from his father. He'd spent some of that time in a hospital, long days that he couldn't remember, when he'd felt like a grey ghost of himself – so he'd wondered if he'd died on the front and was existing in some sort of limbo before being assessed and despatched to either heaven or hell.

He hadn't expected to come home from France to an empty house, the windows boarded up and his father's coffee cup with dried dregs in it still on the bedside table next to the bed where he'd died. He understood that his father's lawyer had seen to the other things, the funeral the headstone and the estate.

He had sat in the empty cavern of the house in the dark, feeling as though he was in a tomb too. And he'd dreamed of the blood and gore, of the burned and dying flesh and pleading eyes of those he couldn't help – and it had brought him screamingly awake and shaking, and thinking he was in hell. One night he'd got up and had begun to drag all his father's stuff from the house into the garden, where he'd intended to set fire to it.

His neighbour had called the police, who had taken him to hospital.

'I wanted to see what hell was like,' was all he could say.

'Hell . . . You've already been there, haven't you?' It had been a sympathetic psychiatrist who'd reminded him of the fact. Little by little Hugh Cahill had become his shoulder to lean on, become his friend. Little by little the man had pushed and pulled, made him keep a diary of his thoughts and dreams and encouraged him to discuss them until he was unable to stand his own self-pity and had begun to rationalize what had happened to him in his own mind. Only then was he strong enough to begin to stand on his own two feet.

'Go home, Martin. Take your pills, find a good woman and have some children to give you purpose. Live your life for all the others who lost theirs,' Hugh had said.

Only he hadn't taken the pills. They'd made him feel flat and strangely muted. Like a piano that hadn't been cleaned or issued a sound for several years, he was completely out of tune. As for women – he'd found women who could make his body function, but he discovered he was unable to participate with them on an emotional level. Perhaps it was just as well, for a man who didn't feel anything apart from the need to satisfy his body, would probably make a lousy husband.

Work had been hard to find too. Even if someone had been willing to take him into partnership as a GP, Martin knew he wasn't ready to return to doctoring yet, especially surgery. If he ever thought he was, he'd do a refresher course. Too many of his patients had died, and although he knew they'd been past saving, he couldn't quite trust himself now. He gazed down at his hands and experienced a fine tremor that always came when he concentrated on them. Inwardly, he cursed them because he knew that nothing was physically wrong with him.

Martin gazed at Benjamin. He'd forgotten there were people who cared about what had happened to people like him. 'I'm very grateful for this chance, sir. Your letter came out of the blue. I was surprised you didn't take the candidate before me. He looked very smart and confident.'

'He is smart and confident. That was Latham Miller and he wasn't after a job he was after my factory. He wants to buy the building and put me out of business. There weren't any other candidates. I wondered what had happened to you, and heard that you were in trouble. It happens that I need a manager, and I knew you'd experienced factory life. I'm sorry the pay isn't better, but times have been hard.' The man lumbered to his feet and patted him on the shoulder. 'I'll take you on a tour of the factory and introduce you. My daughter should be here by the time we've finished. She's looking forward to meeting you.'

'I believe I may have met your daughter when we were children . . . in Bournemouth,' Martin said.

'Ah yes . . . We came down from Waterloo on the train. Julia was excited at the thought of building a sandcastle. She was only five then and you were just a lad.'

Martin's mouth twisted into a grimace. 'I was eleven, and rather superior, I'm afraid. I put a worm down the back of your daughter's dress and made her cry.'

The old man chuckled. 'You gave her quite a fright and she kicked up a fuss, as I recall.'

'And kicked me in the shin for my trouble. Perhaps I should apologize.'

'Oh, Julia never holds a grudge. I imagine she's forgotten about it. Besides, if she kicked you in the shin I think that would have satisfied her five-year-old sense of honour at the time.'

The factory building was three stories high. Benjamin introduced him to everyone as they went, using the familiarity of first names. The ground floor housed jigsaws and stamping machines, plus the packing benches. In the corner the manager and the clerk's offices took up space. The only difference, the clerk's office had a caged aperture that offered a semblance of security, for the wage packet could be pushed through a gap at the bottom and signed for.

Next to that was a small showroom that displayed the various goods for the buyers. The first floor was overflowing with bolts of cloth and stacks of cardboard. The top floor acted as a warehouse. There were stacks of boxes containing jigsaw puzzles, snakes and ladders and other games. A goods lift which was operated by a hand winch and supported by thick ropes, was lowered down through a shaft to the bottom floor.

Martin frowned. 'You seem to have a lot of stock left for this time of year.'

'Yes . . . Sales have slowed down considerably. I was thinking of donating some of the goods to charity.'

'Better for the business if you try to sell them off cheaply and recoup production costs. Most toy factories have outlets in Curzon Street.'

'We can't afford it, since wages have gone up, and so have rents.'

'Do you have figures from the last stocktake?'

Benjamin was puffing from his stair-climbing exertions. 'I haven't done one since before the war. It's probably in the clerk's files.'

They worked their way back down to the office, stopping to chat as he was introduced to various members of the workforce. One or two of the older workers addressed Benjamin familiarly by his first name, something Martin disapproved of, and some stood around talking.

Martin's first instinct was strong. The factory was overstaffed and it was bleeding money. 'I'll need to speak to your salesmen.'

'Salesmen?' The man smiled. 'Toys from the Howard factory speak for themselves. We're renown for quality and use only the finest materials and workmanship. I don't hire salesmen; the customers come to us. That's why we have a showroom.'

Which was empty of possible customers – and that was another reason why they were losing money, Martin thought. This place was a challenge and it was obvious that his role to manage would be hampered by the owner's sentiment.

'I'd like to look over the staff files.'

'You might as well know that I have no intention of dismissing any of them.'

'Yes, you've made that quite clear, sir. I was thinking more along the lines of having a catalogue printed up and sending a couple of the younger men out with samples to hand sell the products to shops and department stores. They could sell on a commission basis, you know. The more they sell the more they will earn.'

Benjamin gazed at him for the moment, then he smiled. 'There . . . I knew you'd come up with something. As long as they have a basic wage to rely on first.'

This was no businessman, this was a philanthropist, and Martin's heart sank.

When his pocket watch chimed, Benjamin took it out and gazed at it. 'Three o'clock. My daughter will be here in a moment or two. We'll take the lift.' He opened the concertina door to the lift and they stepped inside. Operating it by way of the ropes and pulleys they rumbled down to the ground floor and stepped out.

A woman was standing outside the door with a smile on her face. Martin was overwhelmed by an impression of elegance, beauty and an elusive fragrance. His senses sucked her in and breath left his body in a rush.

'There you are, Daddy, you're five minutes late,' she exclaimed.

'Am I dear? My watch must be slow. How was lunch?'

'Enormous. I shall have to walk home to burn it off.' A pair of green eyes surrounded by dark lashes flicked his way.

'This is our new manager, dear, Dr Martin Lee-Trafford. You might just remember him from childhood . . . our holidays in Bournemouth.'

'Yes, of course, how could I forget that when it was the first time I'd ever been to the seaside? But Lord, how you've changed.'

'Have I?'

A practised smile spread across her face. 'You were beastly the last time I saw you, and acted rather superior. You dropped a worm down my dress and I've been scared of worms ever since.'

He felt uncomfortable. So much for her not remembering! Julia Howard was fashionably thin and expensively dressed. Her make-up was perfection, her jewels classy. She reminded him of his mother, who'd been too shallow for words. He preferred less emaciated-looking women, and raised an eyebrow. 'I recall that you were a spoiled little tattle-tale.'

Her eyes widened a fraction and she said lightly, but with what seemed a blatant attempt to goad him, 'Are you suggesting my parents didn't raise me properly?'

He remembered his manners just in time. 'Of course I'm not. I was about to apologize for that incident.'

Too late, for the air was suddenly filled with frost. 'Oh, you really needn't bother, Dr Lee-Trafford. I'd quite forgotten about it until I saw you.' She kissed her father. 'I don't think I'll take tea with you, Daddy, since the pair of you will have plenty to talk about. I'll collect my parcels from the office and be on my way. I've brought your favourite cake, as I promised.'

'Thank you, dear. Excuse me a minute, I need to talk to Sam,' Benjamin said, and he moved off, leaving Martin with room to negotiate with Julia Howard in private.

Martin put a detaining hand on her arm. 'Sincerely, Miss Howard, I'm sorry. We got off to a bad start so don't leave on my account, else I'll feel guilty.'

She shrugged. 'I shouldn't have said you were a beast.'

'I don't see why not, since I've just proved I am still one.'

A slight grin edged across her face at his honesty. 'Yes . . . I suppose you have, but you apologized nicely.'

'You'll stay then . . . please?'

'Since you ask . . . all right, I will. When you see the amount of parcels I have you'll be perfectly justified in your description of me as being spoiled and quite comfortable with the label you've hung on me.'

'What about the tattle-tale bit?'

'Oh, don't worry, I shall observe everything you say and do, and I'll give Daddy my considered report over dinner tonight which will qualify that remark. That's really why I came – to look you over, Dr Lee-Trafford.'

He laughed at that. 'I'd better behave myself then.'

'Oh, my father won't take any notice of my opinion. He makes up his own mind about people and won't allow me to sway him one little bit. He thinks that most women are scatter-brained, this one in particular. And yes, he does spoil me, because I'm his daughter and he loves me. I'm not about to deny him that pleasure, or myself the pleasure of spoiling him in return, since he's all I've got.'

He glanced at her hand. 'You're not married then?'

'I was engaged to a man called Dickie Henderson. He was lost in the war, missing, presumed dead. I was dreadfully upset at the time, but it all seems so remote now. Life just goes on for some, and we have to leave them behind.'

'I'm so sorry. There are still many soldiers missing, or bodies without names. I doubt if they'll all be found, or identified now . . . though some of them might.'

'How sad that they fought for their country and died unrecognized. Sometimes I imagine Dickie might still be alive somewhere, or I wonder where his body is, and—' She shrugged. 'It doesn't do to imagine the unpleasant aspects, does it?'

Something Martin had already learned to his cost, but he doubted if this young woman's imagination would stretch to how bad things could actually get. It was a conversation he could have done without, and being the comforter when he'd so recently been the comforted, didn't sit easy with him. 'He deserves a decent burial; they all do.'

Abruptly she changed the subject, placing a slim, cold hand on his and saying softly, 'But you've been there, haven't you?'

He noticed that she had blood-red nails – sharp and oval-shaped, like scalpels.

'Shall we go to the office?' she said. 'It's warmer there with the gas fire on, and I'll make the tea.'

Anger flared sharply at the gesture. What did this beautiful young woman in her expensive clothes and sparkling diamonds know about the war? So she'd lost her fiancé, he thought, but thousands of women had lost their men. She needed the closure of a burial and a funeral to make things neat and tidy – they all did.

What if she saw Henderson's body smashed and bloody, covered in stinking mud and smelling of gangrene? But she wouldn't. If the man were ever found she'd never see the face of that death. She'd visit his grave for a year or two, say a prayer for his soul and place a red rose on his allocated plot. She would find herself a new man before too long – one who could afford her, for her father would want her to move on up the social scale.

Martin didn't want her pity. He moved his hand away from under hers, for it had begun to tremble, and he put those images he didn't want to remember from his mind. It was gone – behind him – like she'd said earlier.

As they moved off, she said, 'Tell me, Dr Lee-Trafford, what do you think of the factory?'

He swallowed his ire, reminding himself that she was the sum of her upbringing, and was not to blame for the war. He was being totally unfair. Cautiously, he said, 'One factory is very much like another. I do have some changes in mind, but I need to think them through carefully. If you don't mind I'd rather you didn't address me as Doctor.'

He held open the office door for her and she wafted through it in a subtle fragrance of something expensively French – though like nothing he'd ever inhaled in his time there. It reminded him at first of spring, and of drifting blossom, only there was a piquant undertone to it that hit him after the first impression had faded.

He looked round as she put the kettle on a gas ring. There was a bit of a pop as she lit it. One corner of the office had become a depository for paper carrier bags with quality names on them – Harrods, Selfridges, Liberty.

She turned and gazed at him in surprise. 'Oh . . . why ever not use your title? My father introduced you as doctor . . . I understood that you were one.'

'I am, but no longer practise medicine, and nobody but my mother and father ever called me by my first name of Martin. Lee-Trafford will do.'

'Lee-Trafford? That has a typically male, arm's-length quality to it? Martin is such a nice name. If you connect me to your mother you might relax a little.'

'On the contrary, Miss Howard . . . from what I remember of my mother, she's the least relaxing person I know.'

'She's not deceased then?'

He gave a tight smile as he considered, his mother could well be dead, but anyway she didn't live for him. She hadn't for a long time now. 'Not to my knowledge.'

'Oh, good . . . for a moment I thought I'd put my foot in it.'

Although she didn't know it, she had. It was hard to ignore her smile and the quiet chuckle she gave, but he managed it, for the sad thing was, he hadn't meant to be funny.

She must have sensed it for her smile faded and she said airily, 'Oh . . . I see. You won't mind, *Mr* Lee-Trafford, will you?' and she made it sound like an insult. 'You may call me Julia if you wish. Please sit.' Her glance met his, all at once confrontational and he noted a faint flush of anger on her cheeks. Under her calm exterior was a passionate core. 'Perhaps you'd care to take the seat behind the desk and try it out for size. If it doesn't suit you I'm sure daddy's finances will stretch to a new one.'

'Here will do fine. After all, I'm not in charge yet.' He took the seat he'd used during the interview with her father.

She turned a stiff back towards him and busied herself setting out cups and saucers on a tray. Water was poured into a plain white teapot. Steam writhed out of the spout as if a genie was about to appear. She replaced the lid with a definite clink, and, sliding a beaded cover from the milk jug, slanted a pair of startling green eyes his way. 'Milk?'

He'd upset her. 'Thank you, yes. Miss Howard, I—'

A plate supporting a small chocolate cake decorated with icing and cherries was in her hands when she turned. He nearly ducked, thinking she intended to throw it at him. Instead, she set it down on the desk, picked up a knife and stabbed it in the middle. Steadily she carved two even wedges from the round. She set cup and cake in front of him and placed the sugar bowl nearby.

'You're not having any?'

'I don't eat much cake . . . besides, I'm still full from lunch.'

He must apologize for his churlishness. 'Miss Howard—'

'Oh, do stop being so formal.'

The door opened and there was all at once a sense of busy relief about her. 'Daddy, did you forget that you had a new employee to show the ropes to?'

Neat retribution. Even though he hadn't physically taken the managerial seat, she'd set him firmly in the place he had taken.

'I'm here now. Sam wanted to show me a photograph of his new grandson. He's a bonny lad. One of England's future.'

'How lovely. I must congratulate him on the way out.'

'You're leaving already? But you've only just got here.'

'Nonsense . . . it's been half an hour, at least. I just remembered that I've forgotten something. I meant to buy some of those sweet little chocolate soldiers from Harrods for the Christmas tree. I'll see you later. Don't work too hard.' She kissed her father's head and looped her many carrier bags over her arms.

Martin was halfway upright when she said, 'Don't bother to stand.'

He straightened anyway, opening the door for her.

She nodded, said, 'Mr Lee-Trafford,' and her eyes speared him with her angst.

He wanted to smile. 'Good afternoon, Miss Howard. It was nice to meet you again.'

'Was it?' When she gave a soft snort he couldn't help it. He chuckled.

She swept away, leaving him to close the door behind her. He stood, watching her go from the open doorway, waiting for her to look back. She knew he was still there watching her; the self-conscious way she moved told him that. Besides, men would always watch her. But she stopped to talk to the man called Sam, inspected the photograph of his grandson, and moved on.

Behind him, Benjamin gently coughed. 'Well, what do you think of my daughter now, Lee-Trafford?'

Martin still thought she was a spoiled, skinny brat. He also thought she had a sharper mind than she let on, and she certainly wasn't short on wit. Julia Howard was an exquisite creature, a beauty with a vulnerable, fragile air to her. She was, in fact, a woman with elegance and style, and more strength that she'd first appeared to have.

He closed the door and went back to his cake and tea.

'What do I think of her? That she must take after her mother for looks,' he said, and Benjamin burst into laughter.

'Where are you staying?' Benjamin asked him a few moments later.

'I'm occupying a small space in a friend's flat. Arthur Feltham was a stretcher-bearer attached to my hospital. He's in Brighton at the moment, but even when he does return I can stay there until I find a place of my own to rent.'

'My mother would expect my body to be handled with respect, so if I ever catch a bullet or a bayonet I want you to look after me,' Arthur had once said to him.

Odd that such trivia should come to mind. Martin managed to stop himself from retreating into the past and concentrated on what his employer was saying.

'I know an estate agent who owes me a favour. I'll give him a ring and see if he's got anything half decent on his books, as long as you're not too fussy.'

'That would be kind of you, sir.'

It didn't take long. The next day Martin was the tenant of a sparsely furnished, but roomy basement flat in Finsbury Park, which had its own entrance at the bottom of a flight of steps from the street.

'The last tenant took some of the furniture,' the landlady grumbled, 'not that the bed was much good after he finished with it, and with you being a doctor and all you wouldn't want to sleep in somebody else's bed. He left the place dirty. I've got all the rubbish out, but I haven't had time to clean it yet. And the curtains need washing. If you take them down I'll do them for you.'

'I'll give the walls a lick of paint while they're down if you don't mind.'

'As long as it's tasteful, mind. This place used to belong to an aunt of mine. She'd turn in her grave if she saw it like this. There are some ladders and things in the garden shed. They belonged to my Bert . . . not that he ever used them, the lazy bugger.'

'Was Bert a casualty of the war, or was it Spanish flu?'

'Neither . . . He ran off with some floozy who worked at the Dog's Dinner and is working as a bookie. She's welcome to him.'

Martin didn't know whether to laugh or not, so he smiled. 'If you know anyone who will come in once a week to clean I'd be grateful.'

'I'll do that, sir, for a few shillings extra, and your laundry as well, if you like. It will be handy for us both since I live upstairs. But I'll get it clean for you to move into first. And I'd be grateful if you didn't have any noisy parties, though I've got no objection to you entertaining . . . friends. When do you want to move in?'

'I'd appreciate it if you let me have a key now, so I can move bits and pieces in, and get the walls painted. I have to buy bedding and pots and pans, and it would be easier to bring them here than move them twice.'

He settled a month's rent on her and then had a busy two days, shopping and painting.

A knock came on the door on the afternoon of Christmas Eve. It was Benjamin Howard.

Martin stood to one side and let him in. 'I was just about to hang the curtains. You can pass them up to me if you don't mind.'

'I came to see if you'd like to spend Christmas Day with us.'

Martin hadn't gone to any trouble for Christmas, since he'd intended to celebrate it alone, and eat out of tins. 'That's kind of you, but won't Julia mind?'

'Why should she mind? In fact, it was her idea in the first place. It's on account of the turkey.'

'The turkey?'

'It's twice as big as she expected it to be. The two of us won't be able to eat it by ourselves easily, and that means a week of eating leftovers until it reaches the inevitable soup stage, by which time I'll never want to look at a turkey again, let alone eat one. Julia is a wonderful cook. I can thoroughly recommend her.'

Martin chuckled. 'Then yes, thank you, I'd be glad to help you out. I haven't had a decent home-cooked meal for ages.'

'Good.'

'I can't offer you a drink, I'm afraid. As you can see, I'm not properly moved in yet. I've decorated my bedroom and this living room, but intend to do the kitchen next. Then I'm going to try and get down to Hampshire and bring a few furnishings back to make the place look a bit like home. Not that I can carry much, but I can send a couple of trunks by rail. The rest of the personal stuff will have to go in storage for a while until I decide what to do with the house. Lease it furnished for the time being, I imagine. The weekend after New Year I'll move in here. The rest of the redecorating can be done while I'm *in situ*.'

Benjamin handed the first curtain up. 'You're doing a good job with the paint-brush.'

'I'm quite enjoying the exercise, though artistically I belong to the basic, slap it on and slop it around, school. The last tenant left the place in a mess, but my landlady seems to be very helpful and is working with me to set it to rights.'

When the task was completed, his guest gazed around him, admiring his handiwork. The flat smelled fresh and clean. The curtains were dark blue, and a good contrast against the pale-blue walls.

'You know, Lee-Trafford, you could take my Morris and motor down to Hampshire. She needs a good run and you can load stuff in the back seat then.'

'That's very kind of you. I might take you up on that offer; it looks as though the foggy weather we experienced last month has lifted.'

'November was the worst month for fog that I can remember. It lingered all day and nearly brought the entire transport system in this country to a standstill. I hope we don't get a repeat of that at any time soon. It's bad for business.'

Martin finished hooking the last curtain on to the rail, descended the stepladder and reached for his jacket. 'Thank you for your help, sir.'

'Oh, I daresay you'd have managed without me.' The older man rubbed his hands together. 'It's getting cold. Can I give you a lift anywhere?'

'Thank you, but there's no need. I welcome the exercise and I have some shopping to get done before the stores close down for Christmas.'

'Then I'll leave you to it. I'm off to the factory to give the staff their Christmas bonuses, then they can go home early.'

No wonder Howard Toys was running at a loss, Martin thought, as he watched Benjamin head up the steps to where his bull nose Morris was parked. His employer hadn't said how much debt he was in, but it would be considerable, he imagined.

If he couldn't turn the downward trend around and get the stock shifted then he wondered how long he'd remain employed, especially if Latham Miller was after the place. Not that Martin had ever met Miller, except for that chance encounter, but his wealth and reputation was legendary.

But his employer hadn't seemed bothered about Miller's desire to buy the place, so neither would he be. He thought instead of Julia Howard, and wondered, what did one buy a girl who seemed to have everything?

Three

'You invited Lee-Trafford for Christmas Day! Oh, Daddy, how could you when he's such a misery?'

'I felt sorry for him. I told him the invitation came from you so he wouldn't feel awkward.'

Julia offered him a stern look. 'You feel sorry for half the population of England, so I hope you haven't invited them, as well.' A sudden thought brought panic racing through her. 'Goodness, we haven't got a gift to put under the tree for him. Whatever will he think of us?'

'Yes . . . we have. I bought something on the way home.'

'What is it? Let me see.'

He shook the bag he was carrying. It gave a solid thunk rather than a rustle. 'It's a pair of socks.'

She caught his grin and held out her hands. 'He must have very large feet then.'

The bag her father placed in her hands contained a brown leather attaché case.

'I thought it would be useful now he has a new position and purpose. He can take his lunch to work in it, if nothing else.'

'It's perfect, you clever old thing,' she said, and held it to her nose. 'I love the smell of new leather, don't you?'

'Not particularly; you're probably inhaling the chemicals they use in the tanning process.'

'Ugh! How horrid a thought . . . almost as bad as your cigars then.'

'Which I've more or less given up on doctor's orders.'

'More more, or more less?'

He smiled. 'A man can't give up all his pleasures, and I no longer smoke at home. I am trying.'

'I know. I've bought you a cigar to enjoy on the way to the midnight service. And I've made a holly wreath to put on mother's grave, so remind me to find the torch before we leave.'

He sank into his chair. 'I'm tired. I'm going to visit your mother in the morning, when it's light.'

'Then I won't be able to come with you, since I've got dinner to prepare.'

'I know, but you visited her on her birthday, and I'm sure she knows you think of her. Martin Lee-Trafford is a nice young man, don't you think?'

'I've only spent a few minutes in his company and he didn't make much of an impression on me.'

'But wasn't it you who just referred to him as a misery?'

'Yes, I did, but then I remembered that he'd been ill, so I expect he was feeling sorry for himself and will improve on further acquaintance. And since you'll have more to do with him than I will, all that matters is that he suits you.'

She gazed at the insignia on the attaché case. Insall and Sons of Bristol. It was a rather expensive gift for a new acquaintance. Had it been left to her she'd probably have bought him a packet of handkerchiefs or a leather card case. Well, it was too late to take it back to the shop and exchange it for something cheaper, so she would go and wrap it.

She carried the attaché case off, wrapped it in some green crepe paper and tied it with a red and gold ribbon. She hesitated over the Christmas card, one that had been surplus to her needs. It had a Dickensian scene of rosy-cheeked children gazing in round-eyed wonder at a flatulent-looking Christmas pudding of gigantic proportions. An uncompromising 'Have a Happy Christmas' was printed inside the card in black. It was more like an order than a sincere wish, but the card would have to do.

Her father's new manager had made it very clear that he didn't welcome familiarity from her, so he probably wouldn't notice anything unfriendly about the card. As for the rest, she wouldn't be dictated to over what she should call him, but would please herself. He'd just have to put up with it.

She uncapped her fountain pen and wrote swiftly, *For Martin, with best wishes from Benjamin Howard and Julia.*

Before she put the card back in the envelope she gazed at the message again and an imp of mischief grew in her. She grinned as she added at the end *(beware of the pudding!).*

★   ★   ★

Martin's nostrils were filled with the delicious aroma of roasting turkey as the door to the Howard apartment opened and a woman dressed in outdoor clothes let him in. His stomach rattled with hunger as she showed him to the sitting room, saying, 'Miss Howard will be with you in a moment, sir.'

The whispered conversation that took place in the hall just after she left, easily reached his ears.

'I'll be off then, Miss Howard. Your gentleman is in the sitting room.'

'Thank you, Jean . . . Have you got your Christmas envelope?'

'Yes thank you, Miss. Happy Christmas.'

'And to you.'

The outside door gently closed.

The mansion flat was warmed by radiators. Even so a coal fire burned in the grate, so the room was welcoming as well as warm.

A Christmas tree hung with gaudy baubles and twinkling with artificial frost stood in the far corner of the peach and grey sitting room. Martin's lips twitched. There were no chocolate soldiers hanging from the tree – such were the things excuses were made of. He placed his offerings with the other parcels, a bottle of single malt for his host and a box containing a small porcelain figurine of a woman dancing. It had reminded Martin of Julia with her slim body and bobbed hair.

He gazed at the tree, smiling as he inhaled the scent of pine and instantly recaptured a snatch of a Christmas past.

He'd been a boy. His father had been bristling with smiles and excitement as he'd blindfolded him and led him up to the attic. There had been an odd noise, he'd remembered. When the blindfold had been removed he'd seen a clockwork train speeding around the track.

His father had said, 'I made the countryside myself, while you were at school, out of papier mâché.' There were stations with people waiting and fields with sheep and cows. Martin and his father had spent hours up there in the attic, and had given all the people names and made the appropriate chuffing and shunting sounds and conversation. That was the last Christmas he'd remembered his parents being together, and happy.

★   ★   ★

He touched a fingertip against a tissue paper lantern, spinning round guiltily when she said from the doorway, 'Merry Christmas, and welcome to our home.'

She came in, her socially practised smile appearing on cue. Yet it possessed enough distance to keep them strangers. She was struggling to untie the strings to her apron, which had somehow become knotted. He imagined that she wasn't used to wearing one often. He told himself to stop sitting in judgement on her. 'Am I too early?'

'Of course not.'

'Can I do that for you?'

'If you wouldn't mind . . . It seems to have knotted itself, such a nuisance.'

It took him a few moments to unravel the mystery of the apron strings as he stood within the expensive and fragrant space her body occupied. She emerged from it in a cream, two-piece outfit consisting of skirt and long tunic made of a knitted material so delicately patterned as to appear cobwebby. He could see the outline of the lace on the silk lining beneath it. A thin gold belt circled her hips and matched her shoes. His mouth dried and he took a quick step backwards. It was not the type of outfit to cook the Christmas turkey in. There was a flash of impatience in him, not only because of her impracticality, but because he could see no flaws in her.

'Would you like a sherry, or would you prefer something stronger?'

He swallowed his annoyance; something he wasn't entitled to have, since he wasn't here to pass judgement on her. 'I'd actually like a glass of beer if you have any.'

'We do. Daddy likes to have one occasionally. I can make myself a shandy at the same time.' She moved towards a cupboard, which opened into a mirrored interior lined with glasses and bottles and liquor.

'The tree looks pretty,' he said as her many mirrored images went about their task.

'Thank you . . . It makes Christmas seem real, though I imagine it's a sad time now for so many families. The next generation might be able to celebrate it with more pleasure.'

'As each Christmas takes them further and further away from

the war, people will begin to heal.' His words sounded unreal, hypocritical even. There had always been war, and always would be.

She opened a bottle of Whitbread's pale ale, neatly foaming it into the slanted glass, so there was half an inch on top when she finished.

'You would make a good barmaid.'

She gazed at him, her expression bland. 'Would I really? I must bear that in mind.' Hardly any of the beer went into her own glass, just enough to colour the lemonade. She raised her glass to her lips, murmuring her approval as she took a swallow and put the glass down. 'My father has gone to the cemetery to place a wreath on my mother's grave. He should be home soon.'

'How long has she been gone?'

'About three years; it was Spanish flu. I understood the disease took your father, as well. It's sad when you lose a parent.'

Martin hadn't known about his father's death until he'd returned to England after the war. His father's letters had found their way home, full of encouragement and plans for the future. Even though he was an adult, he'd felt cheated.

It had been a surprise to discover his father was no longer alive. When he'd come home it had seemed too late to grieve for him, as if the mourning period had passed and was buried under the layer of stale dust in his childhood home.

His father's lawyer had arranged everything. All that had been required was Martin's signature and what had once been the sum of his father's life had become officially his. The train set was still up there in the attic, he imagined – the train waiting to pull out of the station with its load of passengers and the same sheep still grazing in the same fields.

'Mr Lee-Trafford?'

He pulled his thoughts into the present. 'I'm so sorry, I was wool-gathering. Yes, it is sad, but our parents gave us life and they expect us to enjoy it while we have it – so we must.'

'That sounds a little bitter. Do you enjoy life?'

'I try to.' She was circling him, looking for an opening and getting too close. He didn't want to talk about what was past or the effect the war had on him. They'd given him a medal he didn't deserve, for he didn't have the courage to face himself in the mirror some mornings. He shrugged. 'I enjoy life in my own way, I suppose. I take pleasure in small things. It's obvious that you enjoy being alive—'

'How obvious?' Colour flamed in her cheeks, as if he'd slapped her. He'd intended to tell her that she had a happy disposition but she'd cut him off, so he was not about to elaborate. He must learn not to say the first thing that came into his head, he thought.

There came the sound of a key in the door and relief flooded through him, bringing an involuntary exclamation. 'Oh, good . . . your father is here.'

'Saved by the bell.' Over the layer of her chagrin, her green eyes were cat-like and filled with the instinct to claw and bloody him. 'Could you at least pretend to like me a little when my father comes in?'

He didn't know whether the shock of that undeserved reprimand showed on his face or not, but guilt roiled inside him. He'd deserved it. His remark about her father's arrival had come across as sarcasm as well as a dismissal of her. It had been unforgivable of him. To make his apology and depart at this point would only add fuel to her fire.

'I beg your pardon, Miss Howard. Is the hope that you'll forgive me a non-existent one, perhaps?'

To which she smiled. 'Nothing is entirely unforgivable, and you are a guest. Let me put my cards on the table. I disapprove of you just as much as you seem to disapprove of me, but for the sake of my father can we try to get on with each other? Can you manage that?'

'Of course I can manage it, and dare I say that you're wrong about one thing? I don't dislike you; how can I when I hardly know you?'

Amusement flooded through him and he eyed a bunch of mistletoe hanging from the decorations overhead. Now there was an invitation, and he had an irrepressible urge. One step forward and he stooped to capture her mouth, just a short, sweet caress that caught her unawares, for she responded for just a second before she remembered she didn't like him.

'That was underhand of you.'

'Oh, I don't know. I thought that was why you were standing under the mistletoe. If you stay there I might perform an encore.'

She moved swiftly, stepping back, and Martin smiled, mostly at the annoyance in her eyes. 'Happy Christmas, Miss Howard.'

Benjamin came in, surrounded by an aura of cold. His face was pale and slightly haggard – his mouth had a faintly blue tinge and he was breathing heavily.

She was at his side in an instant. 'Are you all right, Daddy?'

'I should have taken the car, it seemed further than I remembered.' He sank into an armchair near the wireless. 'I'll be fine after a rest. A cup of coffee with a small measure of brandy in it would go down well, my dear.'

'I'll make you a cup.'

'Lee-Trafford, you're here. I'm pleased to see that you made it. Has my daughter been treating you well?'

'Miss Howard has been kindness itself.'

She threw him a scornful glance over her father's head before she disappeared through the door.

He crossed to where Benjamin sat, took the man's pulse, then gazed at him and said quietly, 'Have you been running out of breath and experiencing pains in your chest and arms?'

'Oh, now and again. It's nothing much and goes away if I rest.'

'Do your ankles swell?'

'On occasion.'

'How long has it been going on?'

'A couple of years. I'm getting older, that's all.'

'We're all getting older. That doesn't mean the quality of our lives should be allowed to deteriorate without making some effort to stem the tide. I advise you to make an appointment with your doctor and request a full check-up. The least he can do is give you some pills to relieve the pain.'

He nodded. 'I will, but don't tell Julia.'

'I won't have to tell her if you carry on as you are. You'll drop dead at her feet and that will certainly attract her attention.'

Benjamin smiled rather uncomfortably at him. 'Your bedside manner is effective, but it leaves much to be desired.'

'I don't suffer fools gladly. If something isn't working properly, then you should find out why and either make adjustments or repair it.'

Martin moved away as Julia came back in with her father's coffee. He examined a photograph in a silver frame on the mantelpiece.

A smaller Julia in a smocked dress, her head a riot of tossed curls and a smile on her face, was seated between her father and a woman he only just remembered. Her mother. Julia resembled the woman a lot.

'I was three when that was taken,' she said, moving to his side.

'You were a pretty child.'

'Thank you.'

'Now you're a beautiful woman.'

'When I said we should pretend to like each other for the sake of my father, I didn't mean we should get too familiar.'

She was referring to the kiss, he thought. 'What exactly do you expect from me, Miss Howard?'

'To start with you could drop the formality. You're not at the vicar's tea party. We have an hour before dinner. Shall we open our Christmas gifts?'

He fetched the gift he'd brought for her, smiling a little as he handed her the beribboned box and saying, 'I hope this is informal enough.' The label read: *To Julia, because it reminded me of you. Martin.*

Removing the lid and a layer of tissue paper, she gazed down at the dancing girl. Tears touched her eyes. 'It's sweet, and you've made me feel mean, which is too bad of you. Thank you so much. Look, Daddy, isn't this lovely? I have just the place for it on the mantelpiece.'

Martin enjoyed receiving the handsome attaché case, and the note she'd put on the card. He would indeed beware the Christmas pudding.

The dinner was perfect. Afterwards Benjamin fell asleep in his armchair while listening to a carol service on the wireless, the blue cashmere scarf Julia had given him for Christmas wrapped around his neck.

Martin helped her carry the dishes from the dining room back to the kitchen. She gazed at the remains of the turkey as she tied the apron around her waist once more. 'Will you be kind and take some of this home with you, otherwise it will be wasted?'

'I'll be glad to help out. I enjoyed my dinner. Who taught you to cook?'

'My mother did. She enjoyed planning dinner parties and cooking. So do I. Cut the remains of the bird in two. I'll wrap it in that muslin cloth and place it in a paper bag ready for when you leave.'

'Can I help you to wash up?' he said, when she filled the sink with sudsy water.

'You can dry up if you wouldn't mind.'

He grinned. 'Literally or figuratively?'

'It would be too much to hope for the latter, I suppose.'

He laughed as he picked up a tea towel.

It wasn't long before the kitchen was clean and tidy.

'Would you like another drink?' she offered.

'I had enough wine at dinner. I think I'd prefer a cup of tea.'

'So would I.' She put the kettle on and readied the tea tray. 'Can you manage a mince pie or a slice of cake . . . or both?'

'Are they as dangerous as the Christmas pudding?'

She laughed. 'That was disgustingly rude of me, wasn't it? I made the pies and cake myself.'

'Then I'll have both.'

'It will be at your own peril, then. Daddy said you're taking the Morris to Hampshire for a run in a day or two.'

She made it sound as it he was going to exercise a dog. 'I intend to sort out my accommodation before I start work.'

'May I come with you? I can help, and I promise not to be a nuisance.'

He couldn't really refuse her, since he'd be using her father's car, so he nodded.

A smile lit up her face. 'I'll pack us a picnic basket.'

He sighed, then said, 'It's a working trip, not an outing.'

'We still have to eat, don't we?'

Martin had pictured a rustic ploughman's lunch of Stilton cheese, pickles and a thick slab of crusty buttered bread washed down with a glass of ale, and eaten before a roaring fire in some country pub. 'Yes, I suppose we do, but I do hope you're not hankering after a deckchair on the sand at this time of year.'

'I'm not quite as silly as you seem to imagine.'

'Actually, I don't imagine you are as you imagine I imagine you to be, especially silly.'

Laughter trickled from her and made him chuckle.

There came a knock on the door and she gazed at a dainty marquisite watch on her wrist with a faintly suspicious frown. 'I wonder who that can be?'

'If you open the door you'll find out,' he suggested with an abruptness which earned him a raised eyebrow as she left.

'Oh, hello, Mr Miller,' he heard her say. 'Daddy's sleeping his dinner off. Come into the kitchen and meet Martin Lee-Trafford, the new factory manager. He joined us for Christmas to help us eat the turkey.'

Formally introduced, the pair shook hands.

'I was just going to make some tea. Will you stay, Mr Miller?'

'No, I was just passing and I dropped in with a gift for you. I saw it in a jeweller's window and thought it matched your eyes. The cigar case is for your father, of course.'

'Oh, how nice of you, but you really shouldn't have. And Daddy—'

'Of course I should have.' He placed the flat box in her hands and kissed her cheek. 'Seasonal greetings, my dear. Irene tells me that you'll be at her New Year party, so I'll see you there, I expect. Lee-Trafford, I'm very pleased to meet you. No doubt we'll bump into each other again before too long.' He nodded, and was gone.

Julia opened the box and gasped. Nestled in a bed of cream satin was a delicate pearl and peridot necklace set in filigree gold. 'Oh, how exquisite it is!'

She was a lady who had no scruples about accepting expensive gifts from older gentlemen, Martin thought, and he was just wondering what Latham Miller meant to her when she said with genuine regret, 'It's far too expensive, of course, and I must return it to him.'

'Do you know Miller well?'

'I haven't had much to do with him in the past. Although he seems to know the same people as I do he's a business acquaintance of my father, really. He's awfully well off and people seem to like him.'

The kettle began to whistle and she made the tea.

'Did I hear the kettle?' her father called out, his voice fuddled with sleep.

She chuckled. 'Don't you always hear the kettle boil? You can smell a cup of tea brewing before I've made it . . . be patient, I'll just be a moment.'

Martin carried the tea tray through for her and set it on a side table. A plate of mince pies and cake joined it.

Benjamin looked slightly embarrassed. 'I'm sorry I dropped off to sleep, Lee-Trafford. It was damned rude of me.'

'I often have a nap after lunch myself, especially at weekends. I'm given to understand that it does you good.'

'And anyway, you looked so sweet that we didn't have the heart to disturb you,' Julia said with a smile. 'Latham Miller dropped in with a gift, a cigar case for you and a necklace for me. The necklace will have to go back. I do wish he hadn't put me in a position of having to return something.'

'I'd say that the man was trying to impress you.'

'Well, he won't impress me that way.'

'Would you like me to return it for you?'

'I was hoping you'd offer to play the heavy father on my behalf. It comes in handy on occasion.'

'Remind me of that the next time you tell me that you're all grown-up.'

'You know I am. I just want you to feel useful.' She smiled and kissed him on the forehead. 'Christmas cake or mince pie with your tea?'

'Both.'

Martin enjoyed the by-play between father and daughter, which revealed the depth of the affection existing between them. He'd always enjoyed the time he'd spent with his own father, but had been away at boarding school for much of the year. As for his mother, she'd been a social butterfly – still was, he imagined. He'd arrived home at the end of one term to discover that she'd left. He'd never seen her again. She'd sent birthday cards to his school for a couple of years – then they'd stopped.

Later on he'd been given to understand that there had been a divorce, and his mother had married again and was living somewhere in North America.

'I acted the gentleman,' his father had muttered. 'Less embarrassing all round if the chap takes the blame, since he can get away with much more of that nature. But the woman is no longer your mother, and you must have nothing more to do with her, Martin.'

Later still Martin had realized exactly what his father had meant by that, for he'd found the divorce papers, and the custody agreement that had signed him into his father's care in return for grounds for the divorce. There had been no monetary settlement. She'd been given a clear choice between her lover and her husband and son.

When Martin arrived back at the small flat he temporarily occupied it was cold. He'd enjoyed Christmas Day, he thought, as he lit the gas fire. He set Julia's card on the mantelpiece and gazed at it. Apart from a card from his lawyer – embossed in discreet gold copperplate on white card, and with a sprig of holly for colour – it was the only greeting he'd received.

He knew nobody else except for the former stretcher-bearer who'd been kind enough to give him a roof over his head for a short time.

Briefly, Martin wondered what his own mother was doing. If she knocked on his door he doubted if he'd know her after all this time.

He opened his new attaché case and removed packages containing a quarter of a turkey, half a Christmas cake and six mince pies. He placed them in the pantry. Add a few vegetables and that should keep him nicely fed for the next few days.

Julia was a good cook, and that had surprised him. Not that she was usefully occupied outside the home as far as he could see, so he supposed she needed something else to occupy her time besides shopping.

Beware the Christmas pudding! He grinned. The woman also had a surprisingly earthy sense of humour, but at least she'd spared him from that, for there were no Christmas pudding leftovers to plague him, thank goodness – at least, not yet! They'd eaten it all between them.

He began to laugh.

Four

Julia was out when Latham Miller was announced the day after Boxing Day.

'My daughter has gone to Hampshire for the day,' Benjamin said. 'Come in. I was just about to have coffee. Put another cup on the tray, would you,' he called out to the maid. 'Take a seat, Latham. It happens that I wanted to see you anyway.'

'Oh . . . have you decided to accept my offer?'

'Certainly not; I'm not ready to call it quits. Besides, I have my new manager starting in the New Year. He already has a few ideas for drumming up some business.'

Latham chuckled, and his glance absorbed the room around him. It was comfortable rather than smart. The furniture was outdated and he wondered if the old man owned the place.

'You have a nice apartment, and it's in a good position. You should ask the landlord to modernize it.'

Benjamin didn't bite. 'My deceased wife furnished it, and I have no intention of changing a leg on the table.'

Latham doubted if Benjamin Howard owned the apartment outright. It would have been used as collateral for a loan. He ambled over to the mantelpiece and picked up a figurine that caught his eye.

'Be careful with that, Latham. It was a Christmas gift from Lee-Trafford. Julia is very taken by it.'

He turned it over, examined the maker's mark and grunted. 'I know quality when I see it. I don't mind paying through the nose for something exquisite, flawless and rare, but this is mass-produced by one of the lesser porcelain producers.' It was a duty gift from Lee-Trafford, he thought, not the type of gift a man selected for a woman he was trying to impress.

'Ah, yes . . . but it's not the value of the gift that counts, it's the thought behind it. And that brings me nicely to what I wanted to see you about.' He indicated the jeweller's box on the table.

'There is no easy way of saying this. Julia would rather not accept such an expensive gift.'

The old man was a fool. Placing the figurine back on the mantelpiece Latham managed to find his smile. 'Why not, when I can easily afford it?'

'You know very well why not. Slip it into your pocket, there's a good chap.'

Hiding his anger at the older man's patronizing tone, Latham sprung open the lid and gazed at the contents. It was nothing much, a length of artistically bent metal with a few pearls and semi-precious stones attached. 'It wasn't very expensive, you know, and like you said, it's the thought that counts.'

'And just what is that thought, Latham?'

'My immediate thought is that I feel insulted by having my gift so casually tossed back at me. Your daughter is not a child. She's a beautiful woman, and, considering her age, a slightly naïve one. It's time you loosened the apron strings, Benjamin. Ask me what my motives are instead of assuming the worst. I'm not angling to be her sugar daddy.'

'Courtship? Marriage? You're at least twenty years older than Julia, and have a reputation for preferring younger women.'

Latham shrugged. 'Wouldn't you prefer a younger woman? There are twenty-two years between us to be exact. As you know I'm a self-made man. I would like a family. It didn't bother me much before. When I was busy making my fortune, having a child wasn't quite so important, and Annie was beginning to think she was barren. That's why she was going back to America . . . to see a specialist. Now I've reached middle-age and would like children of my own. Hopefully I will still have some time to watch them grow up. I can give Julia every luxury a woman needs.'

'I see. Julia doesn't seem to be in a hurry to be wed.'

They fell quiet when the maid came in with the tray. When the door closed behind her Latham said, 'Perhaps a little encouragement from you might be in order. Truthfully, would you object to such a marriage, or me fathering your grandchildren?'

'From a personal perspective I don't dislike you, Latham, but I would prefer someone younger for Julia.'

Latham deflected the conversation. 'It seems to me that she's used to the company of more mature men. Besides which, the best of this generation didn't survive the war. In this country alone over 650,000 men died. God knows how many more were damaged beyond repair.'

They sipped at their coffee, contemplating the figure with some awe, as well as sorrow.

Latham replaced his cup in the saucer. 'The truth is, eligible men are in short supply and women are a little desperate. I could take my pick from a dozen women tomorrow. I imagine you could, as well.'

Benjamin chuckled at the thought. 'I'm too old for this fast generation. They wear me out. Why Julia?'

'In whatever guise they appear, I do know the difference between a trollop and a lady. I have a great affection for your daughter, Benjamin. She conducts herself well, and in a manner that does you credit. I can say no more than that.'

Latham could have said more, but it would have shocked Benjamin. He wasn't too proud to admit to himself that he lusted after Julia in a way he'd never lusted after any other woman, not even his late wife. Even in her naivety there was an air of self-possession about Julia, a coolness that kept people at arm's length.

Latham was a self-made man. He'd been ruthless at going after what he wanted, and had learned the power that came with wealth. He wanted Julia Howard, body and soul. She was everything he wanted in a wife, and the need to possess her was strong. He'd buy her if he had to.

'But my daughter has younger friends. Why would she want to marry you?'

Latham didn't allow his amusement to show. 'Youth doesn't always equate with marital bliss. Her friends are a fast crowd, too fast for your daughter, who is hovering on the edges of their society. She'll soon be dragged in, if the Curruthers girl has her way. Irene's private life leaves much to be desired; being a slut is part of her nature. Her brother Charles is a rogue of the first water. He's a disgrace to his parents and I'm surprised he hasn't been sent down permanently. I doubt if he'll ever marry . . . if he does it will be out of duty, and I'll pity his wife.'

'I've heard he's doing well in his studies.'

'Oh, Charles Curruthers doesn't *study* anything. He has a brilliant brain, and loads of charm, I'll grant you that. However, he's lacking in both common sense and self-discipline, so his personal life leaves much to be desired. He'll be burned out by the time he's thirty, mark my words. There's a strong possibility that Irene and Charles Curruthers will lead Julia astray, you know.'

Benjamin's expression said he didn't welcome being reminded of his family responsibilities, and he blustered, 'I trust my daughter.'

'So you should because she's a girl who does you proud. But like the rest of us, she's only human. I'm trying to do this the right way by asking your permission to court her.'

'I can't tell her who to see and who not to see, Latham. Julia is of an age to run her own life so you must sink or swim on your own merits as far as she's concerned.'

Latham sensed the reluctance in Benjamin. There was a vast difference in attitude between those born to wealth – even if it hadn't stuck to their fingers – and those who'd earned their own. 'But you could put in a word for me. She listens to you. I'll watch out for her at the weekend, so you won't have to worry.'

Benjamin sighed. 'I'd be grateful if you would, but I won't endorse you, or anyone else as a suitor. Julia must make her own mind up to that.'

'Fair enough.' Latham snapped the lid to the box shut and placed it back on the table. 'I have nobody else I'd care to give this to. I bought it because it matched your daughter's eyes. Tell her I refused to accept it back.'

'You can't refuse.'

'Yes I can. If she's old enough to run her own life, then she's old enough to hand it back to me herself, not hide behind you.' Standing, he smiled down at his prospective father-in-law. 'Think it over. On the day Julia marries me, not only will I pay you the price you want for your business and agree to your terms, I'll also give you enough shares in my enterprises to ensure that you enjoy your retirement, and have a decent amount left over as a legacy for Julia.'

The man's eyelids flickered. 'You're trying to buy her.'

'I didn't get where I am by taking no for an answer. Like you say, it's up to Julia. I'm just telling you what to expect if she accepts me. Where did you say she'd gone?'

The old man's eyes met his, and there was a malicious amusement in them. 'I didn't say, but she's with Lee-Trafford. They've taken my car to Hampshire to bring back some of his furnishings and to put the rest in storage. They may stay there overnight.'

'You trust him with her . . . a man who's suffered a mental breakdown?'

'Actually, Latham, I'd be more liable to trust Lee-Trafford with her than I would you. By his own admission he might not be quite the man he used to be, but I do know he's a gentleman – and a bloody good man all the same.'

Ah, it was like that for Lee-Trafford, was it? Latham thought, smiling as he let himself out. Lee-Trafford was no competition then, the poor bugger.

'We're not going to finish this and get back to London tonight. I'll ring my father and tell him we'll be staying over, so he doesn't worry. Is the telephone still connected?'

'It should be. Would you like me to ring him? I can book you into a hotel if you'd like.'

Julia smiled. 'Nonsense, no self-respecting hotel would accept me looking as dusty as a tramp. You neither,' and she gazed around the spacious sitting room. 'It's warm in here now you've lit the fire. I'll wrap myself in the eiderdown and sleep on the couch.'

He had to admit that they were both looking a little dusty now. Her outfit was practical enough though, he thought.

Earlier, she'd come down the steps from the apartment block wrapped in a fur coat. Under it was a rather clownish, but charming outfit, a pair of grey slacks with a loose flared ruby tunic over the top. She'd beamed a smile at him. 'How dashing you look behind the wheel.'

Two of the staff from the kitchens had come out after her carrying a picnic basket apiece. They placed them on the back seat.

'Thank you . . . so kind,' she said to them, impressing Martin with her grace and good manners.

He'd abandoned his *dashing* position behind the wheel and had helped her into the passenger seat. 'It's rather a lot of food, isn't it?'

'Not at all, the car might break down in the New Forest, and we might need it. Now don't go all growly on me before we start, else I won't speak to you for the entire journey.'

'That might prove to be a blessing,' he'd countered, smiling at her so she wouldn't take offence.

'It most certainly will not, since there would then be an atmosphere of ill-will and you'd be obliged to humour me, in case I boxed your ears.'

He burst into laughter. 'Or the other way round.'

She'd grinned, revealing an enchanting little dimple to the left of her mouth.

There hadn't been a cross word exchanged all day, just plenty of banter, and although there had been silences between them too, they'd been relaxed.

They were upstairs now. The gaslights gave off a jaundiced glow. From the second storey there was a view during the day of the English Channel, which was an uninviting pewter colour at this time of year. The expanse of dark water was scribbled with a thread of light tying the moon to the earth as it journeyed from behind one cloud to the next. It looked chilly outside and Martin shivered. France was only a few miles across the water.

She broke into his unwelcome thought by drawing the curtains across the window. 'You're flagging. We've done enough for today, I think.'

He turned to smile at her, at the smudges of dust on her translucent cheeks. Reaching out he tried to brush one away, but only succeeded in smudging it more. 'Your face needs washing,' he said. 'Are you hungry? We should get something to eat.'

They went downstairs and he gave in to an urge to slide down the banister, as he used to when he was a child. It didn't seem quite as lengthy as he remembered from his youth. He went too fast and staggered backwards as he shot off the end, ending up sprawled on his backside.

She gave into her amusement, flinging a dollop of scornful laughter his way. 'That serves you right for showing off. Do grow up, Mr Lee-Trafford.' She then collapsed into giggles, making it almost impossible for him to restore his former dignity.

'Investigate that second picnic basket, would you,' she said now. 'There should be two dinners ready to warm up in the oven. I do hope you like roast lamb, mashed potatoes, peas and carrots. The gravy is in a flask, and there's an apple tart and a container of custard to be warmed. We can keep the fresh fruit, hard-boiled eggs and bread for breakfast. We'll have to have lunch on the way home tomorrow. Country pubs are not quite so fussy as restaurants, and they'll think that we're farmhands.'

Anyone who looked least like a farmhand he'd yet to meet. He admitted that he hadn't met any though, just taken it for granted that they existed. He followed her into the sitting room and stoked up the fire, adding more coal before setting the guard in front of it. 'I've never seen a farmhand in a fur coat before. Usually it's the plough horse that wears one.'

'The last horse I saw wore a hair coat. Cows wear . . . hides.'

He snorted. 'That's stretching it a bit.'

'And before you mention sheep, they wear woolly coats.'

'I was going to say rabbits when you allowed me to get a word in edgewise.'

'You're just being aggravating and I won't dignify that with a retort . . . mainly because I can't think of one except that this coat is not lapin, it's silver fox and it belonged to my mother. As a punishment you can cook dinner.'

'And to think I complained about two picnic baskets. You're a genius.'

'Oh, men rarely plan ahead, they just think they know better than women. Go and make yourself useful. I'm hungry, and I'm going to ring my father.'

The cushion he threw at her skimmed past her head as she gave a timely stoop to pick up the receiver. When Martin reached the kitchen he heard her say, 'Hello, Daddy, it's too late to drive back so we'll be staying the night here and will probably leave about lunchtime tomorrow. I didn't want you to be alarmed, and I'll ring you just before we set out tomorrow.'

There was a pause, then she laughed. 'Of course not, we're getting along famously, almost like brother and sister . . . No, we haven't walked along the pier, we haven't had time, we've been working. Now we're going to have dinner, and I daresay we'll find something else to pack into a suitcase before it's bedtime.'

There was a bottle of white wine to go with their dinner, and he poured them a glass while they waited for the contents of the picnic basket to warm.

Martin set the kitchen table with the cutlery and napkins from the picnic basket, then he placed a candle in a saucer. Julia had thought of everything, which was more than he had. Just as he put a match to the gas oven and slid the dishes inside to warm, he remembered his train set in the attic.

The boxes for storage had been picked up earlier. Anything else would have to fit into the car, or be left behind. He was loath to leave it, but remembered that the landscape did come apart. He recalled that there was a box for the train and rails.

He asked her about it over dinner. 'Do you think anything else will fit into the car? My train set is in the attic.'

'We'll make it fit. It's surprising how much can be packed into small spaces if it's done right. We'll have an empty picnic basket to start with.'

'I'm not worried about the train set fitting in when it's boxed, but the landscaping might be a problem. The sections can be unscrewed though.'

'We'll have a look at it after dinner.'

They did. The train set was covered in a dustsheet. Next to it was the old wooden chair his father used to use. On the bamboo table resided a cup with a tea-stained tidemark. Next to that his father's rosewood pipe leaned sideways into the dip of the ashtray. The burned baccy formed a dusty landslide from the bowl. A whistle lay abandoned.

Lifting off the dustsheet Martin gazed at this other world his father had created for him, and the punch to the heart he experienced was unexpected and almost overwhelming.

The train stood at the station, where it had waited since his father's death. The porter on the station had his trolley. The plump woman with rosy cheeks and the same baby in her arms was just behind him. Elsie Carter they'd named her. Up on the hills the same sheep and cows grazed peacefully on the same painted grass.

Something was different about it though. He gazed down at it, the blood pounding in his ears when he spied the extra figures. One stood on the platform near an open carriage door. He was wearing an army uniform. The other one stood on the bridge, waving a handkerchief.

He choked back a sob and turned away, trying to collect himself as he looked for the box to pack it in.

'Martin, are you all right?' she said, and gently touched his arm.

He'd forgotten she was there. 'I'm sorry . . . I'll be all right in a minute.'

'I wonder if it still works.' Behind him, Julia wound the engine clockworks. He heard the faint metallic clunk of the signal from red to green and then the sound of the whistle being blown. The train was set in motion.

He blew his nose before turning to watch it race around the track, a self-deprecating smile on his face. 'I haven't been up here since . . . only God knows when.' He shrugged and sucked in a deep breath. 'Men aren't supposed to cry, are they?'

'It's all right, Martin, I understand.' She kissed his cheek, her mouth like a butterfly settling lightly on his skin before it flew off again.

The train slowed and stopped exactly at the station. His father had timed the clockwork movement to the length of rail to do exactly that. 'It probably needs oiling,' he said.

'See, you came back to him, Martin. He'd have been pleased to know that you survived.'

'Yes . . . I imagine that would have been the case.' He took the figure from the bridge and gazed at it, then stood the two together on the platform and gave a faint sigh. 'I would like to have seen my father again.'

'Yes . . . it's hard to lose a parent. Pass me the box and I'll pack the train set and the figures. It's on that shelf.'

Somehow he found it in his hands, and he gave it to her. There was a picture of a speeding train on the lid with smoke belching out of the funnel.

She gave a huff of laughter and ran her finger through the dust coating it. 'How odd . . . It's a train set made by the Howard Toy factory.'

'I'd forgotten. It's been a long time since I've seen it.'

'Go and fetch the picnic basket, Martin dear; the station and bridges should easily fit in there.'

She had given him time to get a grip on himself, and he was grateful for her sensitivity. An hour later and they were carrying slabs of painted papier mâché landscape down the stairs. It was larger than he'd expected and he expressed his doubt.

'If nothing else we can wrap it in the dustsheet, stand it on the running board and tie it to the door on the passenger side.'

Which was exactly what they did do.

Martin woke her early next morning with a cup of tea, and they packed the rest of the stuff in the car before they ate breakfast. He delivered the key to the letting agent, who would hire a cleaning service and find a decent tenant. Hopefully, the house would rent quickly, and that would bring him in some extra money to help pay his own rent.

The trip back to London was uneventful. Creased and dusty, Julia fell asleep snuggled under her fur coat and a heap of cushions. He was glad, because he didn't much feel like talking, let alone making conversation for the sake of it.

He woke her when he reached her apartment block and she emerged from sleep and the cushions with a startled look and mussed-up hair. Her smile appeared when she realized where they were and her fingers raked her hair into a semblance of order. 'Home already,' and was it his imagination or was there a note of regret in her voice.

'Thanks for your help, Julia. I don't know how I would have managed without you, especially where the eating arrangements were concerned. You're very practical.'

'Thank you, and it was my pleasure. Aren't you coming in?'

'No . . . I've got about two hours left of daylight to get this car unpacked. Tell your father I'll clean the car and take it back to the garage in the morning.'

'Oh, the garage will clean it for you.' She smiled at him. 'It was fun, wasn't it?'

'Yes, I suppose it was.'

'Couldn't you be a little more enthusiastic?'

It had been more fun having her there to talk to than doing it alone, though he'd exposed his emotions when he shouldn't have and embarrassed himself – her as well, he imagined. She'd been surprisingly sympathetic.

'I enjoyed your company . . . and yes, it *was* fun.' He placed a kiss on her peachy mouth, remembered he wasn't ready to get involved, and quickly withdrew.

He left the engine running and went round to open the passenger door for her. When he realized his mistake and turned back, she was standing on the pavement with a grin on her face.

'I can't get out that side, remember.'

'I do remember now.' His mouth dried as he engaged her eyes with their long dark lashes. He struggled with a strong urge to kiss her again.

Her chuckle said she knew it. 'I thought you were going, Martin.'

Then he remembered that it was he who'd set the rules. It would not be wise to become involved with her. If what had happened the day before was any indication, he wasn't yet ready to handle a relationship, or commit himself emotionally to anyone. So he took a step back and inclined his head. 'I am going. Thank you once again; your help was invaluable.'

'Oh, you've stepped back into your business suit, how very annoying of you.' She stepped forward into the space he'd vacated and kissed his cheek. Her eyes glittered like emeralds. 'Take care, and have a happy New Year.'

Everything retreated. Rooted to the pavement he found himself unable to tear his gaze away from hers. A pulse beat erratically against his temple reminding him he was still alive.

There was a sudden swirl of grit and dead leaves around their ankles, carried by a fitful breeze. The lash of it broke the spell between them.

'And you, Julia,' and for some reason he felt like crying again. Sliding back into the car seat he controlled himself for as long as it took to engage the gears and drive off. The road blurred before his eyes as he left her, standing there staring after him.

Five

A second honk on the horn took Julia to the window. She opened it a little and gazed down at the road. Charles, astride their conveyance, was parked in a pool of light under the street lamp.

'I'll just be a minute, Charles. Stop making such a racket.'

'Is that any way to treat a swain? Get a move on, Julia, my love. It's freezing out here.' He revved the motor up.

'In my day, gentlemen escorts picked their ladies up in time and at the door. They also introduced themselves to their parents,' her father said, clearly disapproving. 'Close the window, Julia. You're letting the warmth out.'

'Sorry.' She kissed him. 'Do I look all right?'

'Perfect. You're too good for that ill-mannered young man.' He took her hand in his. 'You will be careful, won't you dear? Charles Curruthers has an unsavoury reputation.'

She avoided his eyes, doubt slithering into her like a stream of cold slush. Talking about losing her virginity was much easier than actually going through with it, and now the time had nearly come she was nervous. Tosh! She thought. Irene had lost hers and was none the worse for it.

'There will be a crowd of us, so no harm will come to me, I promise. Look, if you're really worried I'll stay home. We could play chess.'

'And spoil your New Year celebrations, my dear. Nonsense! I'm just a grumpy old man who has forgotten what it's like to be young, and I wouldn't dream of it. I'm going to put my feet up and listen to the wireless.'

From outside came a series of impatient toots on the horn. The engine revved to an alarming roar, backfired a couple of times, then eased down again.

Annoyance settled on her father's face. 'Go on then, don't keep him waiting any longer, Julia, else I might just take out my pistol and shoot him.'

'Since when have you owned a pistol?' She wrapped herself in the silver fox, tied a silk scarf around her hair, gave her father a final kiss and hurried off downstairs.

'Julia, my angel . . . at last. I was just about to go on my way without you.'

Charles Curruthers was handsome in a boyish sort of way. His golden blond hair flopped over his forehead, his skin was soft and fine and his bottom lip had a natural pout that gave him a slightly sulky look.

He pulled on a flying helmet and gazed through innocent baby-blue eyes at her. His smile was lopsided as he held out a second helmet. 'Dear oh dear . . . Irene informs me that you're still untouched by human hand.'

She blushed. 'Don't tease.'

'I'm not teasing. Don't feel ashamed, Julia; I'll soon have my lascivious way with you and reverse the situation. I won't charge for my service, either. I rather fancy you, actually. I've never had an old-fashioned innocent.'

Her blush became furious and she pressed her cool palms against her cheeks.

He laughed. 'Remove your scarf and put the helmet on, there's a good girl. It will be warmer.'

'But it will flatten my hairstyle.'

'I'm sure Irene's maid will rearrange it for you. Come on, Julia, old thing, stop being difficult . . . do it, just for Charlie?'

Removing her scarf she folded it, placed it in her pocket and pulled on the leather helmet.

'It suits you,' he said, and taking her face in his hands he gently kissed her mouth. He tasted of tobacco. 'Get in the sidecar and I'll tuck the rug around you to keep the cold out.'

They were soon on their way, roaring around the streets with great dash – too much dash for her as she clung to the edges of the sidecar with eyes closed, giving fearful little screams and moans as she was thrown about. It was the most uncomfortable mode of transport she'd ever used. Charles laughed like a maniac as he narrowly missed parked cars and kerbs.

Then they were out in the country. Bounced from one pothole to the next, they headed through a tunnel of light made by the headlights. It was cold, even wrapped in her fur and a blanket.

She sank down behind the windscreen so the wind didn't snatch her breath from her lungs.

Before too long house lights in the misty distance appeared, then a low oblong building that grew into a dignified stately manor as they neared it. They raced around the circular driveway littered with cars, scattering gravel, and drew up outside a porch. Light spilled from the windows and the sound of music came beating from inside the house.

Julia felt slightly nauseated, and was shaking when she climbed out of the sidecar. She could have sworn that every bone in her spine was disconnected.

A window was pushed up and Irene screamed out, 'Yoo-hoo! Julia, darling, I'm up here. It was too bad of Charlie to pick you up late.'

'Felicitations, Sis,' Charles shouted back. 'I was carpeted by pater before I could escape. He said he's holding me responsible for the party, and if any damage is done he'll take the cost of repairs from my allowance.'

Irene laughed unsympathetically. 'As long as he doesn't take it from mine . . . Don't worry, Brother dear, you know daddy is more bark than bite where you're concerned, and you're the favourite son and heir. Besides, I instructed the staff to hide all the breakables that were within reach. Oh, I say . . . Where did that ghastly hat come from, Julia? Take it off at once . . . Come up and show me what you're wearing. It was terribly brave of you to come with Charles.'

Julia eased the leather helmet from her head and threw it into the sidecar, relieved to note that her sick feeling had receded. She shook her head to help settle her hair back into its natural waves.

Charles blew his sister a kiss. 'Nonsense, she was perfectly safe, and all in one piece just as I promised . . . though not for much longer. Like Cinderella, on the stroke of midnight she will be awakened by the kiss of the handsome prince.'

'That was sleeping beauty, you idiot.'

Charles propelled the blushing Julia towards the door, one hand cupped between her buttocks. His fingers applied pressure through the soft fur of her coat. Although Julia's instinct was to give in to the pressure and open her legs a little, she automatically clenched her muscles against the personal intrusion.

He chuckled against her ear and whispered, 'I like a nice, tight arse.'

She felt dubious. 'Perhaps this isn't such a good idea after all, Charles.'

'Nonsense! It's a brilliant idea. I don't know why I didn't think of it sooner.' A cheer went up when they appeared. Charles gave a sweeping bow. 'Miss Julia Howard everyone. Isn't she a peach?'

There was a barrage of wolf whistles. A couple of men advanced to gaze at her, and the one with dark eyes murmured, 'I'll say she's a peach. Adam Oldham at your service, sweets.'

'How do you do?' Julia said.

The other one looked her up and down from slightly hooded grey eyes. He offered Charles a faintly contemptuous smile and drawled, 'Where did you find this exquisite creature? Introduce me at once.'

'Julia, this is Viscount Gyesworth.'

'My Lord.'

Sliding his hand behind her head he pulled her close and kissed her on the mouth. His tongue began to make inroads. When she hastily pulled away she only barely resisted the urge to wipe her mouth on her sleeve. He gave her a mocking look, as if he'd read her mind, and murmured, 'Very tasty, Charles, very tasty indeed, and she's got a full set of teeth. Let's not stand on ceremony, sweetheart; call me Rupert.'

She'd rather not call him anything. 'Excuse me, Irene's waiting for me to go upstairs.'

'Her room is up the stairs. Take the corridor to the right, and Irene's door is the second on the right.' Charles plucked a flute of champagne from a passing servant and placed it in her hand. 'Here you are, Julia. Take this up with you, it will help you to relax.'

She felt the eyes of the three men upon her as she climbed the stairs and couldn't resist the urge to look back, just in time to see the three of them exchange a knowing look, go into a huddle and laugh together.

They knew! Charles had told them. She was peeved by the thought that her intact state was a source of amusement.

Irene was on the landing, looking dramatic in a startling red dress covered in shimmering black beads, and a headband with a waving black feather at the front. She dragged her into the bedroom, lushly furnished in blue and gold and warmed by a fire in the grate. The room was littered with clothing, as if Irene had tried on everything in her wardrobe.

Outlined by kohl, Irene's blue eyes glittered with mischief as she grabbed up Julia's overnight bag and threw it on to the bed. Her lipstick was a scarlet pout. 'I'm glad you're here, at last. I've been waiting for you so we can go down together. Let me see what you're wearing,' and she gave a little scream. 'We must do something about that hair. It's so flat.'

'Charles made me wear a helmet.'

'Just as well, otherwise your ears would have suffered from frostbite in that contraption he drives. I don't know why he doesn't get a car.' She jerked impatiently on the embroidered bell pull. 'Drink your champagne while we wait for Ellen to come and see to you.'

Julia's dress was a turquoise silk sheath. It was less lavishly beaded than Irene's, but delicate sprays of tiny crystals glinted like stardust through its sheer, silvery-white overdress. It wasn't as short as Irene's dress either, which ended just under the knee. Her own finished more modestly at mid-calf. Her new headband had a turquoise butterfly set with crystals to one side.

Irene twirled a long string of black beads. 'You need a necklace.'

'I have one in my bag. Latham Miller gave it to me for Christmas, and he wouldn't take it back.'

'I'm hoping he'll come to the party. His country house is just a few miles away. He said he'd try and get here if he decides to come down from London for New Year. Let me see the necklace.' Diving into Julia's bag, Irene pulled out the jewellery box, opened it and gasped. 'Why would you want to give this back? I wish he'd given it to me. All I received from him was an enamel cigarette case with my initials on it. It's set in silver, though. I fancy him like crazy, you know.'

'No . . . I didn't know. I suppose he is rather attractive in his way.'

'And wealthy. He's a bit demanding though . . . forceful, that's part of his attraction for me. He makes me shiver when he looks at me sometimes.'

'Does he? I hadn't noticed. When I've run into him he's always been very kind and polite.'

'Yes, but you're probably not his type . . . at least, I hope you're not because it would spoil our friendship somewhat!'

'Are you telling me that you're in love with Latham Miller?'

'Oh . . . just a little bit, as much as one can love any man, I suppose. Some women are attracted to men with dark, wicked natures, that's all, and I'm one of them. Latham is definitely wicked.' She lowered her voice. 'Here comes Ellen, so let's not talk about anything private unless we want it to be gossiped about. She spies on me, and tells Mummy everything.'

Irene's critical appraisal of Julia's outfit was part envy when Ellen fashioned her hair back into its style with heated tongs. 'I wish my hair was naturally wavy.'

'Wavy hair is so hard to keep control of. Your hairstyle is striking, like a sleek black cap. It suits your face too. We always want what we haven't got, I think. Thank you, Ellen, my hair looks lovely.'

'Will there be anything else, Miss?' Ellen asked her with a smile.

Irene stared hard at her and asserted her control. 'Yes . . . You can tidy up my room and put everything away, and move Miss Howard's things to the room next door . . . not that she'll be in it much. Come back in half an hour, after we've gone downstairs. We want to talk in private.'

Irene had a bottle of champagne on the table and she refilled their glasses. 'Has anything interesting happened since I last saw you?'

'Daddy hired a manager for the factory.'

'Is he anyone important?'

'I suppose not. His name is Martin Lee-Trafford. He spent Christmas Day with us and I went down to Bournemouth with him to help sort his house out and bring stuff back for his flat in London. We took Daddy's car and stayed overnight.'

'Is this Martin Lee-Trafford old?'

'On the contrary, he's quite young and handsome. He can be terribly stuffy and serious on occasion, then he astounds me by saying something absolutely outrageous, and makes me laugh. I don't think he quite approves of me.'

'Then why on earth did you help him move house?'

'I thought it would help me to get to know him better. He's not been well, you see.'

'What was wrong with him?'

Julia hesitated as she remembered his tears, and pity touched her for all he'd been through. It wasn't her place to gossip about Martin's condition. It would only be conjecture anyway, since she didn't have his confidence, or an awareness of what he'd actually suffered. Depression she supposed. Vaguely she offered, 'He was a casualty of the war. He won a medal for bravery.'

'Oh, there are so many of them with medals. Boring really, since the war has been over for three years, but that's all returned servicemen can talk about.' Irene lost interest in the conversation as she emptied the remaining champagne from the bottle into their glasses. 'Drink up. We'll go downstairs afterwards and mingle.'

By the time they finished their third glass of champagne they were giggling about nothing. Irene posed at the top of the stairs, pulled her skirt up and revealed her garters, black on one leg, red on the other. 'Hello everyone!' she yelled.

A roar of laughter went up. Several of the men ran up the stairs. They lifted her above their heads then ran back down with her. She was tossed through the crowd before she was set down on her feet.

Julia wished she had the confidence to be so out-going. As it was she was chair-lifted by Charles and Rupert. Her hands frantically tugged at her hem as the slippery silk began to slide upwards. Rupert stealthily moved his hand between her thighs and ran his finger along her gusset.

'Put me down,' she said, shocked by the little jolt of pleasure she'd felt.

'Don't be so prim and proper.'

A space had been cleared for dancing in the hall. Charles pulled her into the thick of things, and they joined the others doing the tango. Charles was a good dancer, and so was she. Then the music slowed, his hand slid down to her bottom and he held her close against him.

He smiled calmly down at her when she tried to wriggle away. 'I wouldn't do that if I were you, doll.'

Her blush came as she felt his hardness nudge against her. Oh, my God! she thought with a little thrill of nervous excitement. She couldn't back out now, and was actually going to do it.

She saw Latham Miller on the edge of the crowd, gazing at

her. Unlike most of the people here he seemed totally in command of himself. When he returned her smile she felt guilty about trying to return his gift, and she touched the necklace with her finger, drawing his eyes to it and hoping he'd forgive her for hurting his feelings.

The evening progressed, getting louder and louder. Irene did the shimmy on top of the piano, her hips shaking. You could see all the way up her skirt to her stocking tops.

There was a game of hide-and-seek, but the jazz music and dancing proved to be more popular. Champagne flowed like water. People shrieked with laughter or lost control and were ill. The place was filled with the choking acrid smoke from many cigarettes and cigars. It was fun to watch, but Julia felt sorry for the servants who'd have to clean up after them.

Julia was dancing with Charles again, when Rupert joined them, circling her from behind, so she was sandwiched between them.

Across the crowd she saw Latham Miller. He returned the beaming smile she sent him with a faint one of his own.

They moved towards the stairs and sat down. Rupert left, coming back with a plate of vol-au-vents and more champagne. Adam Oldham joined them; he was swaying a bit as he stared at her. 'Hello, darling.'

'The filling in these vol-au-vents tastes jolly strange,' she said.

'The cook was sampling the sherry when she made them, and she put too many herbs in the mixture.' Charles held another to her lips. 'Wash it down with the champagne.'

She did as Charles told her.

'Has anyone got a gasper?' Charles said.

'I've got a reefer.'

'That will do.'

Adam lit a cigarette, which smelled rather foul, and the three men passed it around between them. 'Want some?' Rupert asked her.

The end was sodden and she shuddered as she flapped the smoke away with her hand. 'I don't smoke.'

It was held against her lips. 'Just one . . . Draw the smoke in and hold it.'

She did as she was told and everything seemed to slow down.

The room swirled slowly around her when she stood, then it shifted back into place. 'I must find Irene.'

'The last time I saw her she was in the supper room talking to Latham Miller. They're probably under the table by now, since Irene's got the hots for him.'

Charles took her hand and pulled her down again. 'Stay with me, Julia darling. It's nearly midnight, and I'll need someone to kiss.'

He'd been fun to be with, and hadn't strayed far from her side all evening.

'You can kiss me any time you want,' Rupert said to him and puckered his lips.

'Not tonight, dear one. I've got a headache.'

Julia giggled. 'You're being ridiculous.'

'Actually I need to relieve myself.' Adam got to his feet and strolled off up the stairs. Not long after, Rupert followed him.

'I feel odd, Charles.'

The room spun again when she tried to stand up. 'Oops, I'm all in a whirl!'

'I expect you've had too much champagne. I'll take you upstairs so you can lie down for a bit if you like.'

'That would be terrific.'

He placed an arm around her as they went up, supporting her against him. 'Thank you, Charles . . . you're so kind. I'm sorry to spoil your New Year.'

'Oh you haven't, dear one. The fun hasn't even started yet.'

'Of course, I nearly forgot . . . there was something we had to do. This isn't my room. I'm sleeping next door to Irene.' She saw Adam and Rupert. Both of them were without clothes. Everything seemed fuzzy. 'I think I'm dreaming, Charles. There are naked men here . . . your friends.'

'So there are, which one do you want after me?'

The alarm she felt was lost in her lethargy. 'I don't think I quite understand.'

'You will in a minute,' and he pushed her gently on to the bed. 'I'll toss a coin, and you can shout out heads or tails. When we've finished with you, your goose will be well and truly cooked.'

'Tails,' she said, with a giggle as the coin spun in the air.

★   ★   ★

Seeing Charles supporting Julia as they went upstairs, Latham Miller headed towards the servants' quarters and beckoned to his man, Robert. He hoped he wasn't too late as he sped off after his prey.

Slamming back the door to Charles' room, he entered, his glance going to Julia on the bed. She was still fully dressed, which was a relief, since carrying a naked female from the house was sure to draw comment.

He gazed from one man to the other. 'This isn't going to happen, gentlemen.'

Rupert stuck a finger in his chest. 'Says who?'

'I do . . . What have you given to her, Charles?'

'Nothing much. We put a little weed in the vol-au-vents and she had a drag on a reefer. Irene made the vols. That's apart from the champagne, of course. What's the harm? She wanted to lose it, didn't you, Julia?'

She wagged her finger at him, and said dreamily, 'Then the lady did, and now the lady didn't . . . *doesn't*, isn't it? Why have those men got no trousers on? They look funny with their little tails, or are they snails,' and she laughed when they covered themselves with their hands.

Charles offered, 'You can have a piece of her too, Latham.'

The clock downstairs began to chime the hour and the count-down began.

'Happy New Year everyone,' Julia said, and turning on her side began to gently snore.

Latham chuckled. 'I'm having all of her, Charles. I promised her father I'd look after her, so I'm taking her away from here right now.'

'No you're not.'

'We can do this the easy way and remain friends, or we can do it the hard way. I could squash you like a bug, Charles, and in more ways than one, so you really wouldn't want me for an enemy. Either way, I'm taking Julia with me.'

When Adam took a step forward, Latham said, 'Robert,' and his chauffeur stepped inside. 'Watch my back. I'm leaving with the lady.'

Robert was a big man and he folded his arms on his chest and stared impassively at the three men while Latham hefted Julia up into his arms.

'Whoops-a-daisy,' she mumbled.

'What's going on, Latham?' Irene said from the doorway.

'I'm removing Miss Howard from the premises. I won't stand by and see her used by three men while I can prevent it. I'd be obliged if you'd fetch her bag and coat and bring them to the car.'

'You don't understand, Latham. Charles was doing her a favour. Julia wanted to lose her virginity.'

'To three men when she's barely conscious, and without her consent? I think not. That's called rape in my book.'

'Why are you being so holier-than-thou about it? It was only a bit of fun,' Charles said sulkily. 'How was I to know she'd pass out?'

'Oh, put your clothes on, will you,' Irene said to the other two, and to Charles, 'Let him take little Miss Innocence with him. She's no fun anyway.' She turned to Ellen, who had just come up the stairs. 'What are you gawping at, girl? Haven't you seen a naked man before?'

'No, Miss.'

'Well, take a good look, because now you can see two of them for the price of one. A bargain, I'd say. Go and fetch Miss Howard's things and take them out to Mr Miller's car.'

'Yes, Miss.'

'Oh, and Ellen . . . if my parents get to hear of this you'll be sorry. Do you understand?'

The maid's mouth tightened. 'Yes, Miss.'

'Good . . . then go.'

Ellen's back bristled with affront as she walked away.

Irene's eyes were glittering. 'You can go out the back way, Latham. Everyone will think you're carrying a dead body otherwise.' Her expression became one of fright. 'Julia is still alive, isn't she? I'll never forgive her if she's died. The last thing we want is a corpse on our hands. The parents would be furious.'

Irene gave a sigh of relief when a small hiccup came from his burden. 'Follow me, Latham . . . and, Robert, please stop trying to intimidate my brother and his friends. Nobody will try and stop you from leaving.'

Adam took a step forward. 'Back off, Adam, you fool. Robert used to be a boxer and he'll break your nose with one punch.'

Irene was an efficient and capable woman, and despite her

appearance, an intelligent one. Even though he didn't altogether approve of her, Latham liked her a lot. They'd always had fun together with no strings attached, and he doubted if she would hold this episode against him. He hoped not, for he didn't want their relationship to end – not yet. If only she wasn't so indiscriminate about her personal affairs . . .

Latham was aware that he'd inherited a streak of Victorian working-class morality from his upbringing, despite employing double standards himself. He'd come from a poor background and his parents had been unable to think further than scraping by on the small amount of shillings they were offered as recompense for their labours.

He remembered his mother offering his father's employer the last piece of bread and butter in the larder to go with his cup of tea, when he'd called to explain why he couldn't keep his father employed at the brickworks. As a consequence of his father losing his job they'd also had to vacate the house he'd rented from his employer. And to think his mother had humbly served him tea. Job and house had gone to a nephew.

Latham had despised his parents' acknowledgement of their lowly position, of the fact that they'd died in the workhouse accepting their lot. They'd left him to make his own way in the world at the age of thirteen, and in the best way he could. He'd sworn there and then that one day he'd be in the position of the master, rather than the servant. And now he was.

Gazing down at the sleeping Julia, he smiled. How perfect a girl, and how helpless in his arms his little turquoise butterfly was – thank goodness he'd been in time to rescue her – that she hadn't been ruined by Charles and his friends.

Thank goodness indeed! It meant that the three men would remain in one piece a little bit longer. And he had yet to punish Irene for her part in the affair.

He placed Julia gently in the back seat of the car and straightened up. 'I believe it was you who doped her.'

'It was just a bit of weed.'

'She's not used to it . . . she doesn't dabble in drugs. How could you carry out such a vindictive act?'

'Julia wanted to lose her virginity, ask her. We decided on Charles. He attracts so many women that I thought he must be good at it. How was I to know that his randy friends would be invited to help him debauch her.' She laughed. 'It's typical of my brother. Stop taking it so seriously, Latham. You could do the deed while she's out of it if you wanted. She wouldn't know the difference.'

It was a notion with some appeal, but he knew he still had enough decency left in him to ignore it.

'I could come with you, and join in. We could be a threesome.'

'Don't be so cheap.' He backhanded her then, not hard enough to leave a bruise, but enough to remind her who was in charge.

'I was only joking,' she said, sounding hurt.

'So was I.' He slid into the passenger seat. 'Take us home, Robert.'

Irene scrabbled at the window. 'When will I see you again, Latham?'

'Tomorrow at noon, when Charles brings you over to apologize to Julia.'

'I won't do that, and neither will Charles.'

'Yes you will.' He didn't bother to look her way, but said, 'Drive on, Robert.'

The chauffeur put the car in motion and they purred off into the night.

Six

Julia woke with a headache. The room she was in was painted a restful shade of warm cream decorated with Japanese-style relief panels in pale fuchsia. A cream wardrobe with storks etched on the mirrors was built against a wall. The bed she was in was wonderfully comfortable, and a feather quilt was piled lightly on her body like a heap of warm fluffy snow.

It was hard to move because her head was thumping so much. She groaned as she made the effort to sit up. Swinging her legs to the floor, her feet sank into the depths of a carpet of a colour to match the wall panels. She wriggled her toes into the luxury of it.

She didn't know where she was, but she did know she desperately needed a pee. She made her way to the door in the corner. Beyond it, a luxuriously appointed bathroom with bath, shower and pedestal was revealed.

She made use of the facilities. Set out on a shelf was a new toothbrush and paste, mouthwash, shampoos and a hairbrush and comb. On the side of the bath stood several bottles of lotions and oils. Thick cream towels were piled high in an open-fronted set of shelves.

She gazed down at herself – at a pair of blue silk pyjamas she'd never seen before. They were too big – men's pyjamas! She turned the cuffs back and rolled the legs up before she turned on the tap.

Water spouted out of the mouth of a golden dolphin. Despite her mystification she was beginning to enjoy the luxury of this place. She poured a fragrant oil into the running water, and it began to bubble and foam.

She gazed at the modern design of a bottle of perfume on the shelf. It was Chanel number five, a perfume fairly new to the market, and Irene's favourite as she recalled. Julia used Emeraude, which she loved. It was cheaper, and made by Coty.

She lay back in the bath, relaxed and feeling pampered, thinking of nothing in particular and bordering on sleep. A knock came at the door.

Who was it? She wondered if she'd locked the door. More to the point, where was she? She remembered seeing two naked men and her eyes widened. She'd lost her virginity! It was an occasion she should be able to remember. Had she really? She couldn't even recall a moment of the event. How disappointing.

The knock came again and a woman's voice said quietly, 'Miss Howard, are you all right.'

'Yes, I'm in the bath. What's your name?'

'Agnes Finnigan. I'm the housekeeper. I've laid your clothes out for you and there's a tea tray on the table. The master expects you to join him for breakfast in half an hour. Is there anything I can do for you?'

'No, I'm fine, thank you, Mrs Finnigan.'

'What's your master's name?' she thought to add a few moments later, but the woman must have left because there was no answer. Just as well really, else she might have got the wrong impression. Mrs Finnigan had sounded like an Irish woman. Was she in Ireland? Charles Curruthers had an aeroplane; he might have flown her there. 'Oh, my God! What if I'm with that horrid leech, Rupert something?' she said in alarm.

Drying herself she pulled on a white towelling robe and went through to the bedroom. The curtains had been pulled back, revealing the view. Sweeps of earth were captured by hedges and combed into brown crumbly furrows in the fields. Mist hovered thinly above the ground, like ghosts without a home to go to. The trees were stark black bones. Beyond the fields, the distance revealed a glitter of cold grey water. A steamer smudged a charcoal line from its stack along a yellow and grey streak of horizon. She could be anywhere.

Somewhere a dog gave a high-pitched yelp, answered by the deeper tone of another dog.

Her bed had been made, and the change of clothing she'd brought with her was free of creases. Somebody had pressed it. Her combinations had been washed and dried overnight. She pulled them on, followed by warm brown slacks and a high-necked cashmere jumper. Over the top went a long cardigan of berry-red cable knit that matched her socks. Slipping her feet into loafers, she tidied her hair, wondering whether to apply make-up. She decided against it.

The hallway outside her door led her past other doors to a

circular flight of stairs. At the bottom she found the front hall. The house was furnished predominately in the same warm shade of cream as the room she'd slept in, only with vibrant colours added to bring it to life. The sound of muted voices guided her footsteps through a lounge room furnished with warm rich reds, and into a dining room of cool blue shades.

A black Labrador thrust its snout into her hand, nudging at it for attention. Whilst she patted it a terrier came to sniff at her ankles, its tail a whipping blur.

A man came in from the room beyond, and smiled at her. 'Leave my guest alone you two. Go back to the kitchen.'

They went off obediently, collecting a pat from their master as they went past him.

'Good morning, Julia, and a Happy New Year.' He kissed her on the forehead before pulling out a chair for her.

'Mr Miller, thank goodness it's you,' she said with some relief.

'I think it's about time you called me by my first name.' His unfathomable dark eyes lit on her. 'Were you expecting someone else?'

She shrugged. 'I wasn't sure where I was. I went to Irene's party . . . I don't even know how I got here.'

'You were unwell and you fell asleep. The party was rowdy and getting out of hand so I brought you here, where you wouldn't be disturbed. How do you feel this morning?'

'Fine, but a little muddled, and my head pounds. I can't remember much. I must apologize to my hosts. Where's *here*, Mr Miller?'

'My home is situated near the village of Tynehill, which is not far from Brighton.'

A thin woman of about fifty, who Julia took to be Mrs Finnigan, came in. 'Is there anything else you need, sir?'

'Some aspirin for Miss Howard, please.'

She was back in a few minutes with the tablets and a glass of water.

'That will be all for now, thank you, Mrs Finnigan.'

'I imagine it was something you ate,' Latham said when the woman left. 'As for your hosts, don't bother about apologizing. They know where you are, and why, and no doubt your memory will return in time.' This was said rather wryly, so she was immediately put on alert.

'Did I make a fool of myself, Latham?'

'Just a little. We'll talk about it after breakfast. Now, take your aspirin so you can get rid of that headache. What will you have to eat?'

'I'm not really hungry,' she said, swallowing two pills down with a shudder.

He began to lift the covers off the dishes. 'The best way to get rid of a hangover is to have something solid in your stomach. Let me see if I can tempt you. How about some puréed apples on a little oatmeal?'

She made a face.

'Just a small portion . . . for me.' He placed a small amount of oatmeal into a dish and spooned apple purée on to it.

It wasn't as bad as she'd imagined it would be, and the apples added a tart flavour that freshened her mouth and tongue. At his coaxing, she followed that up with some scrambled egg on a piece of toast, garnished with a slice of lean bacon. Latham ate the same, only in larger amounts.

'There, that wasn't so bad, was it?'

It had been ages since she'd eaten a good breakfast. 'It was delicious. And my headache has nearly gone.'

'Coffee or tea?'

'Coffee would be nice. You have a lovely home.'

'I like it. I like to think I designed it myself, but I had a lot of help from the architect who drew up the plans. He told me what would work and what wouldn't.'

'And the decoration and furnishing?'

'Mostly mine.'

'You're very talented.'

'I like living in pleasant surroundings and I don't mind paying for objects that have value. I came from nothing, and they remind me that I've made a success of my life. You looked lovely last night, you know, as pretty as a butterfly – too innocent and exquisite to spoil.'

'Can we stop creeping around the subject, please Latham! What did I do last night? Don't spare my feelings.'

'If you want to hear the truth, my dear, you shall. When I found you, you were lying on Charles' bed. Rupert Gyesworth and Adam Oldham were in the room too. They were both naked, and Charles was tossing a coin to see who was to take a turn at you after he'd broken you in.'

She hadn't expected him to be quite that blunt, and the colour drained from her face. 'Oh . . . I see.'

'Take a sip of your coffee, Julia. No harm was done, I imagine, since you still had all your clothes on. Irene told me you were trying to lose your virginity.'

Heat rushed into her cheeks now, so she was forced to press her hands against them. 'Well, yes . . . I suppose I was. I'm so ashamed. I can't remember anything now. Did I . . . well, you know?'

'*Succeed?* I'm assured that you didn't. Irene said it was your idea, and that it had been arranged for Charles—'

'That's probably true. I can't remember whether it was my idea or not. It just seemed a good idea at the time and I got carried along with it.' Julia couldn't believe she was talking to a man like this, but there was something solid about Latham that reminded her of a favourite uncle, and encouraged her confidence. 'I suppose you think I'm stupid.'

'No. I fully understand that women have their needs as well as men. However, you should be a little more discriminating. Men like Charles and his friends are fun, but they live to satisfy their own needs and don't give a damn about anyone else. No man worth his salt would use a woman as sport. As for Irene, be careful. She's just as lacking in character as her brother. She chopped up some marijuana and added it to the filling of those vol-au-vents you ate, so she was probably in on it.'

'Irene did that?' Tears began to trickle down her cheeks. 'How could she when she said she was my friend?'

'Irene is inclined towards spur-of-the-moment actions, just for the hell of it.'

She was crestfallen as she remembered her father. 'Do you think my father will find out about it?'

He came to where she sat, took her into his arms and stroked her hair. 'Don't fret, Julia my dear. If he does, I'll tell him you were with me the whole time and someone was making mischief.'

'Wouldn't that be worse? After all, you're a man, even though you're twice my age.'

'That doesn't mean I don't find you attractive, and I'm not exactly ancient, only forty-three.' He gave a little chuckle, and taking out a white handkerchief, shook it out of its starched creases and dried her tears. 'In fact, I'm a little annoyed that you didn't consider me for that particular little service you wanted done. Sometimes, experience is far better than the vigour of youth.'

She blushed and grinned at the same time. 'Is it? I must admit I'm sick of being innocent . . . or should I say *ignorant* about such matters. But I daresay Daddy was right, and I should keep myself tidy in case I meet a man who wants to marry me.'

'You have met one. I'll marry you if you'll have me, then you can lose your virginity in a manner that would meet all your father's expectations – in the marriage bed.'

She was about to burst into laughter when she saw the seriousness of his expression. 'Surely you don't mean that?'

'I'm not in the habit of proposing marriage to all and sundry. Of course I mean it.'

'But why me?'

'I realized at Christmas that I'd fallen in love with you.'

The baldness of his statement nearly robbed her of breath. 'What about Irene?'

He gave a slight frown. 'What about Irene?'

'I thought . . . she said . . . I thought you and she were *emotionally* involved?'

'That's a rather quaint way of putting it, since my emotions have never been engaged with those belonging to Irene. Look, my dear, I've put my cards on the table, so you'll know exactly where you stand in my estimation.'

Julia found herself looking at Latham Miller as a man now, instead of an *older* man. Forty-three wasn't exactly ancient. He was well muscled and upright, with an aura of power about him. He was not flamboyant. In the city he wore a dark suit, but here he dressed casually in grey flannel trousers and checked, double-breasted sports jacket over a grey knitted pullover, white shirt and tie. Well-worn brogues were a perfect fit on his feet, and a discreet gold signature ring decorated his little finger.

'I'm honoured—'

His chuckle stopped her in her tracks. 'I was waiting for that. Before you add a rider starting with *but* all I'm asking you to do is think about it. I can give you everything you'll ever want or need . . . including children.'

'I hardly know you, Latham.'

'You know me better than you did Charles. I can guarantee that I have all my own teeth. I'm also free of any disease usually attributed to those who make a habit of loose living. Do you love Charles?'

She winced. 'Of course I don't love him. I mean . . . he's all right and is good fun, but I didn't want him for a husband or anything.'

'Did you take the precaution of asking him if he was clean?'

'Clean?' She turned as red as a lobster when she realized what he meant. 'Why . . . no.'

'Then turning yourself into a slut to entertain him and his friends could have turned into a long-term tragedy. It's not in your nature to be promiscuous, Julia.'

She gasped at his plain speaking. If only he knew how promiscuous she felt at times. She told herself that being a woman alone didn't seem natural, and here was a perfectly good man asking her to become his mate and bear his children.

Deep inside her she detected a primitive response at the thought of those children being created. Perhaps she *was* a slut. She tried not to think about it. 'I don't know what my father would say to your proposal.'

'Then ask him, by all means. I've already made it clear to him what my intentions are towards you.'

Her eyes widened at that. 'And he approved?'

'Let's say he didn't disapprove. Quite rightly, he said that you'd have to make up your own mind. And that's what I'm asking you to do. Not now and not even tomorrow. I'm a patient man. In the meantime, allow me to call on you and take you out so you can get to know me a little better.'

He was persuasive, and she was weakening. 'What if we don't . . . *suit?*'

'In what way?' he said, but his eyes showed his amusement plainly.

Her mouth twitched into a grin. He was playing with her, and she liked it. 'You know damned well what I'm talking about.'

'I can't believe that a girl so eager to dispose of her virginity would be a shrinking violet in bed. There was a logical approach to your plan, and I must admit that it surprised and pleased me. It's a pity Charles turned out to be such a cur about it. You could do better than him.'

'I imagine that by better, you mean yourself.'

'I do mean that. Would you like my offer in writing?'

She couldn't quite stifle her giggle at that. 'Certainly not. My father would have a fit.'

'If you'd prefer, you could try before you buy. But I honestly don't believe that's your style. I'd guarantee that none of my friends would be invited to the party.'

She began to laugh. 'Stop teasing me, Latham. Somebody told me you were wicked, but I didn't really believe that until now. If you mention my past indiscretion again I won't speak to you for the rest of the day.'

'Promise you'll take my proposal seriously, and think about it.'

'I promise.'

'Good. Do you fancy a walk? We could take the dogs up to the copse. It's dark and mysterious. Elves and fairies make their home there.'

'I'd rather like to see a fairy.'

'They're hard to find in the winter, on account of them only having wings to keep them warm. We might see an elf, though the last one I ran into told me they sleep during the day.'

She laughed at that. 'How very convenient of them. My fur coat is a bit cumbersome to walk in.'

'Oh, I daresay my housekeeper can lend you something more suitable.'

Rising, he pulled her chair back for her, and when she turned, he said, 'I didn't get a New Year's Day kiss.'

'No, you didn't.'

Her mouth dried when he took her face in his hands. She didn't know whether she should get involved with him or not, but instinct made her turn her head to one side.

'At least try it, my dear.' He brought her face back, and because she'd enjoyed his company and he'd been good to her, she didn't resist when his lips found hers.

The tenderness of the kiss was surprising. His mouth was soft against hers, yet with just enough insistence to indicate his position where she was concerned. Instinct told her that now he'd staked his claim Latham would pursue her to the very end. She shivered.

'Happy 1922 for both of us,' he said.

Julia borrowed a thick woollen coat with a black astrakhan collar, which smelled faintly of mothballs. They set off out, taking the Rolls and parking it on a dirt road at the edge of the copse in case it came on to rain. The dogs leapt from the car to hurry with noisy energy into the undergrowth, their tails thrashing about.

'Well that's frightened the wee folk off, I imagine,' she said.

He took his hand in hers and gave her a sideways glance. 'I have something to confess; I lied about them.'

'That's too bad of you, Latham, when you sold yourself to me as a creature of perfection.'

'Did I sell myself? I wonder . . . ? This way, Julia; we'll take the track to the left.'

The day was cold. Frost lingered in the shade and turned the tough winter grasses into silvery blades. With a brittle brightness the sun came out to paint everything with a touch of sparkle before the frost crystals turned into wisps of steam. Julia could almost believe in his fairies and elves when they came across a bed of bright toadstools sheltered in a knoll at the base of a tree. A shaft of sunlight touched down through the bare branches above, where an icicle dripped.

'Icicles hang where catkins follow,' she murmured.

He gazed an enquiry at her.

'It was a poem called Winter. I wrote it at school when I was twelve. I won an encouragement award for it. I expect Daddy still has the certificate somewhere. He was always proud of me, though I wasn't all that academic.'

'It must have been nice to have a father who encouraged you. Recite the rest of the poem for me.'

She screwed up her forehead, trying to recall it. 'I can't quite remember how it started. . . . *Holly spikes impale the air and lie in wait for drafts to lair . . . talons scratch against the glass to mark the frosted hours that pass.* The rhyme went a bit haywire after that, I recall. *Firelight leans against the cold . . . the hibernation rarely stirs but icicles hang where catkins follow, dusted with pure gold.*'

'Not bad for twelve.'

'Oh, I viewed the world through rose-coloured glasses then. My mother was still alive. I was lucky to be born to good parents, and adored both.'

'And I hadn't long been married then.'

'What was your wife like?'

'The original pushy American with a heart as gold as your catkins,' he said with a laugh. 'She liked to organize people, and I needed to be organized then.'

'I understand that she lost her life when the Titanic went down.'

'Yes . . . We were both booked on it, but at the last minute I couldn't go because I was in the middle of a deal that had begun to go stale.'

She squeezed his hand, feeling a moment of empathy. 'I'm sorry you lost her, but I'm glad you didn't go with her, Latham.'

'So am I . . . now. It took a while for me to think that way, though.'

They fell silent, each with their own thoughts. After a while Latham whistled to the dogs and they returned to mill around, hot and doggy smelling, panting out steam from lolling tongues and in obvious need of a fuss as they leaned against Latham's legs – as though they'd performed some feat that required lavish praise.

'I wonder why dogs feel the need to pee on every tree,' she remarked as they pushed on ahead.

He started to laugh. 'They're marking their territory.'

'Thank goodness we don't have to.'

'But we do; we build walls and fences. We put up signs saying Private Property, Keep Out, or Trespassers will be Prosecuted.'

'I suppose that makes us appear more civilized.'

'Only in our own eyes. Dogs wouldn't mind if we peed on trees. They'd think it was normal behaviour.' He slid her a sideways glance, his amusement plain to see. 'You're good at making conversation about nothing. What's the point?'

Laughter huffed from her. 'I'd hate to be a tree and have a dog pee on me, I guess.'

His arm went round her and he pulled her against his side, as though they were lovers out for a stroll. Only she didn't feel as though Latham was a lover or a friend. He presented a slightly intimidating figure to her, more like a teacher. She didn't like to pull away, but neither did she want to give him false hope by sliding her own arm around him. So they stayed that way, she walking stiffly with an uneven gait until they reached the car and she was released.

The walk had given her an appetite. After they reached his home, she tidied herself and went down for a luncheon of leek and potato soup garnished with bacon and croutons, and served with crisp, home-made rolls. Salad with paper-thin curls of smoked salmon followed. Julia wasn't very fond of smoked salmon. She ate it anyway, because she knew Latham would tell Mrs Finnigan to prepare something else, and she didn't want to put the woman to any trouble. Tea was brought in, accompanied by a plate of almond biscuits.

'Thank you, Mrs Finnigan. Miss Howard will pour it for us, won't you, Julia?' he said.

'Of course.' She busied herself with the teapot.

Mrs Finnigan handed Latham an embossed card. He read it and nodded. 'Ask them to wait in the sitting room until we've finished lunch.'

'Shall I take them some refreshment, sir?'

'I don't think that will be necessary, Mrs Finnigan.'

Another half an hour passed before Latham dabbed his mouth with a napkin and rose. 'Shall we go into the sitting room?'

'I thought you had guests waiting.'

'It's you who is my guest, Julia,' and he held out his hand to her. 'Come on.'

When they entered the sitting room she was surprised to see Irene, and Charles, who was standing by the window, looking out.

He turned when they went in. 'It's really too bad of you to keep us waiting this long, Latham.'

'Oh, do shut up, Charlie, what did you expect?' Irene looked haggard. 'Are you all right, Julia?'

Latham smiled at her. 'Of course she's all right. Did you imagine you might see Julia's body hanging from the rafters?'

Irene's expression was bleak. 'It wouldn't have surprised me, since you're totally unpredictable when you're in a temper.'

Latham ignored her comment. 'I believe the pair of you have something to say to Julia.'

Charles shrugged and sucked in a breath. 'I'm sorry for what happened, old thing. I didn't mean it to go that far . . . it was just a prank.'

Julia felt uncomfortable. 'Oh, you have no need to do this, Charles. It was partly my fault. I just want to forget about it.'

'It was reprehensible of me to turn what should have been a private encounter between us into common knowledge. I shouldn't have involved others. Can you forgive me?' he said with great charm.

She could feel a blush creeping under her skin. 'Of course I can.'

The smile he gave her in return was irrepressible. 'Then perhaps we could try it again sometime.'

Even though Latham grinned his eyes were cold when he said, 'I don't think that's a good idea, do you, Charles?'

Irene stared hard at him. 'Who appointed you *in loco parentis*?'

Unblinking, Latham gazed back at her.

Air hissed between Charles' teeth. 'For God's sake, Irene, why do you have to be so confrontational? Do what we came to do and let's get home. We have guests.'

It was Irene who finally dropped her gaze, but it was an unfriendly one when turned towards Julia. She bit out, 'I'm sorry. We were all as pissed as ponies. I knew you didn't smoke reefers, which is why I put some weed in the vol-au-vents. It was only to loosen you up a bit. I didn't imagine you'd pass out on it.'

'Irene, it's all right, really. I'm sorry I was such a wet blanket. To be honest, I can't remember a thing.'

'Nothing happened to remember. You're still intact . . . at least, you were when you left with Latham.'

'And she still is.' Latham crossed to the bell pull and gave it a tug.

Julia was heartily sick of her virgin state being discussed by all and sundry. 'As far as I'm concerned this subject is now closed.'

'Not quite, my dear. I think they ought to be told that I've proposed marriage to you.'

Irene's eyes widened and she made a strangled sound. 'I thought—'

'What did you think, Irene?'

Her lips tightened. 'Nothing . . . and nothing is what I got.'

Latham gazed from one to the other, his smile bland, his eyes guarded. 'Julia has promised to seriously consider it. In other words, she's off limits from now on. Do you understand, Charles?'

How dare he stake a claim on her in such a manner? 'I'll decide that for myself,' she murmured mutinously, but nobody seemed to hear.

A knock came at the door and he opened it. 'Ah Mrs Finnigan . . . good. Show my visitors out, please.'

Irene's look told Julia that she felt like strangling her as she went by, but she said nothing.

Charles managed a tight grin. 'Well, well, well! Who would have thought an intact hymen would win the bloody jackpot? Good luck, my little honeypot, you'll need it.' Gently, he kissed her cheek.

After they'd gone she rounded on Latham. 'That was outrageous!'

His smile was conciliatory. 'Yes, it was . . . I stepped over the line. I'm sorry if I offended you. I just don't like the idea of you associating with that pair. Neither does your father.'

'Oh, neither of you need to worry, I doubt if they'll *want* to associate with me after this debacle, do you?'

He looked genuinely distressed. 'I really am sorry. I'm used to taking charge of situations . . . not that it's any excuse. How can I make it up to you?'

'I'm afraid you can't.' She would be the laughing stock, and probably dropped by all her friends once the gossip got going. Still, that wasn't his fault, it was her own for getting herself into the situation in the first place. Intuition told her that Latham had been deliberately cruel to Irene, but how and why escaped her. She remembered her manners and sighed. 'You've been very kind to me, Latham, and I'm not ungrateful, but I'd like to go home, please.'

He nodded. 'I was going back in the morning, but if you can't stand my company any longer I'll have Robert bring the car round. I'll ask Mrs Finnigan to pack your things.'

'No . . . don't put her to any trouble . . . tomorrow will be fine.'

For the rest of the time they spent together, Latham went out of his way to keep her amused, and she enjoyed his companionship.

The next morning Latham conveyed her to London. When they drew up outside her home, he opened the car door for her. Gently he kissed her on the forehead, obviously having no intention of going up to see her father. 'Thank you for your company; I enjoyed the time we spent together. Give my regards to your father.'

Her lovely green eyes were suddenly anxious. 'I don't want him to worry. You won't tell him what happened, will you?'

'No, my dear, off you go now; it's coming on to rain.'

Latham watched the doorman open the door for her, thinking that he wouldn't have to tell Benjamin Howard anything, because sooner or later her little escapade was bound to reach his ears.

Seven

It was raining when Latham made his way through the dismal London streets. He stopped at a door set into a recess, and let himself into a small pied-à-terre tucked into a side street not far from Portman Square.

The wireless was playing and his nose twitched as he smelled the stale remnants of reefer smoke.

'Irene?'

'It's a foul night and you're late,' she said sulkily from the bedroom.

She was lying on the bed dressed in silk pyjamas. The ashtray was overflowing. Wrinkling his nose he moved it to the dressing table, along with half a bottle of wine that stood next to it.

'Do you have to be so fastidious?'

'Do you have to be so slovenly?' he countered.

'It's only ash. Must we argue, when we're here for a different purpose altogether?'

She was right. 'Sorry, my dear. I was held up.'

'By darling Julia, I suppose.'

'You suppose wrong. In actual fact I dined at my club with Alec Mailer from the ministry. We had business to discuss.'

He began to undress, folding his dinner suit carefully over the back of a chair.

She left the bed, turned the wireless up and began to shimmy to some jazz music. Her hips were a blur and her pyjama bottoms gradually slid down her legs to her ankles. Moving out of them she unfastened the buttons on her top, then lifting her arms she began to prance around the floor, the bare cheeks of her bum quivering. The front opening revealed a dark tuft of hair cheekily trimmed into a heart shape.

Dropping his trousers and underwear to the floor he reached out for her.

She gave a little squeal as his hands closed around her waist, wriggling away from him. 'Your hands are freezing.'

'I'm going to warm them on you.' Grabbing her up he tossed

her on to the bed and joined her, spreading her wide. Her pupils were enlarged and dreamy, and there was a sweet smell lingering in her hair. 'Have you been smoking opium as well?'

'Just a little, Latham. I was upset after last weekend. Rupert gave me some. I only smoked a little. It calms me.'

He sighed. 'I don't like to see you doped up, like this. You know opium is highly addictive.'

'Oh, it's just a craze . . . everyone smokes it . . . or pretends that they, do.'

'Where's the pipe? I'm taking it with me.'

'Latham, don't be such a crosspatch. I won't touch it again, I promise. Kiss me.' She closed her eyes when he leaned forward and when he kissed her tiny breasts he reared against her stomach.

She laughed, bringing her legs up around him and making sensuous little movements while they wrestled into position. 'You're the only man I know who prefers small breasts.'

'Shameless hussy, you've known too many men,' he said, and drove into her.

With no make-up on she looked older than she actually was, and there were faint traces of a white powder around her nostrils. Fast living would probably kill her, and he had a twinge of remorse as he began to explore what was on offer. Irene definitely knew how to use her body to advantage them both.

When they had satisfied the first urgent frenzy, she sat astride his stomach, pulled the quilt around her shoulders and gazed down at him. She traced a finger over his chest. 'You're not serious about marrying Julia, are you?'

'Of course I am . . . I want children.'

'Then marry me. I could give you a child.'

His eyes narrowed. 'You're not the marrying kind, Irene, and you're too irresponsible to be a mother.'

'How do you know? I love you, you know. Besides, look how good in bed we are together.'

He pushed her aside, sat on the edge of her bed and began to pull on his socks. 'I need a wife who will run my house, and who I can introduce to my friends without having to wonder how many of them she's fucked. I want any children I have to be able to look up to their mother as a shining example. Is that a description of you, Irene? I think not.'

'I can change.'

He shrugged. 'You can't change the past. Let's not argue. You are what you are, and you'll never change that.'

'Oh, fidelity is all in the mind. Julia was quite happy to be initiated by Charles, and was looking forward to it. You spoiled it for her, and didn't even give her one that night to make up for it. What if she turns you down?'

He turned to gaze flatly at her. 'She won't, because I'll find the right opportunity . . . failing that, I'll create one. I love and respect Julia, and I won't have you talking about her like this. We're through if you do. If that's what you want, just say so.'

She stretched like a cat. 'You know, Latham, you're right about me making a lousy mother, but I'd still be willing to give you a child. Who knows, I might even grow to love it. After all, my mother loves my youngest brother, though Nicholas has always been a nauseating little creep. We could always hire a nanny to teach our offspring some manners. Come back to bed; I'll do something nice for you.'

'What?'

'Come here and I'll whisper it in your ear.'

He laughed when she did, flipped her over his knee and smacked her bare bottom.

Martin tried to settle into his new job, but unfortunately Benjamin seemed unable to tear himself away completely, for he dropped in every day to chat to his employees and linger over a mug of tea.

The visits were a nuisance, since they tended to undermine Martin's need to assert his own authority. He had the feeling that Benjamin was looking over his shoulder. It wasn't until the end of January that he found the courage to point this out to his employer.

'They need to accept me as the manager, and so do you, Ben. We both know that changes have to take place. At the moment I'm clearing out the storage areas and doing a stocktake. I intend to send out a catalogue detailing goods that are reduced in price. I've also appointed Gregson as my assistant manager, so we work more closely together and I'm kept aware of the financial situation.'

'Gregson is good at his job . . . Did you give him a raise?'

'No, just an increase in responsibility.'

'I'd like to see him rewarded.'

'He will be, when Howard's Toys is in a better position to do so. We need to get the overdraft down. Two of the employees have handed in their notice, and I'm not going to replace them.'

'Oh, who are they?'

'Young Dobbs is one. His brother is going to open a garage, and Dobbs is going to take up a mechanical engineering apprenticeship with him.'

'He's good with his hands, so should make a fine mechanic.'

'Mrs Brewster is the other one.'

'Mrs Brewster? But she has a family to support.'

'And is expecting another. She and the children are going back to live in her parents' home. Besides, the other workers resent her. In line with general sentiment, they think she's keeping a man out of work.'

'She would be if her man was employable. What will happen to her husband? Did she say?'

'She was forced to take two days off work last week after he took a stick to her. The neighbours called the police and they kept him in the lockup until he'd calmed down. They should have called a doctor to give him a sedative. He'll end up in prison, or even an asylum if he continues to be violent.'

'You said Eileen is expecting a baby. Oh, my goodness, I thought . . . her husband was gassed, you see. I didn't think—'

'That doesn't mean the urges are dampened. Violence is often a release for frustration, and sometimes the two go together.'

'Quite . . . but she could work a little longer, surely.'

'She doesn't want to. She's had enough.'

Benjamin looked genuinely distressed. 'She used to come to work with bruises, and once she had a black eye. She said she'd walked into a door. I didn't believe her, but didn't probe any deeper . . . none of my business really. I'll talk to her on the way out. Are you settled into your flat?'

'Oh, I've finished it. You should come over for dinner . . . Sunday perhaps, unless you're busy.'

'I usually spend a quiet day with Julia.'

'She's welcome to come too. Believe it or not I can cook. I'm not as good as your daughter, but can manage a roast beef with Yorkshire pudding, vegetables, and probably a trifle.'

'A trifle.' Benjamin's face brightened. 'I haven't had a trifle since . . . well, for a while, anyway. Thank you, I'm sure Julia would like that. Come to think of it, things have been quiet for her on the social scene since New Year. Latham Miller has taken her out to dinner, or escorted her to the theatre a couple of times.' Benjamin held out his hand and smiled. 'Dinner on Sunday it is then. I'll try not to be such a nuisance to you from now on, and I'll cut my visits down to one a week to give you some breathing space. Rest assured, I do trust you. It's just that it's so damned hard to let go.'

Benjamin stopped outside the office and took out his wallet. He extracted ten pounds and folded his fingers over it. No need to ask him who the intended recipient was, Martin thought, as Ben ambled towards the packing bench where Eileen Brewster worked. His employer was generous to a fault.

The two had a short conversation, then Benjamin slid the money into her hand. Patting her on the shoulder he walked away. Mrs Brewster watched him go then took a handkerchief from her pocket and dabbed her eyes. Telling Gregson to make her pay up, he called her into the office.

'We're sorry to lose you, Mrs Brewster. You needn't work your notice out, since there's not enough work to keep you occupied. It won't affect your final wage.'

'That's right kind of you,' she said wearily. 'I know you would have had to get rid of me sooner or later, so me leaving now saves you from going to the trouble.' She took the money from her pocket and laid it on the desk. 'I reckon I should give Mr Howard this back. I don't want you to think I took advantage of his generosity.'

Martin pushed it back towards her. 'This is nothing to do with the factory. It was a personal gift from Mr Howard, so put it back into your pocket.'

'My Jack . . . he was all right before the war, you know.'

'Yes, I imagine he was.'

'Aye, I reckon you do, at that. I can see it in your eyes some-times, the despair . . . only Jack can't put it behind him. He has to lash out.' She shrugged. 'It's the children, you see . . . they shouldn't be made to suffer.' Her hands went to her stomach. 'Jack's been strange of late . . . I've got to put the children first, especially this new life. He wants me to get rid of it, but babies are precious.'

'And the procedure is not only illegal, but dangerous to the mother.'

Which was all right for him to say, when he would never be in her position, Martin thought, and he wanted to hug this careworn woman. He was seeing one of the aftermaths of the war – a different victim. Fate had not been kind to her. The war had sucked her man into its maw, voraciously ground him down and spat him out damaged beyond repair. He couldn't get involved, only fob her off with a little extra in her pay packet, an extended hand and his words as sincere as he could make them. 'Good luck, Mrs Brewster. I do hope all goes well.'

On Sunday they went to the morning service. Afterwards, Julia drove her father's car carefully through the streets to Martin's flat in Finsbury Park.

Martin came up the stairs from the basement to greet them. He had a grin on his face, and was wearing a striped apron of the type butchers usually wore. 'Was that you I saw behind the wheel, Julia? I didn't know you could drive.'

'Oh, I'm just learning.'

'Latham Miller's chauffeur is teaching her. Latham said it would keep his man occupied while he's abroad. Robert is making a good job of it . . . except she managed to mow down Nelson's column on the way over.'

Julia giggled. 'I did not. Robert says I have aptitude, but he always grins when he says it, so I don't know if I can believe him or not. I must say I like driving, and it's quite easy when you know how.' She shooed him towards the door. 'Go indoors and take Daddy with you. I'll be there in a minute; I've got a house-warming gift for you and need to get it from the back seat. I hope you like it.'

'I'm sure I shall.'

Julia wasn't at all sure, but she could only try as five minutes later she handed over her offering, a pair of tabby kittens in a wicker basket, to which she'd tied a red bow. 'A boy was trying to sell them in the market, and he was so hungry-looking that I felt sorry for all of them. You will take them, won't you, Lee-Trafford? Once they're house trained they'll be company for you in the evening, and company for each other during the day when you're not here. I've brought you some mince to feed them on.'

He looked slightly dubious. 'Are they male or female?'

'How would I know? They're just sweet little kittens.'

'They won't be so sweet if they grow into fully equipped tomcats. And if they're female they'll reproduce rapidly unless they're fixed.' He picked them up, his hands gentle, and lifted their tails.

'Fixed? What on earth do you mean? How . . . ?'

He grinned at her. 'They're boys, and they'll be simple enough to neuter. How? I'll make a small incision in the scrotum, remove the testicles and tie off the ligaments. They look a bit on the skinny side; have you checked them for worms?'

Of course she knew what fixed meant – she shouldn't have asked. Her eyes flew open and her cheeks fired up.

Benjamin guffawed with laughter. 'I've never seen my daughter's face turn quite so red.'

Good job he hadn't been there when Latham had educated her about sexual matters then.

It was true that her face had warmed at Martin's frankness. Though most of her understanding stemmed from guesswork, she wasn't entirely stupid. She spluttered, 'Heavens, how utterly and ruthlessly . . . *surgical* of you. I think I could have done without the tutorial.'

He couldn't quite keep the grin off his face. 'I'm sorry, force of habit. Sometimes it was learn on the job in the army.'

She struggled on. 'I do hope you didn't *fix* your patients in quite the same manner. Could you be kind and allow me to have the last word on this.'

'I've embarrassed you, haven't I?'

'I must admit . . . well . . . poor kittens. Checking for worms sounds entirely disagreeable to me.'

'Never mind, I'll see to it.' One of the kittens began to purr and he stroked its stomach with his forefinger. The other made little squeaks. 'They are rather sweet. Thank you for thinking of me.'

His voice had a slightly ironic edge to it as he slanted his brilliant-blue eyes her way. He had an effect on her without even trying. She had never felt so attracted to a man.

'What would you suggest I call them?' he asked.

'Anything you like. I did think Billy Boy might suit the darker one, since he's a bit of a thug. I was going to call the other one Clara, but now she'll have to be Clarence.'

'You won't mind if I call them both puss, will you?'

'You're perfectly horrid; of course I'll mind. How would you like to be called puss?' and she laughed. 'And what's more you look rather silly in that apron. Is there anything I can do to help?'

'Yes . . . You can put some newspaper down on the bathroom floor for Billy and Clarence, and give them a saucer of milk. The bathroom is through that door over there. The kitchen is in the opposite direction beyond the dining room.' Then in anticipation of her next question, 'They'll be warm in the bathroom; it has a radiator.'

'You can be awfully bossy, you know.'

'I do know. After you've done that, you can set the table if you would. The bits and pieces are in the dresser.'

The whole place was comfortably furnished in a mannish sort of fashion – no frills or fuss. She remembered he'd grown up without a mother in his life.

He gazed to where her father had made himself comfortable in an armchair by the fire. 'Can I get you a drink, Benjamin?'

'I wouldn't mind a small glass of sherry.'

'You, Julia?'

'That would be nice. I'll deal with the cats first. If I leave the basket lid open they can sleep in it for a while and can claw their way in and out if they need to.'

The dinner smelled delicious, she thought, as she bustled about the dresser, opening and shutting cupboards and drawers while she looked for tablecloths, cutlery and cruets.

Martin Lee-Trafford was talented in many ways. He made an expert Yorkshire pudding batter, pouring it into a sizzling pan of meat juices and placing it back into the oven to cook while the meat rested.

'I'm impressed.'

He appeared slightly embarrassed by the compliment. 'I like to eat, so I thought I owed it to myself to learn how to cook. I don't often get the chance to entertain others. I'm enjoying it.'

'Then you'll have to do it more often.'

'I have some fairly good news for your father. I'll tell him over dinner.'

'Oh, good, he seems to have been a bit preoccupied of late. I think something is worrying him.'

Martin waited until they were tucking into a delicious trifle before he told them, 'I've had the twelve versions of the Rosie Doll packaged together as collectors' items. We've catalogued them as a complete series while stocks last for ten shillings per series, and we're beginning to shift them.'

'And if we run out of early models?'

'I'm negotiating with a department store to take the rest to distribute amongst its branches, along with the overstock of puzzles. The outcome will be a reasonably small profit, but at this stage it's more important that we shift the stale stock and re-establish a cash flow.'

'Well done,' her father said.

Julia gazed at him in mock dismay. 'So that's all I mean to you both . . . stale stock?'

Her father patted her hand and chuckled. 'It happens to us all in time, my dear.'

Martin was clearly puzzled as he gazed from one to the other.

Her father enlightened him. 'The Rosie doll was modelled on Julia for all these years. It was a tenth birthday present for her from her mother and I. Julia named the doll after her grandmother, and she designed the wardrobe for the latest one.'

Martin's eyes reflected his amusement. 'I thought the doll looked slightly familiar. Oh, dear, I seem to have stuck my foot in my mouth again.'

'You most certainly have.'

'There's worse to come, and I hope this doesn't hurt your feelings, Julia. I'd prefer it if we dropped that line altogether. We also need to get into cheaper lines . . . soft toys with musical box innards, or automatons. Plastic figures and cardboard dolls' houses rather than expensive wood.'

'Howard Toys are known for their quality. We make the best rocking horses in Europe. They were one of the Howard factory's original products and we exported them abroad.'

'Daddy used to paint the speckles on the grey ones, and sometimes he allowed me to help. Each rocking horse is signed with his name,' she said.

'There's a whole herd of horses living on the third floor of the factory. I agree they're of good quality . . . so good in fact that they'll never wear out or need to be replaced unless they're attacked by woodworm. The last sale of a horse was over a year ago. We must produce lines that have a good turnover, and that will take time to build up.' He fell quiet for a few moments, then said, 'I'm sorry Ben. Perhaps you should have sold the place to Latham Miller after all.'

Julia gave her father a sharp look. 'Latham offered to buy the factory? Why didn't you tell me?'

He shrugged. 'What was the point when I had no intention of selling it to him. Latham only wants the building. The toys are my life, as they were for my father and my grandfather before him.'

'But if the toys no longer produce a profit—'

'You know nothing about business, my dear. Let's drop the subject, shall we? Do what you have to do, Lee-Trafford. When things improve I daresay a better offer will come along. In the meantime, another serving of that delicious trifle wouldn't go amiss.'

Taking up his dish, Julia went to the sideboard and filled it. She was steaming a little at the unaccustomed rebuke from her father. She wished he'd treat her as though she was an adult, especially in company. When she placed it gently in front of him, she said, 'Latham Miller is usually happy to discuss business with me.'

'I daresay he's humouring you when he does.'

'So why didn't he tell me he'd made an offer for the factory?'

'It could be that he's of the same mind as me, that business and women don't mix. You should ask him. Perhaps he's just waiting for the right opportunity to turn up. He's probably hoping you'll turn me to his way of thinking, so he can pick up the place cheaply. Well, I won't let you do that, Julia. Howard's Toy factory is my life. Now . . . I will hear no more of it.'

He'd wounded her, and the hurt she felt spread coldly through her. 'Daddy, that's completely untrue. How can you think that? Don't you trust me?'

He sighed. 'There are two things in life that I love deeply. One is the factory and the other is you, Julia. I'm sorry, my dear, I didn't mean to hurt your feelings. It's Miller I don't trust. Enough now!' He scraped the last remnants of trifle from his bowl, dabbed the napkin against his lips, and sat back, patting his stomach.

'Oh . . .' She didn't tell her father that Latham had proposed marriage to her. On the times when they went out together he was an amusing companion who went out of his way to please her. As he'd promised he didn't pressure her. He was a perfect gentleman, giving her flowers and chocolates, which her father ate, since he'd developed a sweet tooth of late.

When Latham kissed her it was pleasant enough, though not exactly earth-shattering. She sensed about him something of the predator watching and waiting to pounce. She couldn't help being aware of him when they were together, and she wondered how it would be with him. Her head told her that Latham would be a very good catch indeed, and Irene had told her he was wicked. But on the times she'd decided to say yes to him, her instinct stopped her from uttering the word – yet, she couldn't say no, either.

She felt the need in her to become a wife and mother, as her parents had fully expected of her.

Her glance fell on Martin. He'd been watching her, his mouth curved into a soft smile, his eyes faintly sympathetic. 'I'll make us some coffee.'

'And I'll clear the table and help you wash up,' and her voice was thick with tears. 'Your new abode is comfortable.'

'I like it now it's clean and tidy, and it's nice to have some space around me. Although it was kind of Arthur Feltham to offer me accommodation while I was in London, it was rather small for two of us. My house in Bournemouth has attracted a decent tenant, by the way.'

'Oh good . . . Did you manage to find somewhere to set your train set up here?'

'Not yet; I'll leave it boxed for now.'

'What a pity. I was hoping we'd be able to play with it. I imagine Daddy will be asleep when you take the coffee in.'

'Does he sleep much during the day?'

'He drifts off. He says he's getting old.'

'How old is he?'

'Sixty. My mother was ten years younger than him. He seems to have slowed down considerably over the past year, which is why he's retired a little earlier than he intended too.'

'Perhaps you should persuade him to see his doctor and get a check-up.'

Alarm filled her. 'Do you think there's something wrong with him then?'

'I don't think anything of the sort. I'm just suggesting that a precautionary check-up wouldn't hurt a man of his age – any age come to that.' He took the dirty plates from her and set them on the draining board.

'My father can be awfully stubborn at times,' she said when he turned back.

'I've noticed.'

Her eyes sought his. 'You'd tell me if you thought he was ill, wouldn't you, Martin?'

His eyelids flickered. 'I'm not his doctor . . . besides which there's a small question of privacy.' He took her hands in his. 'No medical practitioner worth his salt would break confidentiality between himself and his patient.'

She nodded. 'I understand that, but you're no longer a doctor, you're a factory manager.'

'And as such I'm unable to offer an opinion on anyone's health.'

'Unable, or unwilling?'

'It wouldn't be ethical.'

'No . . . it wouldn't. I shouldn't have been so presumptuous . . . I'm sorry. It's just that I'm a bit worried about him.' Removing her hands she abruptly changed the subject. 'Latham Miller has asked me to marry him. I haven't told my father yet.'

He stared at her, a nerve twitching in his jaw. Stiffly, he said, 'I suppose that's only to be expected. Congratulations.'

'I didn't say I'd accepted him.'

'Will you?'

'I haven't decided.'

'He'd be able to keep you in luxury.'

'Yes . . . I suppose he would; is that why you said it was to be expected?' and she couldn't keep the coldness from her voice. She gazed to where her father had made himself comfortable in an armchair by the fire. 'I don't think Daddy likes him.'

'You're Benjamin's only daughter. He would find it hard to give you away to another man, especially a business rival. But he'd come round because he'd want you to be happy.'

'Latham isn't a rival. As far as I can see, all he's done is make an offer for the business. Daddy turned it down and that's that.'

'It's possible that he'll change his mind . . . in time.'

She doubted it. 'Have you ever considered marrying?'

'I was engaged once.'

'What happened? And before you tell me to mind my own business . . . *what happened?*'

'I went away to war.'

'Wouldn't she wait for you? I would have.' Laughter trickled from her when he grinned. 'What I meant was that if I'd been put in the position of waiting for my fiancé to return, I would have. In fact, I did. I waited for Dickie.'

'Susan waited for me, too.'

Her curiosity got the better of her. 'And . . . ?'

'I released her from the engagement.'

She could hear the pain in his voice, and remembered he'd spent time in a hospital. Tears sprang to her eyes. 'Did you love her very much?'

The kettle had begun to boil and the lid was rattling. 'She was a nice girl, uncomplicated, and marriage was expected of us. She deserved better than the man who came back from the war. It was the right thing to do, and she's married to somebody else and is happy.' He leaned forward and kissed her on the end of the nose, saying gently, 'Don't cry over me, Julia, dear.'

'You should have married your nice uncomplicated girl. She could have looked after you. Can I hug you?'

He shook his head.

She did anyway. Taking a step towards him she slid her arms around him and looked up at him, smiling. 'What will you do now, Lee-Trafford?'

'What you're expecting me to do . . .' His mouth closed over hers in the softest of kisses that carried her into the clouds. The tip of his tongue parted her lips and gently flicked and probed. She moved against his hard body and for a moment they exchanged the close intimacy of their embrace.

There came a moment when his whole body stiffened. He removed her arms, placed her away from him and gazed at her. 'Did you love the man you waited for . . . the one who never returned?'

It was like being doused with cold water. There wasn't much space between them, just a heartbeat or two, but it might as well have been a mile, a stony one littered with barriers. Those barriers clearly told her to keep her distance. What would happen if she crossed them again, kept crossing them?

She knew now that she hadn't crossed them, he hadn't allowed her to. But she'd already made a fool of herself. She gave a light laugh and shrugged him off. 'You're as prickly as a hedgehog.'

'I don't need your motherly hugs, Julia.'

She'd already been bloodied by her father – now this. She hit back. 'Ah . . . yes, you do, Lee-Trafford, you always have. Every boy has the need of a mother to hold him close and comfort him.'

'Not me . . . not my mother.'

'Especially you and yours. You repel affection as though it's a disease, and avoiding it is the manly thing to do. That way you can't be infected by it. What are you scared of, emotional closeness? You've cried before over your father . . . why can't you cry for the loss of your mother?'

'I'm still trying to find out. Until I do I must cope the best way I can. Please don't trample on my toes, Julia. I don't want to hurt you.'

His answer was unexpected, and it was all the more poignant because he'd given her just a glimpse of himself.

A lump gathered in her throat. 'Damn you then; it was only a hug, not a threat . . . until you changed it into one.' On the stove behind him the kettle lid had taken on a furious clackety-clack. Gruffly she said, 'You'd better make the coffee before you run out of steam. I'll go and check on Clarence and Billy Boy.'

Her feeble joke attracted an equally feeble laugh as she turned and walked away.

After his guests had gone, Martin brought the kittens through and fed them. They were as lively as fleas, jumping out from behind the chairs and wrestling with each other, causing him an amusing half-hour before they tired and settled themselves in his lap to knead at his thighs.

He gazed into the firelight, gently stroking them and enjoying the peace of his solitary state.

His conversation with Julia had been enlightening. Not the words themselves, but her instinct to close in on his weakness. He *had* felt threatened by her hug, and not because of his mother, but because any closeness with Julia brought the inevitable reaction. But he had kissed her – and he wanted her – and it was too late because Latham Miller had put his claim on her.

Even so, his mother did come into his mind now, and he allowed her to stay there. He'd never once considered that she might have a side to the story that he hadn't heard. He'd just accepted his father's account of things, and the occasional reinforcement of them. Sharing confidences hadn't come easy to the man, but Martin had always been sure of his affection – or had it been possession?

Moving the kittens to the other armchair he went into his bedroom and fetched a box from the top shelf of the wardrobe.

The box housed family records such as birth and death certificates, the deeds to the house in Bournemouth and, right at the bottom, an envelope containing a photograph. It was a studio photograph of his father and mother taken thirty years before.

His mother was seated with a baby in her arms. She was gazing down at him with an affectionate smile on her face. The baby gazed back at her with a contented secure expression, as though he knew he was loved. A small hand reached out from the shawl and was extended towards her face, as though he wanted to caress her. More fool him! His father stood behind, his hand on her shoulder staring at the camera. He looked rather stern.

Flipping the photograph over Martin read the inscription, written in his mother's handwriting. He'd not known the photograph existed until after his father had died.

My dearest Martin's christening day. June 12th 1892.

He stared at it for a long time. His mother was wasp-waisted, due no doubt to her rigid corset. She wore a flowing dress with leg-of-mutton sleeves, high collared and trimmed with lace, and a wide hat decorated with flowers. She looked quite beautiful with her dark hair framing her face. He wished he could see her eyes, but they were looking into his and shaded by her eyelids, and he was too young to recall that moment of connection with her.

He knew he wasn't being, had *never* been, fair to his mother. She didn't look like a woman who'd abandon her child easily. Her father said he'd done the right thing by her under the circumstances – that men could. But was it right to deprive a woman of her son – and that son of his mother?

'My dearest Martin,' he whispered.

He began to wonder – was she still alive?

Reaching out he picked up the telephone receiver and held

it against his ear, swiftly replacing it in the rest again. He didn't want to do anything he might come to regret. He must think about it first.

Somewhere inside him a small voice told him he'd more likely come to regret it if he didn't make an effort, and that perhaps he was being too cautious. Julia had been right. He had cried for the loss of his father but he couldn't remember ever crying over his mother, because she hadn't been allowed to exist.

Picking up the receiver again he gave the operator the number of his father's lawyer, and while he waited to be connected he thought; if his mother couldn't be found, then at least he had tried.

Eight

It was April, and soft showers chased across the Surrey countryside, silvering the spring foliage.

> *Dear Sir,*
>   *I'm writing this letter becus you awt to no that your daughter*
> *Miss Julia Howerd did the wrong thing over New Year.*

Ellen gazed towards the window where her mistress stood in a
cloud of dense cigarette smoke, gazing out. 'Have I got to do
this, Miss?'

'If you want that bonus I promised you . . . and if you want
to keep your job.'

Sighing, Ellen licked the lead at the end of the pencil. 'I don't
know what to say.'

'Goodness, you ignorant little fool. Just say that Miss Howard
was under the influence of drink and drugs and you saw her on
the bed with three naked men . . . You saw it yourself, so you
know it's not lies. Tell him she's now the subject of gossip.'

'I don't know how to spell all them words.'

'It doesn't matter how you spell them. Just do it!'

> *Miss Howerd drunk and took some dope, then she went to bed*
> *with three naked men. Everbody is talking about it, and I see'd it*
> *with my own eyes. Shameful, it were.*

'How shall I sign it, Miss?'

'Anonymous.'

Anoneemuss.

'Now, put it in the envelope and write Mr Howard on it.'

When Ellen did as she was told Irene smiled and handed her
a pound. It was a sum Ellen hadn't been able to turn down, since
she could send it to her mother to help support her young
brothers.

'There you are, you'll be able to buy that nice hat you wanted. Remember, this is our little secret.'

'Yes, Miss . . . Thank you, Miss.'

'And Ellen . . . if this gets out, especially to my mother, I'll know where to look for you and your life will suddenly become hell on earth.'

Nearly in tears, Ellen mumbled, 'I won't say anything, I promise.'

'As long as that's understood.' Irene swept the letter into her bag. 'Take my hat and coat down to the hall, then go and tell the chauffeur I'm ready for him to take me to the station.'

Ellen did as she was told, hating Irene Curruthers for making her do such a mean thing. How could she do this to that nice Miss Howard, who was supposed to be her friend? And she couldn't tell anyone because the letter was in her handwriting, and they wouldn't believe she hadn't written it. Guilt beset her, and she hoped she could lie well enough to escape the eagle eye of Lady Curruthers when she questioned her about what her daughter had been up to.

Irene had no such qualms as she looked in on her parents, who were in the morning room. 'I'm off then.'

Her father barely glanced at her over his paper. He managed a grunt then went back to his reading.

Her mother was chattier. 'I don't know why you have to rush off to London as soon as your father and I get here.'

'Oh, really, Mummy . . . it's been two weeks already, and I told you, I want to go to Aileen's coming-of-age party at the Savoy before I go to Monte Carlo in May.'

'If you see Charles, tell him to work hard this term. And Irene . . . do try and find yourself a nice man and settle down.'

'Yes, Mother. I'll certainly keep trying.' She was meeting Latham in May and intended to get him back. Her glance fell on her younger brother. 'What's the creep doing here, why isn't he at school?' Nicholas looked like their father, rather short, with a long, hooked nose and big ears. He was sixteen, and had spots.

'I told you . . . oh, why don't you ever listen to me? Nicholas is recovering from measles. We decided to bring him home for the rest of the term, where the country air will be beneficial. I'd prefer it if you didn't call him names, Irene. He's sensitive.'

'So am I, but you didn't make such a fuss over me as you do over him. I hope I don't catch his stinking measles. That would be the last straw.'

'You've already had it, dear . . . at boarding school.'

'In that case you can give me a hug, Nicky boy.'

Nicholas complied, his head resting against her breast. There was a sneaky movement as he turned his head slightly and his hot breath fanned over her nipple.

'You dirty dog,' she whispered in his ear, and he giggled.

The train left on time, though Irene was forced to share a compartment with a man who got on at the last minute and couldn't keep his eyes off of her. He was quite handsome, in a dark-eyed, swarthy sort of way. His hair was slicked back with oil.

What was first class coming to, she thought, and wished that the train had a corridor. Oh well, if she couldn't get rid of him she might as well make the most of him, and she hadn't played this game for a long time.

Crossing her legs to give him an elegant expanse of silk stockings to consider, Irene smiled at him, then pulled her fur around her shoulders and turned to gaze out of the window. There she saw only his reflection in the mirror, and grinned when he surreptitiously adjusted his crotch.

There was something exciting about the man's bold stare so she turned and stared back at him, an enquiry in her eyes. 'Did you want something?'

He cleared his throat. 'I'm James. Didn't we meet at a New Year party?'

'I would have remembered if we had. I'm Lola. Have you ever had an encounter with a stranger in a train?'

He laughed. 'Not yet . . . How much do you charge?'

How absolutely priceless; he thought she was a whore! Wait until she told Charles; he'd laugh himself silly.

'You don't understand, James. You're the tart and I'm the customer. How much do you charge?'

'A pound,' he said, then stuttered when she took out her purse and dropped the money into his palm. 'I say, I didn't mean it.'

'I did,' she said.

★   ★   ★

When they arrived in London Irene left a dishevelled James behind adjusting his garments, though she'd been tempted to take his trousers with her. She took a cab to Earls Court. There was a ragged-looking lad begging on the corner.

She handed him the letter Ellen had written and pointed. 'See the entrance door to that building; there should be a porter inside. Hand him the letter. When you come back I'll give you sixpence.'

'What if there ain't no porter?'

'Just throw it on the floor inside.'

'And what if there is a porter and he wants ter know who it's from?'

Irene lost patience and took him by the ear, her nails digging into the lobe. 'Tell him to mind his own business. Look . . . Do you want to earn sixpence or not?'

'Aw right, Miss. Ow . . . let me go; that hurts.'

When she released him the boy scuttled off. He was back within a few seconds. 'Well?' she said.

He grinned. 'Nobody was there 'cepting a young man, not much bigger than me. He looked like a performing monkey in his uniform.

'What do you want, boy? sez he, looking down his nose like I was a bad smell. I handed him the letter. Less of your bleedin' lip and take this, my man, sez I, all grand like.' He held out his hand. 'That will be sixpence, please Miss, and if you or your friends need any more jobs doing, Jake is your man.'

'I'll bear that in mind.' Dropping a coin into his palm, Irene smiled as she walked away.

Later that afternoon Julia placed the post on to the table next to her father's chair and gazed at the book in his lap.

'*Scaramouche by Rafael Sabatini*. Is it good?'

'Excellent. I can't put it down.'

'Latham is taking me out tonight so I'm off to get a bath.'

'Are you going anywhere nice?'

'We're going out to have dinner at *Picardy*, then on to the *Rivoli* picture theatre to see *The Three Musketeers*. If you want adventure you could come with us. I know you like Douglas Fairbanks.'

'No thank you, dear. I saw it when it first came out. I'll stay with my book tonight.' He gazed up at her. 'You're seeing rather a lot of Latham Miller lately.'

'He's asked me to marry him. He hasn't pressed me for an answer though. He said you knew what his intentions towards me were, since the pair of you discussed it. Do you approve of him, Daddy? Sometimes I think you don't like him all that much.'

'He seems to have his priorities in the right place. You could do worse, I suppose.' He reached out and touched her hand. 'I have nothing against the man, Julia, but I want you to be happy. Do you love him?'

'I don't know. I like him.'

'You do realize that because Latham is your constant escort, it suggests that there's an understanding between you.'

'He doesn't put any pressure on me.'

'He does, but it's a subtle type of pressure. He's a powerful man, and it's unlikely that other young men would approach you under the circumstances.'

'I don't know any younger men, except for Martin Lee-Trafford. He can be awfully prickly sometimes, and doesn't seem at all interested in women. Did you know he was engaged before the war? He gave his lady friend her freedom because he was sick. I had to practically chisel that information from him.'

'Martin is discreet about his personal life. Actually he's a fine young man . . . if a little troubled, and one day it's possible that he might get over that. I like Lee-Trafford enormously, but I don't think it would be wise for either of you to fall in love. What about the crowd of people you used to go out with . . . Irene someone and her friends?'

'Oh . . . them. After New Year the friendship faded away, and our mutual friends went with her. I called her a couple of times and left a message with the maid, but Irene never got back to me. She's awfully popular.'

'From what I've heard about them they were a fast crowd anyway, not at all suitable for you to mix with. Good friends should last you for life.'

Colour seeped under her skin as she remembered New Year's Eve. She'd been such a fool. Thank goodness her exploit hadn't got back to her father.

★   ★   ★

Two hours later Benjamin remembered his letters and reached out for them. The first was a regretful letter from the bank informing him that they could no longer service his overdraft, and advising him to clear the outstanding debt as soon as possible. The second was an overdue account.

How the hell had he got himself into such a mess with his finances?

His chin sunk on his chest. Perhaps he should sell to Latham Miller after all. He cursed. Latham was astute – he'd force the price down just because he'd refused his former offer.

The third envelope just had his name on it, written in pencil. It had been spelled wrongly.

Dear Mr Howerd

As Benjamin read the rest of the note a band seemed to tighten around his chest. *'Julia . . . dear God!'* he whispered, and perspiration flooded his body. His fingers clawed at his shirt collar as he tried to loosen the buttons so he could get some air.

He mustn't panic. He mustn't! It was all lies of course. His daughter wouldn't do anything like that. He'd sell the business to Latham, and take her away to live by the seaside, where nobody would know her.

The band around his chest tightened and he tried to stand. It turned into a relentless pain that spread into every nook and cranny of his upper body. Dropping to his knees, slowly he began to crawl through his pain towards the emergency button . . .

Nine

The restaurant in Soho was well appointed and discreetly hidden behind a curtained window. Latham was obviously a regular patron, since the waiter recognized him on sight. So did one or two of the other patrons.

They were shown to a small table in the shadows with a view of the room and a flickering candle in a red vase.

'What would you like, my dear?'

She scrutinized the menu, trying to find something that wasn't too fattening.

She'd learned that Latham liked plain, solid meals without too much fuss attached to them. He made up his mind quickly, and gazed up at the waiter. 'Peppered lamb cutlets, steamed vegetables, and chocolate mousse.'

'I'll have that too, only without the pepper. I'll have Lemon Sorbet for afterwards.'

'We'll have a half bottle of burgundy to go with the main meal; *Côte de Nuit?*'

The waiter nodded. 'Naturally, sir.'

They'd reached the coffee stage when the waiter approached them. 'There's a telephone call for your companion, sir. The caller said it was urgent.'

Julia's face paled as a feeling of dread washed over her. 'Will you take it for me, Latham?'

'Of course.'

His back was towards her so she couldn't see his face. The call was brief. He hung up, paid the bill and strode towards her, his grave face causing her to rise from her seat. 'It was the porter at your building; your father's been taken ill.'

'What's wrong with him?'

'He doesn't know. Your father managed to get to the emergency bell, and the porter let himself in with his master key and found him on the floor. He rang for an ambulance. While they were waiting your father managed to tell him where we were and asked him to call you.'

'Then he can't be too bad if he could still talk. Perhaps it was just a faint.'

His glance met hers; his voice calmed her. 'Yes, I expect you're right. He's been taken to St Thomas's in Lambeth Palace road. I've asked the waiter to fetch your coat from the cloakroom. Come now and wait in the lobby while I get the car,' and his hand slid under her elbow and she was guided expertly and without fuss through the other diners.

Latham was so very capable that it was easy to allow him to take over – easier for her to believe that her dear, lovable father had experienced a faint. He would be sitting up in bed with an abashed smile on his face and would say: Stop worrying about nothing, Julia my dear. I'm fine.

There were several forms to be filled in, giving permission for this and that.

'When can I see my father?' Julia said to the nurse with some impatience.

'You must come back tomorrow at visiting hours.'

Latham took the woman aside and had a conversation with her.

'I'll go and ask the ward sister,' she said and smiled at him.

Still, it was another half an hour before they got to see him. He was in a private room. Face grey, he was propped against the pillows, his breathing harsh.

'Mr Howard is medicated and needs to rest but you can stay for five minutes. Try not to agitate or upset him in any way.'

As if she would. Taking his hand in hers she whispered, 'Oh . . . Daddy . . . you will get better . . . you must.'

'Julia, is that you?' he whispered, and his eyes flickered open.

She kissed his cheek. 'I'm here, Daddy . . . I love you. I can't leave you for five minutes without you getting into trouble, can I?'

'I'm sorry my love. It was just a faint and I'll be better after a few days' rest. Is that Latham with you?'

'Yes.'

'Come closer, the pair of you.' His voice strengthened. 'Latham . . . if anything happens to me, promise you'll look after my Julia.'

'I will, sir . . . if she'll allow me to.'

'Julia . . . I want you to accept Latham's offer of marriage. If I die you'll need him to sort out my business affairs, and he can look after you in the way you're used to, so I won't have to worry.'

Although she wanted to smile at the absurdity of his words a knife twisted in her gut. 'You're not dying . . . don't even say such a horrible thing. It was just a faint, you said. You wouldn't lie to me, would you?'

He sighed. 'For once in your life will you do as I ask without arguing? You need a husband and Latham is in a position to protect you.'

It seemed like an odd thing to say, but she decided to humour him. 'I'm going to look after you when you come home . . . but all right, I'll wed Latham, as long as you can live with us. You need someone to keep an eye on you. Is that acceptable to you, Latham?'

'Yes . . . I can get a special licence.'

'And Latham,' Benjamin said tiredly, 'I've been thinking it over, and have decided you can have the factory at the price I first offered, except without the conditions attached to it.'

'I accept,' he said, and despite the situation of her acceptance of his proposal, he gave an ironic-looking smile. It was restrained though, as if it were a smudged copy of the smile of triumph he really wanted to give.

A nurse came in and bustled about, straightening the sheets. 'You must go now; Mr Howard needs to rest. Come at visiting hours tomorrow.'

'Leave me now, my love. I'm tired.'

She gave him another kiss. 'Have a good night's sleep and I'll see you tomorrow, Daddy; I'll bring your slippers and pyjamas, and your wash bag.'

'You do that.'

His hand came down on Latham's wrist. 'You go on, Julia, I want to speak to Latham privately for a moment.'

She had no choice but to leave them together, and said to the nurse on the way out, 'May I speak to the doctor?'

'He's gone home; he needs his rest too. No doubt he'll speak to you in the morning after rounds.'

'Will my father be all right? What's wrong with him?'

'That's not for me to say, Miss. The doctor will talk to you tomorrow. In the meantime he needs a good night's sleep, and I'm just about to give him some medication.'

'He isn't going to die, is he?'

Sympathy came into her eyes then. 'Good gracious no! He's in no immediate danger, but he does need to rest. Oh, good, here comes your gentleman friend. Do try not to worry, my dear.'

Easier said than done, she thought, and said, 'He's my fiancé; we've just become engaged.'

'Congratulations.'

And that was that. Now she'd said it out loud and committed herself, her being engaged to Latham didn't sound quite so strange.

It had been raining outside, and the air smelled fresh. Light spilled prettily in wet runnels of multi-coloured water across the pavement. The tide was out and the Thames river mud sent a pungent odour of rotting vegetables and other shudderable substances into the night air.

'What did my father want to talk to you in private for?'

Latham gave a faint smile. 'I thought you'd ask. It was just business things. I told him they can be dealt with when he's a little better. You know, he'd be better off recovering at my house in Surrey. I could hire a nurse while he recuperates. We could even get married there, in the little village church, before I go to France on business. He'd like that.'

The image of her father looking so tired and grey had impressed itself on Julia. She stopped being brave and allowed tears to flood her face. 'He looked so old.'

Latham pulled her into his arms and held her close. 'He'll be all right. He'll have the best of attention, I promise. Just leave everything to me.'

'Why are you so good to me, Latham?'

'Because I love you,' he said, and handed her his handkerchief. When she'd dried her eyes he slid his hand inside his coat and brought out a ring box. 'I've been carrying this around waiting for the moment when you'd say yes. I wish the circumstances had been better. I do hope you like it.'

How could anyone not like an emerald embedded in diamonds? she thought when he slipped it on her finger. But then, how could an emerald set in diamonds feel like a manacle on her finger?

Latham took Julia back home, where he thanked the porter and slipped him a tip. 'Miss Howard has had a shock and I'll be staying a little while to keep her company,' he said.

He made some coffee, added a good dash of brandy to it and took it to where she was seated. 'Sip this slowly. It will help to relax you.' He removed her shoes and placed her feet on an ottoman. 'It's been quite a night.'

She sipped the brandy, her hands curved around the cup, and her eyes closed.

The piece of crumpled paper he must find and keep from her was near her father's chair. Latham picked it up, read the first few words then pushed it into his pocket. The content was exactly as Benjamin had described it.

'You did look after her at that party, didn't you, Latham?' Ben had said at the hospital.

'Of course I did. Take my word for it; the letter is malicious lies. Julia was with me from midnight on, and in plain sight before that.'

'Julia mustn't see it. Find it before she does, and destroy it. I think I dropped it on the floor.'

Latham smiled to himself. The wily old bird had taken advantage of the situation to get the price he'd wanted for the factory by making his daughter part of the bargain. Only Latham didn't intend to destroy the letter; he intended to find the person who'd written it. He crossed to where Julia sat and took the cup from her hands. Taking her chin in his finger and thumb he gently kissed her tender mouth. She gave a bit of a sigh and her eyes opened. Her mouth twisted into a smile. 'Do you want to make love to me, Latham?'

So it had come down to gratitude. 'Always . . . Is that what you want?'

'It's about time somebody did. I need something to stop me from thinking of my father.'

Not gratitude then, but a distraction. He'd thought he had thick skin, but she'd managed to leave a sting embedded there. 'Perhaps you'd prefer a performing seal?'

'You haven't got one, and your elves and fairies live in a Sussex copse. Did I make that sound like you were only a distraction? How horrid of me. I didn't mean to.'

'It was *horrid* of you, but I'm not too proud to dismiss your offer out of hand because of it, despite the motivation.' He reached out and touched her breast through the fabric of her tunic, caressing it with his thumb. The nubs hardened and surprise filled her eyes.

'You do realize that I'm a complete novice at this?' she said.

'Of course you are.' He wouldn't be marrying her if she wasn't, though she wouldn't be a novice after he'd finished with her, and this time she wouldn't escape. He kissed the other nipple and when she gave a little shiver he laughed and scooped her up in his arms. 'In which direction is your bedroom?'

The little carriage clock on Julia's dressing table gave a muted chime. One a.m. A faint cool breeze came through the window and her body prickled with goose-bumps. She was aware of herself as she'd never been aware before.

Latham had broken her gently, but there was a dull ache where he'd thrust away most of his energy after the foreplay. Although she didn't love him, her body had needs, and as they lay together in her bed, he had tickled her just where she needed it most. His member came erect and he kissed her. 'Tell me what you want.'

'I'm not sure . . . I don't know.'

'Then I'll have to guess.'

His guess was to eventually please himself. When he began to caress her she pushed against his hand. As she enjoyed the sensation he grew rigid against her buttocks. He was bigger than she imagined a man could be.

He turned her towards him then rolled on to his back and sat her across his thighs. 'Take me in your hands, Julia. Play with me.'

His skin was silky soft and taut, ridged along the length of him, and she felt shy. 'I can't . . . not yet.' She suddenly remembered. 'We haven't got . . . *protection*.'

'We don't need it; we'll be married next week and I want a child, anyway.' Hands scanning her waist he flipped her on to her back, threw back the covers and switched on the bedside lamp.

'Can't we do it in the dark?' she pleaded.

He gazed at her, his eyes darkly aroused. 'We could, but the only way for you to lose your shyness is not to give in to it.'

'What if I don't want to do it?'

'If you didn't want to do it you shouldn't have led me on. Come now, Julia. Stop being so bloody silly.'

His mouth sought out her most intimate of places. She was still shy about exposing her naked body and tried to wriggle away from him, but he trapped her arms above her head with one of his hands and he was insistent and a little rough when she struggled, and he got his way with her by using his strength. Eventually, she gave a long, shuddering cry and he spread her apart and drove into her. She was dragged down into a whirlpool of painful pleasure.

'I love you, I didn't mean to hurt you, and it will get better when we get used to one another,' he said afterwards. But it hadn't felt like love to Julia, more like she'd been used, even though she'd instigated it.

It was then that she saw Latham for what he was, and knew she *had* been used.

He dressed himself and when he bent to kiss her she turned her face away, and she buried her face in the pillow and cried herself to sleep.

Her father came home a changed man. He had a bad heart, the doctor said. There were nitroglycerine pills that he must carry on him at all times, one to be melted under the tongue to ease the pain if it came again. He seemed to have shrunk and there was a tiredness lingering about him as though his illness already had him beaten and he was just marking time. He moved more slowly, breathed more heavily, and Julia's heart ached for him.

Latham came with his lawyer. There were papers for him to sign.

Julia hadn't been alone with Latham since that night when his ruthless side had been revealed to her.

Even so, now the physical relationship between men and women had been revealed to her she felt more confident, and she accepted the kiss he'd pressed on her mouth.

There was plenty to do before they moved, and little time to do it in; accumulated rubbish to be thrown out, treasures put aside to be stored, and things they needed to take with them.

The day arrived.

Robert arrived to help the porter take the luggage down, and the big man wheeled her father down to the Rolls and tucked a blanket around his knees, as gently as though he was a baby. There, a nurse waited, as grey as a dove but pleasant enough and respectful towards her father. In Surrey her father would occupy the guest quarters, which were on the ground floor. They were self-contained and separated from the main house by a pair of doors with coloured glass panels.

His accommodation couldn't be faulted. There were two bedrooms with a bell to summon the nurse if need be. They were on the sunny side of the house and looked out over the garden that contained a pond with plenty of bird life coming and going.

His armchair and personal belongings were strapped on to the Morris. The Rolls would go on ahead and they'd follow in the Morris. 'We'll leave the Morris in Surrey so you have a car to get around in when you're down there.'

'Where else would I be when I'll be looking after my father?' she said.

His dark gaze had contemplated her for a few seconds before he smiled and said quite gently, 'You'll be where I expect you to be, Julia, by my side. You'll be my wife, remember?'

'Yes, of course.' She'd forgotten that small detail.

Latham would see to everything else in that calm way he had. He'd arrange for things to be put in storage, see to the lease. She wouldn't come back here again – wouldn't have to worry about a thing. He'd got what he'd wanted – her. He'd waited, and had used her father's illness to push her further than she'd really wanted to go.

'Is there anyone you'd like to invite to the wedding?' he said now.

Her glance wandered to the figurine Martin Lee-Trafford had given her.

Crossing to the mantelpiece she took it down and wrapped it in a piece of newspaper. But she didn't really want Martin there at the wedding. There had been a special moment when she'd shared his tears, and she didn't now want him to share hers. He'd know she wasn't in love with Latham.

The blue eyes that so clearly revealed his feelings would

condemn her for what she'd done. And that couldn't be undone. Not now.

She turned to find Latham watching her. 'Has anyone told Lee-Trafford about Daddy?'

'Yes . . . I asked him to keep it quiet until I get back to London. I'll address the factory staff myself.'

'Did you tell him about . . . *us*.'

'I didn't consider it to be any of Lee-Trafford's business. Is he important to you?'

'I hadn't had time to get to know him very well, but he would have made a good friend. I liked him and we got on well.'

'Did you love him? I can see why you would, since he has the ironic air of a romantic hero about him.'

She felt annoyance. 'That's a rather cynical remark to make about someone you hardly know.'

'Yes, I suppose it is. I wouldn't mind, you know. I'd expect you to have romantic feelings towards a man at your age.'

'If I had romantic feelings towards Martin I certainly wouldn't have made them obvious. It would have embarrassed him no end.'

'He would have kept you at arm's length I expect.' Latham pounced then. 'He wouldn't have been much good to you as a man, anyway. The war saw to that, I'm given to understand.'

Julia experienced a jolt of shock, and pity for Martin. No wonder he'd let his fiancée go. All the same, on behalf of Martin she felt angry that Latham would betray him by telling her.

'Surely you could have afforded Martin some personal dignity by keeping that to yourself,' she said, and she turned away from him.

He turned her back. 'You *do* care for him, don't you?'

'He's the only person I know who has integrity.'

'Well, at least I don't have to worry that you might stray in that direction now. Shall I invite him to the wedding?'

She felt like slapping him. 'No . . . There's nobody I wish to share my wedding day with . . . and to be honest, that includes you at the moment. You're the most ruthless man I've ever met.'

He laughed at her small flare of temper. 'I wondered when the gloves were going to come off. You can't expect to use people and not pay something in return. Your father was on the verge of bankruptcy. You and he would have lost everything, including the shirt on his back and the roof over your heads. I've baled him out, and bought you as part of the package.'

'Thank you for being kind to my father, at least,' she said to him, even while knowing it was a means to an end and she'd pay a heavy price for it with the loss of her freedom.

'It wasn't kindness; it was business. Now, come here. Let's kiss and make up so you'll know what you're made of.'

Now she shook her head and she turned away from his kiss, feeling nothing for him but revulsion by his attempt at possession. And Latham, perfectly aware of her reluctance, threw her belongings on to the couch and bore her down to the floor.

There a silent skirmish took place, with him using his knowledge of her to make her feel what she didn't want to feel, and her fists thumping at him at first, then her fingers digging into him because she couldn't stop herself from wanting what he was doing to her.

Finished with his assault on her, Latham rose and buttoned his trousers. He held out his hand to her. 'Get up, it's time to go.'

She did as she was told, ignoring his hand, and stepping into the illusive protection of the underwear he'd pulled from her and abandoned. He had ripped a length of lace from one of the legs. She straightened her skirt and took her handbag from him.

'You have long, shapely legs,' he said, and grinned.

He closed the door behind them and they went down to where the Morris waited. She said goodbye to the porter as though nothing had happened.

She didn't speak a word to Latham, not even when she remembered she'd left Lee-Trafford's Christmas gift to her lying on the sofa.

Damn Latham! she thought, and hoped the removalists would find it and pack it safely.

Three days later she and Latham were wed in the small village church. Julia dressed in a creamy silk gown with lace-trimmed georgette panels. She wore a cream hat with pale-pink roses and carried a floral spray. Latham and Robert were in formal grey suits with top hats – they looked almost like brothers. Apart from her father, who was similarly garbed for his duty of walking her down the short aisle to the altar, his nurse and Mrs Finnigan were the only people she knew. The fact that several strangers were in attendance to celebrate Latham's marriage to her, came as a surprise. They were business friends of Latham's, she supposed.

She wished she'd paid a little more attention to her appearance. But no, she hadn't had to, for she couldn't have looked more perfect according to Latham, who had provided this wedding finery for her. Not only was Latham's taste impeccable, his organizational skills were too.

She wished now that she'd invited some of her old friends, and Martin Lee-Trafford. It seemed wrong now, not inviting him and she felt a sick panic rise inside her as she made her responses. She shouldn't be doing this. She should turn and run, find somewhere safe to hide.

'Who gives this woman . . . ?'

'I do.' Her father was smiling at her, reassuring her with love in his eyes and a proud smile on his face. He needed to know she was safe. The smile defeated her, grounded her so her feet were too leaden to move, let alone run.

Latham looked into her eyes when he slid the ring on her finger, and there was amusement in them when he whispered, 'There you are, Mrs Miller, all nice and legal now. Try and look a bit happier.'

She smiled at him then. 'Believe it or not, Latham, I am happy.' But he wouldn't know that it was because he was going to France in two days, and would be gone for the entire fortnight.

They posed on the porch steps for a photographer and she offered the man she'd married her best smile. When they went home the conservatory had been transformed. A buffet had been set out and there was champagne. Latham introduced her as his wife and made an amusing speech. There were congratulations all round. Even the dogs wore bows in their collars. Gifts of silver and crystal had been set out. *Everything that glisters . . .*

Julia was pleased to be introduced to everyone, especially those from the immediate area, who she was duty bound to entertain from time to time. She had a naturally gregarious nature, made even more so by two glasses of champagne. By the time she'd got around to everyone she'd made several friends. As none of Irene's family had turned up for the event, she wondered if they'd been invited.

Finding her father missing she went in search of him.

'It's been a long day for him,' the nurse whispered. 'He's taking a rest.'

Julia went back to her husband's side, picking up a third glass of champagne on the way. He looked down at her as if surprised to see her there, and she giggled.

He took the full glass from her and handed it to a maid. 'Bring Mrs Miller a glass of lemonade, would you.' Threading her arm through his he kissed her ear and whispered, 'I love you, Mrs Miller.'

She wished she could say the same to him – she really did.

Her father died in his sleep the day after Latham arrived back home from France. Julia was almost inconsolable with grief. Latham made the arrangements.

'I reserved a place for him to be buried next to your mother. He expressed a wish . . . well, I thought it would please you,' he said.

'Thank you, Latham, that was thoughtful of you.' It was also cold-blooded, and she wondered if her father had known that Latham had planned his funeral in advance.

'You don't look too happy about it?'

'It's not exactly a happy occasion. May I ask you something . . . Have you planned my funeral in advance?'

'Now you're being childish, but I know you're grieving and upset so will ignore it. I've called the undertaker and he's on his way down for the body. We can go through the arrangements with him together if you like. I'm doing this because I don't want the arrangements to be a burden you must bear alone.'

Julia felt guilty as well as numb, and she agreed to everything Latham suggested; after all, he was paying for it.

'He looks peaceful,' she said when it was time to say goodbye to her father, who was lying on his bed still dressed in his nightwear.

'Yes . . . he does.'

She touched Latham's black tie with a fingertip. 'How very odd. I've got nothing black in my wardrobe, while you seem to always be prepared for every eventuality.'

'Don't worry about it. I'll get something suitable sent down.'

She kissed her father's cheek, her lips warm and alive against his cold, unmoving face. 'Goodbye, my darling man; give Mummy my love.'

Her father was placed in the plain casket by the reverential undertakers, and carried out to the hearse, his best suit of clothes, clean shirt and newly polished shoes wrapped in tissue paper and placed carefully on top. Her father would not be allowed to go into the hereafter looking shabby.

There was a faint smell of tobacco smoke lingering about the hearse, and she had visions of the two men loosening their black ties and lighting up their gaspers as soon at they got out of sight of the house. She tried not to smile at the thought.

A black dress, a coat with fur-trimmed hem and a wide-brimmed hat with a draped hatband appeared in her wardrobe two days later. The clothing was a perfect fit. Julia felt pale inside it, as if the black had drained her of colour.

Latham pinned the brooch he'd given her to her lapel. 'Diamonds always look perfect against black; they relieve the severity of it. '

'You told me they were crystals.'

'Did I? I must have lied. It doesn't seem an appropriate time, but I brought you some matching earrings from Cartier while I was in France. I'd like you to wear them.'

He stood behind her, clipping them to her ears, stars dangling from the curve of a crescent moon. His eyes met hers in the mirror, he smiled and one hand slid under her chin. As he pulled back her head and kissed her throat, she thought: *Not now, Latham . . . please, not now! I don't want to remember the day of my father's funeral as one of being forced into having relations with you.*

But even Latham wasn't *that* insensitive. To her relief he moved away, but he picked up her pot of rouge and gently dusted her cheeks with the puff to give them some colour.

'We'll be staying two weeks in London. I think that will be enough time in which to explain the legalities of the financial situation, and get your signature on certain papers.'

'I haven't packed anything.'

'Everything you need is right there in your wardrobe.'

So she had a London wardrobe as well.

She'd never been to his London house. *Their* London house, she corrected herself, though it was more his because she'd never lived there, while Latham spent most of his time there, and his weekends in Surrey.

Her father had always liked May because it was the month he and her mother had married. When she and Latham left the Kent house, the day had a polished glow to it. The air was a faintly humid caress against her cheek, and perfumed with hawthorn blossom. Arum lilies grew in the damp places. Campion, hyacinth and buttercups displayed their wilder beauty amongst the grasses, and crab-apple blossomed in hedgerows.

The funeral was well attended, for her father had made plenty of friends and acquaintances during his lifetime. She'd asked for red and white roses for his casket, and Latham had somehow provided them. She intended to plant a red rose bush on her father's grave, and a white one on her mother's now they were together.

As the reverend droned on Julia glanced up and her eyes met those of Martin. The impact in her stomach was like being hit by a train. Her breath exited her body in a great rush, leaving her feeling disconnected from anyone but him. For one long moment their eyes clung, and she saw in his, not the disdain she'd expected, but a kind of sadness.

I love Martin, she thought with a sudden shock and experienced a sense of wonder.

Beside her, Latham gently cleared his throat.

A little later she thought: how odd to come back to a house she'd never been in before, one that was her home. It was not too large, and not too far from where she'd lived in Earls Court. Latham was discreet. Everything about him spoke of money, but he wore his wealth without ostentation. She was his wife, and she didn't know where the bathroom was. A man couldn't be more discreet than that.

One of the older maids took her coat and hat and directed her. 'I'm sorry about your loss, Mrs Miller. Such a sad day for us to meet.'

So the woman knew who she was. 'Thank you, Mrs . . . ?'

'James . . . Mary James. I'm the housekeeper here.'

'Thank you, Mrs James; which is my bedroom?'

'Follow me, Mrs Miller. I'll show you.'

Her room was at the front overlooking the street. Standing open, an adjoining door led to Latham's room. On the mantelpiece stood a silver-framed photograph of them on their wedding day. That must have been how the housekeeper had recognized her.

Doing what she had to do she tidied her hair with an initialled silver-backed brush she'd never seen before, on a dressing table she'd never seen before either. The wardrobe was full of clothing she'd never seen before. The drawers held neatly folded underwear of every description. She transferred the brooch from her coat to her dress.

At the bottom of the stairs Latham stood in wait for her. 'You look pale, Julia; are you all right?'

'I'm a little tired.'

'People won't stay long, my dear, then we'll be alone.'

There were sandwiches and fruitcake, tea and sherry set out on a buffet. A maid stood in attendance.

'Mrs Miller, may I express my condolences?'

It was Martin, his voice a caress against her ear.

'I must go and talk to Hollingsworth for a moment before he leaves. I'll leave you in Lee-Trafford's capable hands for a minute or two.' Kissing her cheek, Latham was gone.

Julia turned, taking his hands in hers and trying not to make her smile too wide at the sight of him, considering the occasion. 'Martin . . . thank you . . . I'm going to miss my father dreadfully, you know. How are you? It seems ages . . .'

His eyes had never been bluer to her, his mouth never so soft. Her hands moulded into his as though they'd been designed to fit together.

'Oh, Martin . . . When I saw you today . . .'

'I know . . . Don't say it . . . It's been too long.'

She let out a shaky breath. 'How are the kittens?'

'You know what felines are like . . . they're damned nuisances, but they're good company.' His thumb brushed against her palm. 'Are you happy, Julia?'

'Latham is good to me.'

'That's not what I asked.'

'I know, but you have my answer.'

The air quivered like a bowstring with everything that needed to be said, but it remained unspoken between them. The few inches separating them might just as well have been a mile.

'You take my breath away,' he murmured, almost to himself.

He'd been with her long enough to satisfy convention and he released her hands. 'May I fetch you some refreshment, Mrs Miller . . . some tea, perhaps?'

She turned her head slightly to find Latham's attention focused on them, and smiled at him before she said, 'Thank you, Mr Lee-Trafford, that would be kind of you.'

Even though Latham didn't regard Martin as a threat, he made his possession of her perfectly clear when he approached them. 'You look tired, my dear. It's about time you went upstairs and rested. I'll send the maid up with your tea.'

So, she was not to have friends either, unless he'd hand-picked them. She wasn't going to miss a second spent in the same room as Martin. She might just have something to say about that, she thought.

'I'm perfectly all right, Latham. People are here to pay respects to my father and I need to be here for them. Please stop fussing.'

His eyes narrowed a fraction. For a moment Julia thought he might insist, in which case she'd have the choice of doing as she was told or creating a scene. He made no reaction, just gazed at Martin and said, 'We must talk, Lee-Trafford. Now Mr Howard is no longer with us I intend to convert the factory to domestic ware.'

'But you promised my father—'

'Any agreement I had with your father was binding only while he lived, my dear. Please don't comment on something you know nothing about.' He beckoned to the housekeeper. 'Fetch Mrs Miller some tea please, and make sure she has a bite to eat.' He placed his hand on Martin's back to guide him away. 'Lee-Trafford?'

Martin nodded to her, sympathy in his eyes. 'Mrs Miller, it was nice to see you again despite the sad circumstances. Your father was a fine man.'

A hand touched her arm as she watched them walk away. It was a woman Julia had met before at her wedding to Latham. She was the wife of a politician in opposition to the government. Her mind scrambled for a name. 'Mrs Oliver, I'm so pleased you came.'

'I'm sorry we had to meet again on such a sad occasion. I didn't know your father well but he struck me as being a nice gentleman.'

'Yes . . . he was a nice gentleman.'

Now her father was where he'd always wanted to be. But he'd done his duty first. He'd brought her up with love, made sure she received a good education and married her off to a successful man before joining her mother in eternity.

Attacked by a sudden feeling of loneliness, she thought: What more could a woman need or desire?

Her glance fell on Martin Lee-Trafford.

Ten

They stayed in London for two weeks. Despite her grief over her father's death Julia found she was expected to entertain on several occasions.

They joined a party for the theatre on the second week. Among the many gowns inside her town wardrobe was a black-beaded gown with a velvet cape.

Latham wound a long string of flawless pearls with a pear-shaped diamond drop around her neck, and he clipped pearl drops to her ears, saying, 'I must hire a maid to look after you.'

She applied her lipstick, a startling red that made her face look pale. Latham had bought it. She stared at her image. She looked like a living parody of the doll her father had invented. Not Rosie, the wholesome child in her sailor tunic – or the teenager with her ringlets and bows. Not Rosie, the perpetual virgin with the simpering smile, who knew nothing about herself, let alone life. Her glance slid to Latham then skittered away again. She was Rosie, the battered bride in a black gown, a woman whose eyes had lost their innocence.

The paper doll looking back at her through disappointed green eyes from the mirror was in mourning for the man who'd invented her. She was a treasured possession handed over from one man to another for safekeeping – only she was learning that Latham was unpredictable, and she wasn't always safe. She was wary of him, but she couldn't live her life in fear, and her eyes lifted to his. 'I'm quite capable of looking after my own appearance, Latham.'

His eyes met the reflection of hers in the mirror. 'I want you to be perfect in every way, Julia. You're elegant and well mannered. Men envy me and women are jealous of your looks and your style.'

'It's not my style; it's yours. I can't live up to such perfection, and I don't give a damn about other people's jealousies.'

'You can be perfect, and you will be. These people we mix with, you're every bit as good as them . . . better.'

'I never imagined I was any different. It's you who seems to feel inferior, Latham.'

He reached out for her, and even though she'd half expected it, she jumped.

'Latham, please don't. I'm dressed ready to go out.'

'I know,' he said, and he pushed her down on the bed and ripped the gown down the middle. Beads scattered everywhere and he used his thumb to smear streaks of red lipstick across her face. Pulling her upright his arms came round her from behind and he turned her to face the mirror. She looked like a clown.

His thumbs caressed her bared breasts and she shivered.

Julia wore a dark-blue silk gown with sleeves to the theatre. It had sleeves to hide her bruises. She smiled until her jaw ached, when really she felt like crying. She could smell Latham's possession on her as she sat next to him, her mind in a ferment of hatred.

On the other nights of their stay in London he went out by himself. A couple of times he returned in the early hours of the morning with the faint scent of perfume about him. It was an exquisite fragrance, one she'd smelled before, in the guest room she'd used on New Year's Eve.

Surely Latham didn't wear perfume, though she'd heard that some men did. It was an interesting development, but no – it was Irene's perfume. He'd been seeing her. Either way, Julia found she didn't care all that much.

They went back to Surrey together in the Rolls. Julia liked Latham better there. He was more relaxed.

There were answers to the condolence letters to write – even the ones from Charles and Irene Curruthers. It was unexpected hearing from them after all this time. She missed seeing Irene, who'd always had an air of craziness that had made Julia laugh. Julia didn't laugh much now, and she had an odd thought that marrying Latham might have aged her – suddenly turned her into a forty-year-old matron.

The dogs greeted her with the same enthusiasm they offered everyone, but they obeyed Latham. When he made a fuss of them they responded with delight.

She went to visit her father's quarters. Julia had expected it to be exactly the same as she'd left it, but the bed by the window, photographs of her mother and herself on the mantelpiece, the little pieces of memorabilia special to him were all gone. His favourite chair was gone too. The place had been wiped clean of her father's presence and the guest quarters were as neat and comfortable as a hotel. The bed and mattress that had supported the weight of her father's laboured last breaths had been discarded and replaced with a new one. Even the nurse had departed. It was as if nurse and patient had never existed.

She went to see Latham in his study. He was seated behind a blond-wood desk, reading a letter. He turned the paper against the blotting paper, looked up at her and smiled. 'Julia, I must teach you to knock at doors. What can I do for you?'

'I wondered where my father's things had gone?'

'I left instructions for them to be stored in the attic while we were away; I didn't think you'd be up to doing it yourself. If there's anything you particularly want Mrs Finnigan will find it for you.'

'Thank you.'

He rose and held a chair out for her. 'Stay and talk to me, Julia?'

'About what?'

'Anything.'

She shrugged, knowing she had nothing much to say. She searched her mind. 'I'm bored, Latham. Would it disturb you if I learned to type?'

'Probably. Why do you want to learn to type?'

'It might come in useful one day.'

'And it might not.'

'I wouldn't practise it when you were here, only when you're in London.'

'I can understand why you're bored. You must please yourself about the hobbies you adopt when I'm away. I'm much too busy to get bored myself.'

She'd not given his working life much thought. He was wealthy, yes, but he had to earn that wealth. Suddenly she was curious. 'What do you actually do for a living? Tell me about it.'

He gave a faint smile. 'It's nothing that would be of interest to you. I have five factories, including the one I've just bought. During the war my factories mostly produced weapon parts. Now I'm making domestic appliances.'

'China and stuff?'

'No, I don't run a pottery. Three of them produce gas appliances such as cookers and water heaters. There's a big demand for such items now. One produces a range of goods such as baking tins, copper pans, jelly moulds, biscuit tins, scales, etcetera.'

'And the factory you bought from my father? What domestic goods will you make there?'

'Army and navy supplies.'

'I thought I heard you tell Mr Lee-Trafford it would be domestic ware.'

He laughed. 'Servicemen don't use their fingers as spoons and forks unless they have no choice. It's cutlery, canteens, tin plates and other goods. I also need storage space and the Howard factory is central and on the river. Your father made me pay through the nose for it, you know.'

'Will you keep his former staff on?'

'I see no reason to lay good men off if they're needed and can do the work. I'll consult with Lee-Trafford on that. He's got a good head on his shoulders.'

Now it was her turn to smile. 'Yes . . . he has. My father was very attached to his workers.'

'I know, but that's what got him into such a hole. Lee-Trafford has been whittling down the staff by natural attrition.'

'What does that mean?'

'That when they leave they're not being replaced. Once your father's debts are cleared what's left will go to you. By the way, there has been a good offer for your flat, so the mortgage will be finalized with some left over.'

'Will it be much?'

'The amount will be enough to help clear his other debts. His affairs are complicated. The moneylenders were irresponsible in furnishing large loans on a failing business. Unfortunately, people of your father's era operated on the old school tie and a handshake principle, and unsubstantiated small debts keep coming out of the woodwork. Right now I'm negotiating with his bank on the overdraft interest. I think they'll come to understand that it's better to forgo some of the accumulated interest than have the debt left on their books as a monument to their bungling.'

'I'm sorry you have so much of my father's business to clear up as well as doing your own.'

His head cocked to one side and he gave a soft chuckle. 'I enjoy the cut and thrust of business and I'm pretty certain I can save some of your father's estate for you and leave his reputation intact while I'm doing it.'

At that moment she felt closer to him than at any time during their short marriage. 'Thank you. My father's reputation means a lot to me, as it did to him.'

'I know. If you'll allow me to invest any monies left over, it will amount to a tidy sum in the years to come.'

She nodded.

'I'm going to take the dogs for a walk; would you like to come with me?'

'Not today, Latham; I feel a bit off colour.'

His expression questioned her. 'Time of month?'

When she nodded he looked disappointed.

'Goodness, we've only been married a few weeks,' she said, making light of the moment as best she could. Julia would have loved to be able to tell him she was expecting a child – he might stay away from her then.

Latham was off walking with the dogs one day, when Irene was announced.

'Please show Miss Curruthers into the sitting room, Mrs Finnigan. I'll join her there shortly.'

Julia went upstairs and combed her hair. She didn't really want to be pleasant to Irene, who had snubbed her since the day of the apology, but she supposed she must.

Irene looked fabulous in a dark-blue crepe-de-chine frock and flat walking shoes. Her hair was a dark cap with perfect scimitar curves pointed against each cheek. She was as thin as a reed. Her smile was wide, but there was a hollowness to her eyes when she said, 'Darling Julia, marriage to Latham obviously suits you.'

It didn't suit her at all! Julia took a moment to remember that as much as Irene could love anyone, she had loved Latham, and she felt a twinge of remorse. 'Irene, how lovely to see you again, to what do I owe the pleasure?'

'Liar to the first . . . curiosity mostly to the second.'

Julia laughed; she couldn't help herself. 'You haven't changed, have you?'

'Not in the least.'

'Would you like some coffee?'

'Of course I would. I'm absolutely parched after that walk. I've never liked the country much, except when we have a party, then its perfect since the neighbours are too far away to complain about the noise.' She eyed Julia up and down. 'Oh, for crying out loud, come here and give me a hug . . . Hating each other is stupid, especially because of a man.'

Irene was wearing the same perfume that Julia had smelled on Latham in London. 'I don't hate you, Irene . . . actually, I haven't given you much thought.'

Irene's eyes flickered. 'When you take the gloves off you really take them off, don't you? Do stop being such a bitch, Julia, though I suppose I deserve it.'

Julia rang the bell and ordered some refreshment before asking, 'Why are you really here?'

'I wanted to say how sorry I was about your father.'

'You sent me a card.'

'I know I did. I only met him twice but he was a nice old duffer . . . decent, you know. Oh hell, Julia, I used him as an excuse to come over and visit you. Besides wanting to commiserate with you, because I know you adored your father, I wanted to apologize for what nearly happened at New Year.'

'You did apologize.'

'Latham insisted so it was under protest then. Now I really do feel guilty about it, and I'd like us to put it behind us and remain friends.'

Astonished, Julia stared at her, then she shrugged. They were bound to run into each other socially, and it would be silly to ignore each other. 'Of course we can still be friends. I never blamed you, you know.'

'No, you wouldn't have . . . You're so noble that sometimes I could kill you. The hug, please? I warn you, there's only so far I'm going to crawl before I give you a good slap or puke all over your carpet. I've just about reached that limit.'

Julia laughed as they gently hugged and kissed the air at the side of each other's cheeks. She doubted if she'd ever trust Irene again, even though she'd missed her company. 'Exquisite perfume,' she said.

'Chanel number five. It was a gift . . . I take it you finally lost your virginity, and to Latham. Was the experience as good as you expected?'

'Better.'

Irene looked her straight in the eye and answered the lie with one of her own. 'I'm so glad.'

Fifteen minutes later Julia heard the distant bark of the dogs. Latham was on his way home. This could prove to be interesting.

He came into the sitting room just as they'd finished their second cup of coffee, a bunch of bluebells in a small vase. 'Look what I found in the woods. I picked you a bunch and put them in water . . . and I found a four-leafed clover.'

Julia couldn't resist it. 'How sweet of you, Latham,' and she turned her face up to be kissed. The touch of surprise in his eyes at her wifely gesture was gratifying.

It didn't fool Irene. 'How touching . . . Latham Miller, with a jam jar full of bluebells and a kiss for his lady love. Good Lord, Latham, your background is showing,' she drawled from her position in the other chair.

His eyes flew open in shock, then shuttered down. It was almost an anti-climax as he turned towards her, his voice flat: 'Irene . . . What are you doing here?'

'Visiting your wife, of course . . . You can't keep her in seclusion, you know, and you are by far the most interesting people in the village; everybody says so.'

'Why?' Latham said.

'You seem so ill-matched.'

'We're perfectly matched. I was asking: Why are you here?'

'I'm delivering an invitation from the parents to come to an informal lunch on Saturday.'

'I'll check my diary.'

'Several people will be there who might be useful to you, and Charles of course. I thought we might make up a four for tennis.'

'Charles is coming down?'

'He's been sent down for the rest of the term. Father is furious, of course, so Charles has been summoned and will get a fearful wigging. Lord . . . I've never seen Daddy so incensed.'

'What did Charles do this time?'

'Apparently he buzzed the chapel in his plane with Rupert standing on one wing and Adam standing on the other . . . both of them debagged.' She gave a gurgle of laughter. 'They must have frozen their arses off.'

Latham laughed and even Julia giggled at the picture Irene presented.

'Pater has threatened to ground Charles' plane. It's terribly inconvenient, since we had plans to go over to the continent next month. I suggested to Charles that he lands on your meadow. You won't mind, will you? It won't be the first time, and they'll think he travelled down on the train.'

'It's too late if I do mind.'

'Don't be such a meanie, darling.' She stood, smoothing down the skirt of her dress. 'Julia, you look marvellous. Marriage must agree with you. No, don't get up, dear. Latham can see me out . . . Let's go up to the meadow and wait for Charles, shall we, Latham? He won't be long. Do put those flowers down on the table. You look slightly ridiculous holding them, just like a lovesick schoolboy. How terribly boring of you.'

They went out together, Latham closing the door behind him. Julia wished he'd left the bluebells behind in the woods because they were already beginning to wilt and would be dead by nightfall. And there was the four-leafed clover. Perhaps it would bring them luck – perhaps she would learn to love Latham. She took it upstairs and placed it between the pages of a book to dry.

The sun came out from behind a cloud and she saw her husband's shadow, and that of Irene. The two merged together for a long moment, then they moved apart as the couple strolled away from the house, Irene chatting and laughing, the gap between them left deliberately wide in case the truth of the relationship was detectable by closeness.

Irene had separated her from Latham, making her prior claim on him perfectly clear with a gesture so manipulative it took Julia's breath away. She didn't care if they were lovers, but Irene had lied to her. She hadn't come to visit her, she'd come to see Latham. She wouldn't sit meekly by and be made to feel like an interloper in her own home.

She'd discarded hard black mourning for casual wear at home.

Pulling a pale-green cardigan over her charcoal slacks she ran downstairs and caught the pair up. The gap between them was big enough to slide into, so she claimed it, saying, 'I do wish you'd both waited for me. I've never seen an aeroplane up close.'

Latham slid his arm around her and pulled her against him. She felt like provoking Irene. This time her arm went round him. He looked down at her, smiled and kissed her cheek.

A breath hissed between Irene's teeth and she shrugged. 'You should have said you were coming with us.'

'Why . . . do I need your permission?'

'Enough, Julia,' Latham said, and Irene raised an eyebrow and offered her a smug little smile.

Julia heard the plane before she saw it. The three of them stood together and waved. The wings waggled as it circled the house and grounds then it came in to land, skimming the hedges and touching down to bump over the tussocks. It trundled down a slope out of sight of the house, and the sound of the engine died away.

Charles had a smile on his face as they drew near to the plane. Looking every inch the handsome fly-boy hero, he stripped off his blazing red scarf, leather helmet and jacket and threw them into the plane before he swung down to the ground. The breeze ruffled sunlight through his hair.

'Hello, Sis – and to you as well, Latham.' He shook Latham's hand, then his glance came her way and his smile became all charm with just a hint of mischief. 'Why if it isn't the delectable Julia Miller. What a corker you are. If you feel like eloping with me just say, and we'll fly off into the sun together.'

'And like Icarus your wings will melt and you'll crash into the sea.'

For some reason a chill ran through Julia at Latham's words.

'What trouble are you in now?' Latham said.

Charles' smile faded. 'I imagine Irene has told you. I got a blistering lecture from my tutor. I expected him to gate me, but he sent me down for the rest of term, pending consideration of making the arrangement permanent. I'm dreading seeing my father, who will probably stomp all over me like a herd of rampaging buffalo. It was just a prank!' Another smile crept across his face, wider this time. 'It was a damned good one actually. I say, Latham, you know my tutor quite well; could you convince him that I won't do it again? In fact, I'll knuckle down and act like a parson for the rest of the year, and make him proud of me.'

'Is that a promise, Charles?'

'Cross my heart and hope to die,' and he placed his hand against his chest and looked so sincerely holy that Julia giggled. Charles sent her a gratified look. 'I think my tutor was more worried about the spire being left intact than seeing Rupert and Adam with their shirt tails blowing in the wind.'

'I'll get on the telephone and see what I can do.'

The breeze carried the smell of hot oil to Julia. 'It must be exciting to fly an aeroplane,' she said. 'What does the ground look like from up high?'

An indulgent smile came her way from Latham. 'Perhaps Charles will offer to show you, after all he can't get up to anything improper in an aeroplane.'

'I wouldn't put it past him,' Irene murmured.

Charles was all enthusiasm. 'I'll say. Everything looks small; the buildings look like dolls' houses and the people like fleas. I'll take you up in her tomorrow if you like, that's if pater hasn't thrown me into the dungeons. You won't mind that, will you, Latham?'

'I daresay she'll enjoy it. Come about eleven, Charles; I might have some news to butter your father up with by then. You and Irene can join us for lunch afterwards.'

'Will do. I'd better get off home now. If I'm late he'll work himself up into a bigger ferment. As much as I dislike the miserable old codger, I don't want to be the cause of him having a seizure, especially since I'm his heir. I'm not responsible enough to take over the ancestral pile yet.'

The flight the next morning turned out to be more exciting than Julia had thought it would be. She couldn't imagine how anyone would have the courage to stand on the wings and hold on to the struts.

Despite the wild ride in Charles' motorcycle and sidecar, Charles flew the aeroplane with a steady hand, taking her in a wide circle.

As soon as Julia felt secure she began to enjoy the sight of the countryside below. The buildings did resemble dolls' houses and the fields seemed stitched together by the hedges to form a patchwork quilt. They flew out over Brighton and the channel, where he took the plane down to skim just above the water. The shadow of the aircraft formed a dark cross on the water. People in a boat waved at them.

Ten minutes later they swept rapidly upwards, so the breath left her body with the excitement of it. Heading back over land they followed a car along a road. Charles banked the plane a little and they turned and began to follow a train, the funnel puffing out a plume of smoke that disappeared into the air.

The scene reminded her of Martin's train set, and she wondered if he'd set it up yet. There was a great longing inside her to see him again, though she knew they could never be anything but friends now.

Perhaps Latham would take her back to London with him if she asked.

They gradually lost height, a pulse beating in Julia's throat as they neared the ground and began to leapfrog over the hedges, frightening a flock of sheep who raced in all directions. But she needn't have worried. Charles had a wonderful sense of timing. There was hardly a bump as the wheels touched the ground. They came to a halt, the propellers barely stirring the air until they gave a final cough and became still. They had been in the air for an hour.

Once again there was the smell of hot oil in her nostrils.

When Charles helped her down she beamed him a smile. 'Thank you so much, Charles. That was the most exciting thing I've ever done. I'll never forget it.'

'It's the least I can do, kitten, since Latham has saved my bacon again.'

As they neared the house Latham appeared. His face was slightly flushed and she could smell Irene's perfume on him.

Julia could hardly contain the flare of anger she felt – not at him for cheating on her, but because he chose to insult her by doing it in the home they shared.

When the Currutherses had departed she knew she was braving Latham's own anger by bringing the subject up, but she did anyway, saying: 'You're making a fool of me, Latham. Please conduct your affair with Irene in a place where I don't have to be an onlooker, and where the servants won't gossip.'

Julia could feel the tension growing in her as he stared at her, and she knew full well that he'd strike, and quickly if the mood took him.

She stared defiantly back at him, but jumped when he suddenly leaned forward and said, 'Are you jealous, my Julia?'

She wanted to kick him. 'She's welcome to you.'

He laughed at that. 'I can have her anytime, anywhere. Irene's like me. She's a slut.'

'Then why didn't you marry her?'

'That is why. Besides . . . I love you. You know that. The rest is nothing to me.'

She felt like kicking him. 'Well, I don't love you. I only married you because my father wanted me to. If he knew how you were going to treat me he wouldn't have been so keen.'

He scooped her into his arms and against his chest. 'How do I treat you, my darling? Tell me!'

She tried to struggle out of the embrace but he was too strong. 'You rip my clothes and you hit me. I want a divorce. You do realize you're giving me grounds.'

'Try and prove it in a court of law.' He tipped up her face and gazed into her eyes. 'Come, my dear, you're being a little drastic, since we've only been married for a short time. I provide your clothes, and I only rip the ones you look like a trollop in. I married you because I love you, and I want children with you. No more of this nonsense now. Let me know when you're able to resume our relationship.' When he tenderly kissed her Julia began to hate him all over again.

Lunch with the Curruthers family was hardly lively; the talk was mostly political. Lady Curruthers was aloof, and didn't bother to be pleasant. She wore a disapproving expression reserved especially for Irene's friends, if Irene was to be believed.

However, Irene was wicked with her wit, and Charles all charm.

Julia had found a white tennis outfit in her wardrobe. The tennis game had obviously been taken into Latham's estimation of what she might need for living in the country when he'd bought her wardrobe. He'd crowed with success when they had beaten Irene and Charles at tennis, and had thrown his arm around her and kissed her cheek.

Winning seemed important to Latham, even a silly tennis match. 'I didn't know you could play tennis,' he said.

'I was the school champion for two years in a row.'

'I must set up a tennis court for you to practise on.'

It was not as though a school tennis match was Wimbledon. And she'd laughed and said, 'There's really no need, Latham. I don't like the game that much.'

'I will, anyway.'

That same evening he told her he was going to France again. He'd be away for a month. He didn't offer to take her with him, but said he'd telephone her every night. A week later he was gone, leaving her light-hearted, but bruised.

Irene was gone too.

Eleven

Summer came with a vengeance two weeks later. Everything was bursting at the seams. The air was languid and filled with the fragrance of roses and the buzz of bees.

Although Julia was still officially in mourning she decided to take the train up to London. 'If my husband calls tell him I've gone to London to arrange for some rose bushes to be planted on my parents' graves, and to get my hair cut.'

'Certainly, Mrs Miller. Will you be staying at the London House? If so I'll ring them and tell them you're on your way.'

'No, I'm sure that's my husband's business address.' She would go there only as a last resort.

Agnes Finnigan shifted from one foot to the other. 'Mrs Miller, I wanted to let you know that I'm going to look for a new position.'

'Oh, Agnes, I'll be so sorry to lose you. May I ask why, when you've been working here for several years? Is it me?'

She drew in a deep breath. 'Oh, no . . . you're the nicest person I could ever have for an employer. It's just—'

'Go on.'

'It's personal, you see. I'm going to be truthful . . . Sometimes I hear you cry out and I see your bruises. Although Mr Miller is a good employer for most of the time, and I have the greatest respect for him, I can't bear to think that he's treating you badly.' Her face went bright red and she folded her arms on her chest. 'There . . . I've said it, and I daresay you won't want me to stay on now, because what you do in private isn't any of my business.'

Tears pricked Julia's eyes. To say that she was mortified was an understatement. 'That's true, of course. But you're wrong about me not wanting you to stay on. I'd miss you if you left, and I *would* like you to reconsider your decision, especially since jobs for women are hard to come by. As for the other business, my husband is a little forceful by nature, but doesn't really hurt me. I bruise easily and I'd rather you closed your ears and mind to it.'

'If you say so, Mrs Miller.'

'Mr Miller has offered to hire another maid, one to look after my clothes and help out generally. She'll be able to relieve you of some of the work. And I'll see if I can secure a raise in your salary. Please stay, Agnes. The time may come when I need a friend.'

Mrs Finnigan said staunchly, 'I'll stay, but only because you want me to, and for no other reason. As for a maid, Ellen from the hall is looking for another position.'

Julia smiled. 'I know Ellen, and yes, I'm sure she would be suitable. When my husband gets back from France I'll tell him about her and he'll probably make arrangements for an interview. It will be up to him if she's hired or not.'

Latham wouldn't like her going to London without his permission, but Julia didn't care. She booked herself into a small hotel called *Clements* before going to visit the cemetery. Once there, she discovered that the roses had already been planted and were covered in tight buds.

There was an air of frustration inside her, because Latham, with his usual efficiency, had already arranged something she'd wanted to do herself. She hated the fact that he hadn't bothered to tell her.

She'd managed to get a hairdresser's appointment for later in the afternoon, then rang Irene's house. A woman answered, a maid, she thought. 'Miss Curruthers is in *Monte Carlo*, and is unavailable. Who shall I say called?'

About to blurt out her name, she remembered that Latham was in France as well. She imagined the pair of them were together. 'Oh, it doesn't matter, I'll call Irene when she gets back next week.'

'That will be in ten days' time,' the woman said before she hung up.

Julia had her hair trimmed, washed and styled, and wondered what to do next. She bought herself a dress. It was low waisted with capped sleeves, and was made of a pretty pale-green silk. Red poppies grew around the hem. Sitting in a hotel room with only herself for company wasn't very enticing, neither was going to the theatre. She doubted if she'd get tickets on a Saturday, anyway.

Martin came into her mind and she smiled as she checked her

watch and said out loud, 'I'll go and visit the cats . . . and I'll call in on the market on the way there, and I'll cook Martin his dinner when I get there.'

About to leave, she decided to change into her new dress. She didn't like herself in black.

Martin gazed at her in amazement when he opened the door. 'Julia, what a surprise and how wonderful to see you.' He looked past her shoulder. 'Are you alone?'

'Latham is in France,' and she sent a beamer of a smile at Martin. 'I was in London to get my hair cut, so I used it as an excuse to visit the cats and cook your dinner . . . unless you've already made arrangements.'

'No, I was just thinking of heating the leftovers.' Holding the door wide he captured her hand, pulled her inside and closed the door behind her.

'Puss, puss, puss!' he called, and within seconds the cats streaked in to thread through and around her ankles, purring loudly.

'Gracious, look how big and glossy the pair of you are. I told you that you'd find a good home here.'

'They're very efficient mousers, but they like to show off their hunting skills. If you see any dead mice don't be alarmed.'

'I'll be more alarmed if I see a live one.'

He took her bag from her and she and the cats followed him into the kitchen. 'What have you planned for dinner?' he asked.

'Chicken casserole and vegetables. Apple crumble and custard.'

Placing the bag on the bench he turned to her and scrutinized her face. 'Are you happy, Julia?'

A lie would embarrass him less than the truth, even though he'd know she was lying. 'At this time, with you, I've never felt happier.'

He reached out and touched her face and she turned her face and kissed the palm of his hand. 'A couple of weeks ago I went up in Charles Curruthers' aeroplane. We followed a train along the line and it reminded me of you.'

'Ah, I see . . . the day in the attic. That flowered dress you're wearing is pretty; it's too good to cook in.'

'I just bought it. I know it's frivolous. I'm supposed to be in mourning, but black is so draining, and wearing it makes me feel sad and dreary.'

'Like a wet afternoon in London.'

'Exactly.'

'Come here.'

They were both playing the evasion game.

He placed an apron over her head and tied the strings in a bow at the back. She shivered as his soft breath caressed the skin at the nape of her neck. She wanted to turn in his arms and hold him close. But she must remember that Martin had been injured and could only be her friend.

'I miss my father. I'm lonely without him and I imagined how it must have felt for you thinking that your father would be waiting, and coming home from the war to an empty house.'

'You have a husband, you shouldn't have been thinking of me at all,' he reminded her.

'So I do, but thinking about you makes life bearable.' Even though her heart was breaking she managed a brilliant smile, and her thoughts were so clear she felt as though she'd spoken, *and it's you I love, Martin, I want you to know that.* 'Now, where do you keep the casserole dish?'

'It's on the bottom shelf in the overhead cupboard. Would you like me to peel the vegetables?'

She nodded. 'The apples too, if you would. Oh . . . and you can peel and chop the onions. They always make me cry.'

'It's the sulphur in the gas.'

'Onions have gas?'

'Propanethiol s-oxide is released when an onion is cut. It's caustic, so we blink, which produces tears to wash the irritant away.'

He grinned when she said, 'Stop showing off, professor.'

'It's elementary science. Allow me to show off a little more.' He skinned and diced the onions under water, waited a couple of minutes then tipped them into a colander to drain.

There was not a tear in sight.

Now it was her turn to grin. 'I'll remember that trick.'

'It's not a trick, it's common sense.'

'Yes . . . it is.' And if she had any she wouldn't be here with him, torturing herself.

'Would you like a glass of white wine?'

'That would be nice.'

They worked well together, and soon the casserole was in the oven and the table was set. Martin fed the cats. After grooming themselves they went to sleep in an armchair, cuddled up to one another.

'I have something to tell you,' Martin said after dinner. 'I've made enquiries about the whereabouts of my mother. I found a photograph of us all together amongst my father's things. I rang the lawyer who handled the divorce. He doesn't know where she is, but said he'd make enquiries to try and locate her address.'

'Can I see the photograph?'

He nodded, and rising from the sofa took down a silver frame from a shelf and handed it to her.

'Your mother is lovely. A woman who looks at her baby like that wouldn't have willingly abandoned him. You have the same shaped eyes as she does. I imagine they were blue like yours. Will you write to her when you find out where she lives?'

'I'm still thinking about it, and have discussed it with my lawyer. I'm wondering if it's worth the effort. It might not be a wise thing to do, since after all this time we'd be strangers to each other.'

Julia's eyes were getting damp. 'But you've taken the first step, though.'

He caught a tear on the tip of his finger, and smiled as it trembled there like a glittering dewdrop. 'You're not going to cry all over me, are you?'

'Probably . . . oh, I know you've been ill, and you were injured and you're not quite . . . well . . . you know . . . *manly*. But that doesn't mean you can't love somebody on a platonic level.'

His eyes flew open. '*Not manly? Platonic?* What the devil are you talking about, Julia?'

'Latham told me you'd been injured during the war. That's why he doesn't mind too much if I see you.'

His smile was a cross between a grin and a grimace as he took her by the hands and pulled her to her feet. Placing her arms around his neck he slid his hands under her buttocks.

'Martin, what on earth are you doing?'

He looked her straight in the eye. 'So . . . you're under the impression that I can't function as a man should.'

'Well, yes, but there's no shame—'

'I never thought I'd ever need to prove I can function as a man, but under the circumstances . . . ?' She was pulled against his body and his mouth took hers, tenderly at first, then with more passion as she responded. Julia knew what an aroused man felt like, especially one as close as this one was, and Martin was certainly not lacking in any manly qualities.

She grinned at him when he pulled away and pulled him back again. 'I got that wrong, didn't I?'

'With a vengeance,' he groaned. 'I've been crazy about you from the first time I set eyes on you. I was trying to keep you at a distance.'

'Why?'

'Because you made me feel more than I wanted to; and I didn't know if I could handle it. I was going to wait until I was sure.'

She hugged him tight. 'You do realize that I'm in love with you, don't you?'

'I knew there was a connection between us and hoped it would progress to something more in time. When you married Latham Miller and I lost you I couldn't believe it.'

'My father wanted me settled. He was in debt, and needed to know I was going to be looked after. I couldn't bear seeing his distress. And Martin . . . you haven't lost me . . . unless that's what you really want.'

Taking her face between his hands he gazed into her eyes. 'What are you suggesting, Julia?'

'You know what I'm suggesting.'

'That we should become lovers? You're my employer's wife.'

'The alternative is that we never see each other alone again. Latham won't suspect anything while he believes what he does. Besides . . . he has a mistress . . . more than one, I suspect.'

'That doesn't mean—'

'The marriage was a mistake. I've already told him I want a divorce.'

'You know, Julia, I never thought I'd ever make love to another man's wife.'

'You haven't made love to me yet,' she pointed out, 'so if you want to indulge in guilt, wait until you have.'

She glanced at the window, which opened on to a terraced back garden. It was still light outside, but the sky had a faint, peachy bloom of dusk that would deepen before too long.

'Can you stay the night?'

'I have every intention of staying the weekend.' She kissed a pale patch of skin where his hair curled darkly against his neck and sent her fingers running through his hair. He shivered, and she smiled.

He took her hand and led her towards his bedroom. Once there, she began to unbutton his shirt.

'Lift your arms,' he said, and gently pulled her dress over her head when she complied.

When she stood there in her lacy waist petticoat, camisole and drawers, he drew in a breath.

'My turn.' She pulled his shirt from his shoulders and threw it on to a chair.

Her petticoat went next, leaving her in her drawers, camisole and stockings.

She exchanged the drawers for his vest. Martin's body was lean, firm and muscular, and his arms were lightly tanned, as though he'd been gardening with his shirt off.

'Sit on the bed,' he said, voice gruff.

When she did he knelt and took up one of her legs. He threw her shoe aside and began to roll down her stocking. When he kissed the arch of her foot, a riot of nerves made her body convulse and she giggled. 'I have tickly feet.'

'So I notice,' and he laughed. Standing, he stripped naked, joined her on the bed and kissed her.

'I still have some clothes on,' she pointed out.

'I was saving those until last.' Her camisole was soon removed and she was left wearing one stocking.

But Martin wasn't looking at her charms, he was gazing down at her with a slight frown. 'How did you get those bruises?'

She avoided his eyes. She'd forgotten about the bruises. They were old, yellowing ones. Usually Latham slapped her, which didn't leave any bruises. On a couple of occasions he'd lost control and used his fist. 'I fell over.'

She shivered when he leaned down and gently kissed the bruise on her breast, then his mouth grazed over her skin to her stomach, and kissed the second bruise. He murmured, 'You must have fallen over twice, because one bruise is fresher than the other. And you must have fallen on the same thing because the bruise is the same shape . . . like a set of knuckles.'

'I fell on the carved wooden bit on the arm of the chair. I tripped over the rug. It was an accident. I don't want to talk about it, Martin.'

'I could kill him,' he said savagely.

Her arms slid around him and she snuggled into his warm body. Making her voice as even as possible she lied, 'There's no need to . . . I told you, Martin, it was an accident. Now, let's forget everyone else and just enjoy each other.'

He gazed down at her then. 'Are you sure?'

Sure of what? That her bruises were caused by an accident? That she wanted him to make love to her? 'I'm very sure that I'm in love with you, Martin. If we can only meet this once, then that will be a precious memory to keep you close to me, always.'

'There's that.'

'I'm still wearing one stocking.'

'I forgot it.' He sat up and gazed at it. 'You look sensual in one stocking . . . sort of dissolute and rumpled.'

'Rumple me a bit more.'

Martin obliged, his tongue running little circles over her skin. He took his time, his fingers working magic on her body, his kisses deep and loving. Julia caressed his silky skin until neither of them could contain the half-crazy sensation that sent any thought of caution fleeing from their heads.

He was gentle, his touch sensual as his fingers absorbed every hurt Latham had imprinted on her body and left in its place a loving caress. Where she'd once been reluctant she was now eager to love and be loved.

Soon, she was rising to meet his thrust, her legs anchoring him to her body as she discovered several new dimensions to the depths of her feelings.

'Oh, hell, I've forgotten . . .' Martin whispered, as if the thought of protection had suddenly occurred to him. But it was too late and his words were lost in an explosive, shuddering finish.

'Don't worry about anything,' she murmured against his chest. 'I've been to that Marie Stopes clinic and got one of those rubber cap things.' She didn't tell him it was still in the bottom drawer, where it had been since she'd bought it.

Later, heart beating fast, Julia dared to open her eyes, to find his glance soft upon her face. He smiled at her, and she chuckled.

'I suppose you think I'm frightfully forward.'

'I think you're lovely . . . I adore you, and I adore your belly button. It's so neat and pretty. Can I kiss it?'

She giggled when he did. 'I'm glad, because I feel the same about you, and need to know you better. Tell me about yourself, Martin . . . What has prevented you from going back to your profession for all this time?'

'You really want to know?'

She pulled the sheet over them both and snuggled up to him. 'Yes . . . tell me.'

'Put simply, there was too much blood and gore in my life . . . too many appalling injuries that couldn't be repaired . . . too many casualties who couldn't be saved. Everything became too much for me. I couldn't eat, couldn't sleep. My hands began to shake every time I saw blood, and I couldn't trust myself. I began to believe I was killing more people than I was saving.'

'Poor you.'

'It wasn't true, of course. I became depressed and spent some time in a mental institution, and two years seeing a psychiatrist trying to come to terms with myself. I magnified things out of all proportion.'

She slid her arms around him. 'Oh, Martin . . . how awful for you.'

'I'm almost better now . . . though I do suffer from bad dreams at times. I can cope with those. Your father helped me to believe in myself by offering me employment.'

'Will you go back to doctoring eventually?'

'I'm beginning to think about it, though I'll have to be passed as fit first. I doubt if I'll ever perform general surgery again, but I might enter some other branch of medicine.'

'If you're attracted to belly buttons perhaps you could deliver babies. Bringing new life into the world might compensate for those people you tried to save, and lost.'

How simple the solution was to her, yet there was a certain amount of merit in her suggestion since he'd thought about studying obstetrics before the war had intervened in his training.

So he held her close and smiled as he murmured, 'Now there's a thought . . .'

Twelve

Julia took the afternoon train home. She'd barely closed the door behind her when the telephone rang.

It was Latham. 'Where were you last night when I called, Julia?'

'I was in London. I did leave a message with Mrs Finnigan.'

'Yes, I received it. For what reason did you need to go to London?'

'Do I need one? Actually, I had a hair appointment.'

'Surely you could get your hair done at that place in the village.'

She laughed. 'The woman who runs it shears sheep in her spare time. I prefer to see my own hairdresser. I also bought a dress I liked.'

'Where did you stay?'

'In a cosy little hotel in Kensington. Goodness, Latham, why the interrogation?'

'The name of it?'

'*Clements*, I think it was called. It's perfectly decent. In fact, it only caters for respectable unescorted women. Does it matter?'

'Why didn't you use the London house?'

'Oh, it's a little too grand.' Besides which the staff would report everything back to him. 'The hotel was rather homely, and it's not far from the hairdresser.'

'Next time, stay at the house, please; then I'll know where you are.'

'Where were you last night, Latham?'

'Pardon?'

'You heard me. If I'm expected to account for my every movement then you must do the same . . . and why did you have those rose bushes planted on my parents' graves without telling me? I wanted to choose them myself.'

'Now you're being childish. When I get back we'll see about getting you a maid who knows how to dress hair then you won't have to dash up to London every time you need a haircut. As for the rose bushes, I thought I'd save you the trouble.'

Now he'd mentioned a maid it wouldn't hurt to mention that Ellen was looking for a new position. 'There's a maid who works at the hall who's looking for another position. Her name is Ellen.'

'Ellen? The name's familiar.'

Julia heard a frantically whispered conversation in the background, and Latham making shushing noises. She smiled to herself. 'Oh, I'm sure you'll remember Ellen, Latham. She's Irene's maid when she's at home in the country, and was there when you rescued me from the big bad wolves.'

'I doubt if Irene will want to part with her.'

'Oh . . . she will. Irene doesn't like Ellen because she tells tales to her mother. Shall I interview her?'

'That can wait until I get back.'

She felt like provoking him. After all, he couldn't hurt her on the telephone. 'Nonsense . . . you're too busy to bother with domestic matters. I'm perfectly capable of interviewing her myself, then the next time I feel like going to London in your absence I shall take her with me so you won't have to worry.'

'Julia. You're to stay home. Do you understand?'

'Perhaps it's you who should learn to understand something, Latham . . . I have a mind of my own and will do as I think fit. If I want to go to London, then I will. In fact, I'll catch the train in the morning and stay there for a whole week.'

He lost his temper and shouted, 'Julia, you will stay where you are until I get back.'

She felt strangely reckless and said, 'I certainly will not. Give my best wishes to Irene.' She hung up on him.

Ten minutes later the phone rang again. She approached it with caution. 'Yes?'

'I'm sorry, Julia. Will you forgive me?'

'Since we're married, I suppose I shall have to.'

'Listen to me, my dear. If you want to go to London I won't stop you, but I want you to stay at the house so I won't have to worry about you. I'll tell my secretary to get you some theatre tickets, and I'll ring Lee-Trafford and ask him to escort you to the theatre.'

She wanted to laugh with the childish glee that surged through her. Instead, she said, and in a rather off-hand manner because she didn't want to sound too eager, 'Martin Lee-Trafford has a life of his own, I imagine.'

'Not while his salary is being paid by me, he hasn't. As for the maid, allow me to sort that out. I'll need to get a reference from the girl's employer.'

'Oh, I don't suppose that will take you very long,' she said. 'And I'll give you a reference, since she did my hair perfectly. In fact, she'll suit me, and I want her in my employ.'

'Why Ellen in particular? There are other maids.'

'Truthfully . . . ' and she grinned, because she knew that this he'd understand. 'It's because it will piss Irene off.'

She knew she'd won when he began to laugh.

'Goodnight, Latham,' she said, and hung up.

Martin rang her half an hour later. 'Latham called me.'

'Yes . . . he said he would. How are you, my darling?'

'The same as I was when you left this morning . . . except I feel more alive.'

'I'm coming back up tonight.'

'You can't, there's no train.'

'I have my father's Morris. They're not expecting me at the house until tomorrow, so we'll have all night together.'

'You're taking a risk.'

'I know . . . but I happen to think you're worth it.'

'I love you . . . You do know that, don't you, Julia? I don't want you to think that I'm using you.'

'Yes, I do know,' and she wanted to cry because she'd been too hasty when it had come to planning her future, and her father would never have pushed her into marriage with Latham if he hadn't been desperate. Her poor father who was barely cold in his grave would be resting uneasily if he knew what she'd been up to – and was prepared to continue with.

The trip back to London was uneventful. She remembered to pack the pregnancy preventative device she'd bought from the clinic – something she'd practised setting into place, but had never used.

If Agnes Finnigan was surprised she was leaving again so soon, she didn't show it, but merely said, 'Enjoy the play, Mrs Miller.'

'Oh, I will. I'm staying at a friend's house tonight.'

When she got to London she went straight to Finsbury Park

and threw herself into Martin's arms when he opened the door. He laughed and twirled her around when she said, 'I missed you too much to stay away.'

The night they spent together was perfect. The next morning she presented herself to Latham's London House, and she gave a wry grin at the notion that she thought of it as her husband's house rather than hers.

Latham's clerk, who had a little office at the back of the house attached to Latham's study, was taken aback when he saw the car. 'We expected you to arrive by train, Madam, and have sent the lad to the station to fetch you.'

'Then he won't find me.' She handed the keys to the man and scrambled through her memory for his name. 'Perhaps he'd like to take care of my car when he comes back, Mr Allan.'

The clerk looked gratified that she'd remembered his name. 'At Mr Miller's request I've acquired some theatre tickets for *Phi Phi,* which is on at the Pavilion Theatre. He thought you'd find the play amusing.'

'Thank you. Mr Lee-Trafford will be calling for me about seven.'

'So I'm given to understand, Madam. At Mr Miller's request I've taken the liberty of booking a table for supper at the restaurant across from the theatre. He has an account there.'

'Did my husband order our supper by any chance?' she couldn't resist saying and the man looked surprised.

'Why, no, Madam.'

'Ah, here is Mrs James,' and Julia smiled at the housekeeper, even though she was furious with Latham for arranging her night out so thoroughly. 'I'm tired after the drive; I'm going to take a bath and rest until lunchtime.'

'Yes, Madam. Shall I run it for you?'

'No . . . I can manage for myself.'

'Just ring the bell if you need anything, and I'll come straight away.'

After a little while of lying up to her neck in the luxury of warm bubbles Julia relaxed with a grin on her face and thought of Martin. He'd been surprisingly amorous and knew exactly how to excite her senses. He'd welcomed her tentative exploration of him and had guided her hand when she'd hesitated.

Making love with Martin had been fun, and she grinned.

'I could give you an anatomy lesson at the same time if you like,' he'd whispered in her ear.

'Then I'll be forced to attack you with a pillow.'

The room attached to Latham's was ready for her occupancy. Not a fleck of dust marred its perfection. She grinned as she kicked off a pair of pink slippers she'd found in the cupboard, and she flopped into the middle of the comfortable bed.

She'd already selected her outfit, one with a Paris designer label on it. Once again, Latham's taste in clothing surprised her.

As she fell asleep she remembered the contraceptive device, still in her bag. She'd been so eager to fall into Martin's arms she'd forgotten to insert it. For a moment she felt alarm, but then she remembered that Latham never used protection and she hadn't caught. In fact, her last period had been two weeks ago. She hoped she wasn't one of those women who proved to be barren. As sleep began to claim her she thought drowsily that she'd like to have a child of her own to care for, even if it was Latham's.

Dressed in his evening suit, Martin presented himself at his employer's house later that evening.

The air was soft, and was wearing that peculiar sweet potpourri fragrance associated with summer's blending of various blossoms.

Martin felt like a suitor calling on his sweetheart, instead of being the lady's lover, as he was shown into the half-panelled drawing room. Never in his life had he imagined he would find himself placed in such a precarious position, but love had proved to be a stronger attraction than he'd expected.

Unless Latham agreed to a divorce – and from what he knew of the man he wouldn't let go of Julia easily – Martin knew he'd spend the rest of his life living for each moment they could be together. Those would be few and far between.

The room he found himself in was pleasant, with pale-blue embossed wallpaper and an expensive-looking Persian carpet in pastel shades. Wing chairs upholstered in dark-blue brocade and a settee of ivory-coloured Indian cotton were covered in exotic cushions. An oversized, but expensive-looking oriental pot in blue and gold stood in one corner.

His heart nearly exploded from his chest when Julia came in, and he noted that she was careful to leave the door open. She was

exquisite in a dusky purple dress with a beaded bodice, elbow-
length sleeves and a handkerchief skirt that floated around her
ankles. Her wavy hair was kept under control by a band that circled
her forehead. Diamonds twinkled in her ears.

As she advanced towards him her smile brought an answering
one from him, though he tried to keep any intimacy from showing
when her eyebrow raised slightly and she said rather wickedly,
'Martin, my dear, we haven't seen enough of each other lately . . .
how kind of you to agree to be my escort.'

'How lovely you look, Mrs Miller.' He handed her a small
posy of flowers he'd bought from a seller, which she gave to an
older woman who'd followed her in. 'Place these in water after
we've gone, please, Mrs James.'

'Yes, Madam. I'll fetch your wrap, shall I?'

The wrap was fringed silk and as delicate as a cobweb. It settled
over her shoulders like a drifting silvery cloud so she looked like
a moonlit sprite.

'Where shall we go?' Martin said when they were outside.

'I have tickets for *Phi Phi*.'

'I've seen it, but never mind . . . it's enjoyable so I don't mind
seeing it again.'

'Latham has lots of friends, and he has a box, so somebody
will notice if we don't use it, and they'll tell him. And he's bound
to question me about it.'

'Is Latham really that devious?'

'He likes to have control of everything and to know what's
going on. That's his nature,' she said unhappily.

'I'm not a man to pander to your husband's nature.'

'He even got his clerk to book the restaurant for supper. We're
to put it on his account.'

'I think I can afford to buy us some supper.'

'Oh, no male rivalry please, Martin. Let's just accept things as
they are for the time being.'

He waited until they were around the corner then took her
hands in his and whispered, 'But this is so hole-and-corner, and
it doesn't sit easy with me.'

'Nor me . . . but what else can we do?'

'Nothing . . . I doubt if Latham will release you from the
marriage, though I could ask him.'

'I have grounds . . . but you're right. He wouldn't seriously consider divorce, let alone provide grounds. He'd rather break me . . . you as well, if he finds out.'

'You'd need to prove grounds . . . and I doubt if your friend Irene would oblige, especially with her connections. Her parents wouldn't welcome a scandal such as that one would cause.'

'Then *we* can provide grounds.'

He wanted to take her in his arms right here in the street. 'My darling . . . your name would be mud. You'd be ostracized and would probably have to go and live abroad. As for me . . . ?' He shrugged. 'I'd never be able to get a decent job . . . or go back to medicine.'

'I wouldn't mind.'

'I would . . . oh, I know it would be fun at first. But both of us were brought up to live by a certain standard of decency. I couldn't stand seeing you pilloried, and Latham would make sure that you were.' He recalled the condemnation his mother was subjected to by his father, and he knew he couldn't bear that happening to Julia.

'Oh, Martin . . . I'm being horribly selfish. I'm so happy when I'm with you, and that's all I can think about. Let's just do what Latham wants. It will save an argument with me trying to explain why we didn't.'

And mindful of the bruises he'd seen on her, and the doubt he felt over the origin of them, he agreed, though he still intended to retain his independence by paying for their dinner.

Tucking her arm in his they resumed walking. One thing Martin was certain of, they wouldn't fool Latham Miller for long if they kept on meeting. The man was much too astute.

First, they ate supper in Latham's favourite restaurant. There, the waiters fawned over Julia. Not the case with him, though. The change was subtle, from obsequious through to barely disguised scorn. Perhaps his imagination was working overtime but he felt as though they regarded him as a paid gigolo. He squirmed in his dinner suit at the thought. Paying the bill restored his dignity a little.

Latham couldn't have picked a play with more irony to it. It was a musical comedy about a Greek sculptor who fell in love with one of his models – a woman who just happened to be married.

During the interval they were approached by several of Latham's acquaintances, men who exuded power and who flirted with Julia in a respectful sort of manner and acknowledged Martin with a nod of the head, as if he was beneath them. Some of them Martin knew, others Julia introduced him to.

Seated in the red womb of the box, they surreptitiously held hands in the darkness, totally aware of the attraction of the other because the air vibrated around them like an invisible crystal cage. They were also aware that opera glasses were trained on them now and again. There was bound to be speculation.

About halfway through the play Julia tickled the fleshy pad beneath his thumb with a nail painted purple to match her dress. She whispered, 'Shall we sneak away?'

They stole from the box in the middle of a ragtime song by Cole Porter, when the audience's attention was riveted on the stage.

A short cab ride saw them at Martin's flat. He followed Julia inside and a short time later they were making love with a passion that Martin hadn't thought possible. When they were spent, their limbs were tangled around each other.

Martin ran his finger down the length of her nose and her eyes opened. For a moment she gazed at him through dark lashes clumped and sodden with tears. Then she snuggled her soft, translucent cheek against his palm. 'We probably won't be able to see each other again after tonight.'

'I know.'

'Latham would ruin you if he found out. He might even . . . *kill you.*'

He smiled at her fancy, sobering though when he was hit by a flying thought. Latham would be more inclined to kill her. 'You'd be worth dying for.'

'Except I'd only feel half-alive on a world without you, my darling.'

He held her tight and they slept a little. When the clock chimed ten, they dressed. There was a cab rank, and they were dropped off outside the theatre just as the audience began to trickle out.

She turned her face up to his. 'What was the ending like?'

'*Phi Phi* returns from a night with his lover and catches his wife with Ardimédon in a compromising position.'

'And then?'

'He congratulates them for finding the exact pose that he wanted for his sculpture.'

The small huff of laughter she gave had a slightly hollow sound to it.

A few people bade them goodnight.

They waited until their cab went off with passengers, then picked up another one.

'You're a devious man, Martin.'

'I don't want you to be in any trouble, my love.'

'He's bound to go away again, you know.'

In the darkness of the cab he kissed her, then he got out of the cab and went round to open the door for her. He stood and waited while she walked to the door and knocked. How odd that she didn't have a key to her own home.

She turned when it opened, and offered politely, 'Mr Lee-Trafford, would you like to come in for coffee?'

He couldn't flaunt their relationship, especially in Latham's own home. It was asking for trouble.

'Thank you, but no. I have to be at work early tomorrow. Goodnight, Mrs Miller.'

The door closed behind her and the house swallowed her up as the cab drove away.

Julia had never felt so abandoned. She supposed it was a price she'd have to pay for her duplicity.

She tossed up whether to take a bath or not, and decided that she'd better. After all, she'd often noticed Irene's perfume on Latham.

'It was hot in the theatre, so I'm going to take a bath before bed.' She wondered why she was giving an excuse to a servant, when she could bathe twenty times a day if she wanted to. Guilt, she supposed.

'Will you bring me up some hot milk please, Mrs James? Leave it on the bedside table if I'm still in the bath.'

She lay there, surrounded in warm water, waffling between the pleasure of being with Martin, and despair at the thought of not being able to be alone with him ever again. Reluctantly she washed him from her body, dried herself and went through to the bedroom.

She took a sleeping pill with her warm milk, slid between the sheets and fell asleep almost instantly.

When a warm body slid in beside her she thought it was Martin. Turning in his arms she whispered, 'Hello, darling, how did you get here? Am I dreaming?'

'Hello, my love. I thought you sounded upset, so Charles Curruthers flew me across the channel to be with you. I shouldn't have left you alone for such a long time.'

All her nerves went on alert and she wanted to scream with disgust when Latham kissed her. Thank goodness she hadn't stayed at Martin's flat.

'I'm tired . . . I've just taken a sleeping pill . . .'

'Then you'll be nice and relaxed . . . I've missed you, Julia, and he kissed each breast. Just lie there and enjoy yourself.'

Enjoy herself? This would be a punishment after Martin.

' Did you enjoy the play?'

'I just want to sleep, Latham,' she pleaded. She didn't want Latham's hands on her, fondling her roughly and him thrusting himself into her, hurting her inside and out. But she was too sleepy from the pill to protest too much.

Her mind strayed to Martin and his tenderness, as he pushed her legs apart and entered her.

'You're hurting me.'

'Stop whining, Julia . . . I need to hurt you . . . you're much too rebellious and must learn to treat me with respect. Tell me about the play . . . What was the hero's name?'

'Hideous . . . no, no . . . it was Phidias.'

The light was suddenly switched on and she squinted against it.

'I suppose you think that was funny.'

'No . . . it was a mistake, the sleeping pill has made my mind go fuzzy.'

'Never hang up the telephone on me again,' he said, and he slapped her face.

All vestiges of sleep fled, and just in time she remembered not to cry out, so it became a muffled groan. It was bad enough that Mrs Finnigan felt sorry for her without the staff here doing the same.

Eventually, Latham finished his punishment of her, satisfied himself and left for his own room.

Julia quietly cried herself to sleep. There couldn't have been a worse way to end such a beautiful evening.

Thirteen

September and October passed in a swirling glory of metallic colours. Autumn drifted from the trees in bronze, copper, brass and gold shapes and fragments. Nuts fell to the ground, rust coloured and glossy.

Julia didn't have a chance to be alone with Martin again, though she managed to talk to him over the telephone on a couple of occasions.

'I found an address for my mother amongst my father's papers and wrote to her,' he told her. 'Loving you has shown me that emotion is a strong force. I can't condemn her for being human, and she must have wondered about me.'

'That's wonderful, Martin. I'm so pleased, and I hope everything goes well.'

'I'm also making enquiries about what's available to me in my profession. I should be able to get some locum work after I've been cleared as being fit to resume my profession.'

'Good luck, my darling . . . I love you.'

'And I you.'

Latham still came to Surrey at weekends, spending his weekdays in London. Sometimes he spent the weekend behind his desk, or on the telephone, and sometimes he just relaxed, taking long walks with the dogs. People came from the village for lunch or a game of tennis on the newly built court, and she was almost happy sometimes.

Julia realized she'd missed a period, and a little quiver of excitement lodged in her. When she missed the second one she was almost sure.

She woke one morning and went down to breakfast. Agnes Finnigan served her bacon and eggs for breakfast. Julia took one look at her plate and sprinted to the bathroom.

When she returned to the dining room the eggs had been replaced with a piece of toast and some gooseberry conserve to spread on it. Mrs Finnigan had a smile on her face, and Julia grinned. 'I've missed two, so I'd better go and see the doctor.' Her smile faded. 'Then I must tell Latham.'

'Congratulations, my dear. It will be lovely to have a baby in the house. Mr Miller will be pleased.'

The doctor was all smiles as he examined her. 'It seems as though your suspicions are correct, Mrs Miller. Your baby should be born about the end of May. You're a little on the thin side, so you must eat healthy food and drink plenty of milk. My nurse will give you a list of what will be needed for your lying-in. Goodness, that's quite an arrangement of bruises on your thighs. How did that happen?'

'I tripped over a table. I haven't told my husband about the baby yet . . . He might want me to have the baby in London and be under the care of a specialist gynaecologist.'

'You tell him that the country air will do you good, and I've delivered hundreds of healthy babies in my time. Better still, send him to see me and I'll tell him myself. I'll also remind him not to leave any more tables in your way, since we don't want any harm to come to mother or infant, do we?'

She blushed, She should have known the doctor wouldn't have been fooled by her injuries.

Julia's first thought when she arrived home was to telephone Martin, because she was sure it was his baby. But it was Latham who answered. 'Julia . . . how did you know I was here?'

Her heart sank and she thought quickly. 'Didn't you mention it over breakfast last weekend? I've just got back from seeing the doctor.'

'Your voice sounds odd . . . Is something wrong?'

'No, Latham . . . nothing is wrong.' And indeed, she couldn't stop smiling as she blurted it out, because even if it turned out to be Latham's baby she'd still love the child. 'The doctor tells me that I'm perfectly healthy. I'm expecting a baby, that's all, around about May. The doctor said I should give birth to the baby here, since the country air will be beneficial . . . and he's delivered hundreds of babies.'

'I'll talk to the doctor myself, to make sure.' There was a moment of silence then he whispered, 'You've made me a very happy man, Julia. I'll be home early tonight, and you won't have to worry about a thing. I'll hire a nurse to look after you, and I'll have a room turned into a nursery.'

There was a noise in the background and she heard him say, 'Lee-Trafford. I'd like you to be the first to know; Mrs Miller is expecting a baby in May.'

'Congratulations,' she heard him say, and her heart ached and her mind reached out to him.

'You can talk to Julia if you like. I'm going to make sure they get the right balance on that press they're installing. Lee-Trafford wants to talk to you, darling. I'll see you this evening. The car is being serviced so I'll take the afternoon train.'

A few seconds later Martin's voice said, 'Julia . . . he's gone.'

'Oh, Martin. I wanted to tell you first . . . I didn't expect Latham to be there. I'm sure this is our baby.'

'Julia, my sweet. A baby changes things considerably. It will need a loving, stable home and the reassurance of being cared for by its parents. Are you really *sure?*'

'Well . . . no, because there's no way I could know for sure . . . but I wanted it to be ours.'

'Wanting it is something entirely different. Besides, you said you were using that birth control cap . . . You *did* wear it, didn't you?'

She didn't answer. 'What shall we do?'

'We have two choices. The first is that we can tell Latham that we love each other, and you can leave him and move in with me. I'm going back to my profession, and will have to be retrained. I might be able to find another job and put the retraining off until later. It will be hard, but we'd manage somehow.'

She shuddered at the thought of what would happen when they told Latham. 'And the alternative?'

'You know what the alternative is. You must settle down in your marriage with Latham and your child, and make the best of it. What's more, we must never see each other again. I'll probably move back to Bournemouth eventually. We can't go on like we are, Julia. It's not fair to anyone, least of all the coming infant. I wasn't brought up to embrace dishonesty and subterfuge. If you'd seen Latham's face when he told me, he was so proud . . . Julia . . . for God's sake, stop crying, my darling . . . We have to be strong. You never answered my question about the birth control device. We need to be rational, since there is more to this than us. The infant's future should also be taken into consideration.'

If she left Latham and went with Martin she'd be the cause of him having to give up his career. In fact, if she went with him, she would most likely ruin his future altogether. Hadn't he been through enough?

Tears flooded her cheeks as she took the course that would be the most secure for the man she loved. 'I did wear it,' she lied, 'but perhaps it didn't work.'

'That's unlikely. The child is more likely to be Latham's, you know.'

'I know. I just didn't want it to be his. Can I think about it a bit longer? If it's Latham's baby . . . well, it wouldn't be fair to deprive the child of its father's love. I'll be in touch when I've decided, Martin.'

They both knew she would do no such thing and this was the end. 'Once you have your baby in your arms everything will seem different and you'll be able to see things in their proper perspective.'

'Yes, I expect you're right. You won't think badly of me, will you? For coming to you, for loving you so much; I mean . . . I couldn't bear it if you did.'

'Never, Julia. I'll adore every memory of you until the day I die. By the way, the letter I sent to my mother was returned. She hasn't lived at that address for years.'

'Oh, how disappointing. I'm so sorry.'

She didn't want to hang up but thought she'd better get it over with before Latham realised they were still talking on the telephone. 'Goodbye, my love.' And then she gave a watery chuckle. 'We sound like actors in a film . . . a melodramatic story of un-requited love.'

'We *are* a love story, just remember that.'

'Yes, we are,' she whispered as she hung up, 'because I'll never stop loving you.'

Martin knew that the time had come for him to move on. He'd loved and lost – and although Julia was a permanent part of his heart he'd survive the inevitable conclusion to their affair. Knowing she loved him might even have strengthened him.

He would think things over, and come up with a plan before he told Latham. No, this was the incentive he'd needed. He would tell him now, give him time to think it over and get someone else.

He gazed to where Latham Miller stood, hands in pockets as he watched the machine being installed. It would thump all day, stamping out metal objects and gradually causing deafness in the employees.

Martin joined him. 'That's going to be noisy. The workers should be supplied with earmuffs.'

'Factories are noisy places. They'll soon get used to it.'

Latham was an enigmatic man with strength of purpose and a streak of ruthlessness.

'I've decided to retrain and resume my former profession.'

His employer turned, his dark eyes giving nothing of his thoughts away, and making no attempt to retain Martin on his staff, which did little for his pride. 'When do you want to leave?'

'I was thinking that a month's notice would give us both time to make arrangements. I'll stay longer if you get stuck.'

Latham nodded. 'I won't get stuck; I'll promote a foreman from one of my other factories to take over the running of the place as manager. In fact, I'll send him over to work with you so the factory hands will know what to expect when you leave. Some people don't take kindly to changes in management and methods, and that will give them time to get used to a different way of doing things. My staff have always been interchangeable, and the man I have in mind will get the best out of the factory hands. If you decide to leave earlier, I'll still pay you out for the month and will leave instructions with the clerk.' He held out a hand. 'If I don't see you again, good luck, Lee-Trafford.'

His imminent departure was not going to bother Latham Miller one little bit. In fact, Martin had gained the impression that the man was relieved.

Miller was about to walk away when he said, 'Have you got rid of all those toys yet? If not, throw them out; we'll need the storage area in a few weeks.'

'I thought we could donate what's left to an orphanage.'

'A good idea. I'll arrange some publicity in one of the news-papers for the handover day. I'll bring Julia up to London, and they can take a photograph of us with the orphans. It will be good for business. See to it, would you? I'll take one of the rocking horses home for the nursery, too. Julia will like that. Robert will come in for it later. Pick one out and give it a dust off if you would.'

It sounded as though Latham wasn't bothered about him handing in his notice, and indeed, he had taken it into account and planned his replacement. What a cold fish the man was.

'You must be pleased about the coming baby. You're a lucky man to be married to such a lovely woman.'

An expansive smile lit Latham's face. 'It was more judgement than luck. A baby will settle Julia down a bit. She's been restless since her father died, which is why I asked you to take her to that play. Planning for a baby will keep her occupied. By the way, I believe you paid for the dinner yourself . . . You must allow me to reimburse you.'

'That won't be necessary. It was my pleasure to spend an evening in the company of such a delightful woman.' And the nights, Martin added silently, the next moment hating his own hypocrisy.

'I wouldn't trust any other man with my wife's care, Lee-Trafford, so thank you. I'll be able to spend more time with her once this place is up to scratch.'

Martin picked out a grey dappled horse with a dark mane and red leather accessories. It was one that the baby's grandfather had painted the spots on and signed his name to. Martin's fingertips ran over the name. Benjamin Howard. Julia would like that. As he cleaned the dust from it he knew it was one he'd pick for his own son if he had one, and he allowed himself to wonder for just a moment . . . what if? But no, Julia had taken precautions; and just as well in the absence of his lack of foresight. Bringing women home wasn't a habit he indulged himself in.

There was a package of Rosie dolls left on a shelf. He decided to keep those for himself and took them down to the office.

Harold Clapton arrived the following week. He was loud and hectoring, but he knew his job, and Martin found himself almost redundant.

'You've got to make the lazy buggers work,' he said the following day. 'I've got my eye on that spotty young man over there. He's slow, and he needs a boot up his backside.'

'He hasn't had much education and doesn't learn easily, but he's a willing worker when he's shown how to do it. His wage helps to support his family.'

'With respect, Miller Enterprises is not a charity, Mr Lee-Trafford.'

The following week the young man was dismissed without notice. 'I've cleared it with Mr Miller,' Harold said. 'I've got to get this factory into production and showing a profit by the end of next month, else I'll be out of work myself. There's no room for slackers. I don't know why you're staying on to work out your notice. You've cleaned out the toys, and there's nothing left for you to do.'

'Are you implying that I'm a slacker, Mr Clapton?'

He shrugged. 'I know that you're not. You're superfluous to the factory work-force, that's all. I understand you're going back to doctoring.'

'If they'll have me.'

'Thank your lucky stars that you've got skills you can fall back on, otherwise you'd be doing this sort of job for the rest of your life, like I'll have to. This is the best I'll ever be. I was lucky to get back from the war with nothing more than a bullet in my arse. I married a widow to save her and her kids from starving. She's a good woman who rarely complains. Four kids now, and we live in a two up, two down terrace with a coldwater pump and a lavatory in the backyard shared with the occupants of half a dozen other terraces, with built-in rats and cockroaches. If I were a doctor I'd be going to where I could do the most good . . . and not be doing a job where a lesser man could be employed.'

Martin took his advice. He drew his pay, and left.

A few days later he cut a picture from the newspaper. Julia had a wide smile on her face as she supported a newly bathed orphan with a pale skin, stick-thin limbs and starving eyes, who was clutching a soft toy. A glass of milk would have done the child more good.

Harold had been right in that he did possess skills, Martin thought. And he could put them to good use once he'd updated them.

He gazed at Julia again, and could see the tension behind her brilliant smile. She was wearing a saucy-looking hat with a feather in it. Latham gazed fondly down at her, his hand possessing her shoulder.

Separating her from her husband, Martin put the picture in the frame behind that of his parents. It was a pity Latham's hand was still there, keeping her under his thumb.

He had an appointment with Hugh Cahill later in the day. Hugh and two other eminent doctors would comprise his board of examiners.

He was given a physical medical examination and asked questions on various aspects of doctoring, as well as his war service. They quizzed him for an hour, then pronounced him fit to resume his career.

Hugh Cahill invited him to dinner at his club afterwards. 'You look well, Martin. What are your plans now, back to surgery?'

'I've been out of the system too long. I was thinking of gaining some experience in obstetrics and gynaecology, then working as a locum before going into general practice with my own rooms in Bournemouth. I have the premises.'

'A good idea, since there has been a steady upsurge of babies being born since the war ended. I might be able to help you out with both at the same time, if you don't mind moving out of London.'

'To where?'

'The Northeast . . . a slum area. Colifield to be exact.'

'I've never heard of it.'

'It's not far from Newcastle. You'll get plenty of experience . . . and some repair work from the occasional home curettage.'

'You're supposed to report such cases, aren't you?'

Hugh shrugged. 'Sometimes it's better to turn a blind eye. Many of the women have large families, and very little else. Why add to their troubles?'

'But it's illegal and I disapprove of the practice.'

'We all do, and of course it is . . . but the women who decide to go through with the process are usually desperate. They'd have to be to consider risking septicaemia by going to a butcher in a backstreet hovel. It's the person who performs the procedure who needs prosecuting.

'Anyway, it's not your responsibility. They're shunted off to Newcastle Infirmary if need be. You can leave all the paperwork to Jack Tomlinson. His wife helps out on the nursing side. If you take the job, as soon as you learn what's what, he'll be taking a month off come spring. He's worked without a break for four years and is worn out.'

'Friend of yours?'

'We went through medical school together. I thought I'd take him to Scotland in the spring for a spot of fly fishing while the wives get together for a gossip.'

Martin chuckled. 'So, you've got a vested interest in this.'

'I certainly have. Catherine, his wife, is my sister. It will be an eighteen months' contract, by the way. By that time your replacement will be trained.'

Like Hugh said, he'd get plenty of experience. There was nothing to keep Martin in London, except the hope that he might run into Julia, which would torture him even more. A clean break would be better – so why did he feel as though he was deserting her?

A lot could happen in eighteen months. He gave a small huff of laughter at the next ironic thought that occurred to him. He might even get over her. When Hugh gave him a look of enquiry, he said, 'I promise to consider it. Give me a couple of days to think it over. I need to look at my finances.'

'A salary comes with the job, courtesy of the local Quakers fund. It's not generous, but it's enough to live on with a bit left over. Accommodation is free – a two-roomed furnished flat at the back of the surgery, bedroom and living room with gas cooker. You'll be on permanent night call, I'm afraid. The lavatory is in the yard and you'll be provided with a tin tub to wash in. It's a bit primitive from what I gather, but like I said, if it's experience you're after . . .'

A month later and Martin had arranged storage for his goods and was on his way to Colifield, suitcase in one hand and the cats in a roomy cardboard box secured with string in the other. They were a gift from Julia that he couldn't bear to leave behind, even though his landlady had offered to take them in.

There was a branch line that went through Colifield and served the coal industry. A passenger car had been added to the empty coal wagons, and there were two passengers besides himself. The station was black with smuts.

Beyond the houses in the distance was the wheel that supported the miners' cage, but the gates to the pit entrance were padlocked. Beyond that was a towering pile of slag.

Martin understood in a telephone call from Jack Tomlinson that the mine had flooded and now stood abandoned. Some of the younger men had been employed at neighbouring pits, some had not. Some had managed to find work at the ironworks. The smoke from the works sent out a sooty smell and peppered everything with smuts.

There was no one to meet him. It was a wet and miserable day. He asked directions of a lad with a cart and hired him for a shilling. Martin loaded the cats' container and his suitcase on the cart and they walked through the grimy rows of streets to the surgery. It was a red brick house on a corner site, and the ugly building looked as though it had once been a shop, with a window either side of a door recessed into the corner.

The door was open and he walked in, his nose twitching at the overwhelmingly nostalgic smell of disinfectant.

A thin woman with greying hair smiled at him. 'You must be Doctor Lee-Trafford?'

'Yes, I am.' The cats set up a pathetic clamour at the sound of her voice and he smiled. 'I'm afraid they've been travelling all day and have reason to complain. They're hungry, unsettled and a little bit afraid, though being cats they wouldn't admit to the latter. You must be Mrs Tomlinson, Hugh's sister. There's a definite resemblance, but I must say that you're much prettier.'

She laughed. 'Call me Sister Catherine, most of the patients do . . . Bring the cats through, Doctor. We'll have a cup of tea first since I daresay you could do with one. I'll find them some milk and make a fuss of them. They'll soon settle down in front of the fire, and if they can help keep the rat population down, all the better.'

His rooms were small and dimly lit, rather depressing after his London flat, but big enough for himself and his companions. The cats drank their milk, stretched their legs by exploring their new accommodation and lapped up Sister Catherine's attention with appreciative mews of pleasure and chin rubs against her ankles.

'I'd forgotten how wonderfully soothing cats are; they'll be nice to have around,' she said when they finally settled down in an armchair in front of the fire on one of Martin's pullovers. 'There's a yard out the back if they need to go out. I'm sorry nobody was able to meet you. I was doing the afternoon mothers' clinic and Jack was called out to an emergency.'

'Is there anything I can help with?'

'It will be throwing you in the deep end, but would you mind taking evening surgery? It will mostly be temperatures and coughs. Bronchial in the men; some of them have been exposed to black damp, especially those who have been in the pits for a long time. The wet weather makes the condition flourish. German measles is doing the rounds, and there was a case of whooping cough two weeks ago. I've isolated the patient, but she's a baby and will be lucky if she survives. One of the Quaker women comes in to help out in the evening. She mixes the medicines, does the files, cleans wounds and is there in case you need to examine a female patient. She'll show you where everything is kept and will keep you organized. Her name is Joanna Seeble.'

'She sounds like an angel.'

'Believe me, she is. I don't know what we'd do without her. One of her sons will eventually join the practice when he finishes training. Jack takes him out on the rounds with him, when he's home. I think that's about all you need to know for now.'

'Thank you, it was most helpful.'

'I'll have time to cook Jack a decent dinner for a change. You'll join us, won't you? Our last assistant used to eat dinner with us and put towards the food bill. That way you'll get one decent meal a day. You can manage your own breakfast and lunch. We live in the adjoining house, so you won't have to travel far. There's a general store, a greengrocer and a butcher in the next street. I've got the basics for your cupboard and you owe me for that. The receipt is on the dresser. We can take it from your salary if you like.'

It was indeed mostly coughs and colds, boils and blisters, with several blossoming cases of German measles. The women and children tended to be pale, malnourished and anxious looking.

Mrs Seeble was quiet and respectful, and went about her job efficiently.

He got the bulk of evening patients out of the way quickly,

dispensing bottles of cough medicine and diagnosing two preg-
nancies – to which pronouncement one earned him a sour look.

'It's not my fault; you should take precautions,' he said.

'Aye . . . well, that's all reet for thee, mon, but tell it to my
husband and yon pope in his Italian palace,' the woman said.

Just as Mrs Seeble was about to lock the door, a boy came in,
blood flowing from an ugly gash in his arm.

'Joe Harris,' Mrs Seeble murmured, reaching for the iodine
bottle.

'How did this happen, Joe?' Martin asked the boy

'I climbed over a wall and it had broken glass on the top. Are
you the new doctor?'

'I am that.'

'You talk posh.'

'Do I?' He examined the jagged edges of the wound.

'Do you reckon you'll have to stitch it, Doc?'

Martin looked up at him and smiled. 'I reckon I will, at that.
What were you doing climbing over the wall?'

'I got locked out, didn't I . . . sides, it ain't no business of
your'n.'

'Would you prefer me to stitch it with, or without, an injec-
tion, Joe?'

'What's a jection?'

'A needle with anaesthesia in it to numb the pain.'

'I ain't no bleddy girl, and I don't want any jection . . . You
won't get a soddin' yelp of me.'

Martin gave him a sharp look. 'Don't swear in front of the lady.'

'Sorry, Mrs,' and the lad gazed with some alarm at the instruments Mrs Seeble was laying out. 'Ere, what are all them things for?'

'The iodine will sterilize the skin so germs won't enter the
wound. This thread is for the stitches, and this needle—'

Joe Harris fainted clean away.

Martin swabbed the wound with iodine. 'Fetch the procaine if
you would, Mrs Seeble. Master Harris isn't as tough as he imagines.'

The woman smiled. 'Yes, Doctor,' then a few minutes later, 'Very
neat embroidery. I'd heard you were good.'

Astonished, he gazed at her. 'Have you? From whom?'

'A man called Stanley Bridges. He said you saved both his legs
and his life during the war.'

'I can't say I recall his name. There were many casualties at the front . . . too many of them to remember names.' *Too many legs, arms, guts!*

'He has cause to remember you, Dr Lee-Trafford. I imagine many other people would remember you, and be grateful for the diligent practise of your profession under duress.'

'I suppose there *would* be people who remember me. How odd, when I only seem to remember the ones who died.' He didn't know why this motherly woman invited his confidence, but she did. 'It all caught up with me eventually, you know . . . a mental collapse. I've only just returned to my profession.'

'Mental turmoil under extreme stress can be expected if a man has any degree of sensitivity. You're being too hard on yourself. You were endowed with the skill to heal and comfort, and that can only be used to the greater good. You were not born with the power to select those poor unfortunates to whom your gift would be of the most benefit.'

Her words gave his spirits a lift as he injected the procaine around the wound.

Half an hour later Joe Harris swaggered off with his arm in a sling and with a reminder to come back in ten days to have the stitches removed.

Mrs Seeble called after him, 'Tell your mother that the bill will be two shillings and sixpence, and you're to bring it the next time you come.'

'It didn't hurt a bit,' Joe bragged, as he went off.

'Wait until the anaesthetic wears off you cheeky little tyke,' Martin muttered and turned to his companion. 'Why do I feel we'll be lucky to see that particular bill settled?'

'It doesn't take much working out. They're poor and the boy thieves. His mother will probably remove the stitches herself, and use dirty scissors. If it gets infected they'll blame us and use it for an excuse not to pay.'

Martin was relieved to discover he'd performed the simple procedure without so much as even thinking about flinching.

He helped Mrs Seeble to clean the surgery and instruments ready for use the next day. 'You needn't do this. You go next door and get your dinner while I wash the floor,' she said.

'I'll make sure you get home safely first.'

'Don't worry about me; my son will be here with the car in a few minutes.'

There was the sound of a car sputtering to a halt, and the door was thrust open pushing a splatter of wet wind before it, 'What ho! What have you done with all the patients, Mrs Seeble?'

'They've all been dealt with, Doctor.'

'Good, because I overtook your boy on the way.' A smile sped across Tomlinson's face when his glance fell on Martin. 'You look too healthy to be one of my patients so you must be Martin Lee-Trafford. I'm Jack Tomlinson. I'm so glad you got here. It looks as though the women got you organized the minute you walked through the door?'

'Yes . . . they did rather, but I'm here to work. I was just going to follow up on my dinner. Sister Catherine invited me to your table.'

'Then follow me . . . I'm starving, and I imagine you are too. I'll be working with you on emergency for the next few days until you get to know the district. It's cold these nights, so it's best to get a good dinner inside you.'

'Goodnight, Mrs Seeble,' they both said together.

'Goodnight, Doctors . . . God bless,' she said.

It was pitch dark outside, except for a sputtering gas lamp on the corner, which acted as an unintentional beacon for the surgery. A car coming round the corner flooded them with light. A horn honked and Jack waved.

Colifield was a far cry from London – or from Bournemouth for that matter, where Martin intended to end up eventually.

Catherine had cooked a solid hotpot with suet dumplings for dinner and Martin's stomach expanded as every nook and cranny of it was filled.

Later, he fed the cats on leftover hotpot, and saw to their comfort, allowing them to explore the yard. He'd just finished unpacking his suitcase and was about to go to bed, when Jack came through the adjoining door in the wall and thumped on the back door.

'One of the patients has gone into labour. The mother's a veteran, so I thought this would be a good start for your first baby. Look lively though, the infant is not going to wait.'

Watched by two young girls of about twelve and thirteen, who bustled about carrying water and flannels for their mother, Martin brought his first baby into the world, a strapping, squalling boy.

'There's a bonny lad,' the woman said. 'Go next door and tell your da he's got himself a son, our Jessie.' She beamed a smile at Martin. 'We've got five daughters, and this is our first lad.'

'He's my first lad too; in fact, he's the first baby I've delivered.' And he felt a wonderful sense of achievement as a result.

'Well, you made a damned fine job of it. I reckon we'll be calling him after you then, as well as his father. What's your name, Doctor . . . out wi' it.'

'It's Martin.'

'Martin it is, then. Martin Bertram Ucklesbury; that's a reet grand name to go through life with.'

Even if that life was short. A few days later whooping cough broke out of its confinement.

As Martin learned that first week, the surgery might be a poor living, but it was a busy one, and just as much a battleground as the war had been. It was just that the casualties were different.

Fourteen

Latham spared no expense when considering the prenatal comfort of his wife and coming child.

Without any more objections on his part, Ellen was hired to take care of Julia's personal needs, and to help Mrs Finnigan in the house. Julia was able to convince Latham that she didn't need a nurse to look after her – at least, not in the early stages.

'I'm not ill,' she insisted. 'This is an entirely natural state for me to be in.'

'I insist on you having a nurse for the last two months . . . you might fall.'

'So might you. Stop wrapping me in cotton wool.'

The good thing was that Latham didn't hit her any more, and Julia thought the doctor might have mentioned her bruises to Latham, as he'd suggested he would. He still paid her regular attention in bed.

'The doctor said it would be all right up to the seventh month,' he told her. 'After that we can find another way to satisfy our urges.' *His* urges, she thought. She didn't have any of note where he was concerned.

There was an air of duty being done about Latham. He developed a schedule where he came down from London on Friday nights and went back on Monday morning. It was clear that he preferred the busy push and shove of London.

She missed seeing Martin, and had a sick feeling in her throat every time she thought of him. In the end she gave in to her resolve not to ring him, waiting until Latham was out with the dogs. At the factory she found it hard to hear against the background din.

A man called Harold Clapton told her loudly, 'Mr Lee-Trafford no longer works here.'

When she rang Martin's flat a woman answered. 'Doctor Lee-Trafford has taken up a medical appointment in the North of England, I understand. A pity, since he was such a lovely tenant. Very clean and tidy.'

Her heart sank. 'Do you know where he went?'

'It was one of the mining towns up North. I can't remember the name. He left a forwarding address in case any mail came for him. Hang on a minute, love.' A few moments later Julia was given the address and phone number of his lawyer in Bournemouth. She wrote them on a notepad kept by the telephone.

She rang the lawyer.

'I'm afraid I can't divulge my client's address, Mrs . . . um?'

She heard a noise from the kitchen and the dogs noisily lapping up water from the drinking bowl. Quickly, she hung up, then she tore the paper with the lawyer's details on off the pad. She stuffed it in her pocket.

Latham came in. 'Who was that on the telephone?'

Guilt filled her. 'I don't know.'

'You don't know who you were talking to?'

She'd learned that he became suspicious in his questioning if she lied, though that could be her own imagination, brought about by her guilt. She wasn't a very good liar, no matter how hard she tried. 'No . . . She didn't give a name.'

'Why did she ring you then?'

'She didn't. I rang her.'

Latham heaved a sigh. 'Julia, are you being deliberately obtuse?'

She didn't want to incur his anger. 'No . . . Actually, I wanted to talk to Martin Lee-Trafford so rang his landlady.'

His eyebrows rose like a pair of grizzled wings on a bird about to take flight. 'Lee-Trafford? What on earth do you want to talk to him for?'

'He was my friend, and I wondered how he was getting on. She told me he'd left London. Did you dismiss him?'

'Certainly not. Lee-Trafford handed in his notice and said he was going back to his profession. I have no idea where he went.'

She was upset by his revelation. 'Why didn't you tell me he was leaving?'

'I didn't think it was that important. People leave my employ all the time.' He took her in his arms. 'I know you thought a lot of the fellow, my love, but perhaps you should ask yourself something. If he was such a good friend, why didn't *he* tell you he was leaving?'

The only thing worse than Latham being mean to her, was Latham being nice.

She felt smothered.

Julia already knew why Martin had wanted to get away from a situation that couldn't be resolved if he stayed. He'd covered his tracks, so she wouldn't be able to find him. There was a bottomless pool of tears congealing inside her for him. Martin hadn't believed that the baby might be his, and she'd encouraged him in that. He'd chosen to be cruel to be kind. She felt abandoned, and wanted to bawl like a baby.

'You're right; I'm a bit out of sorts today,' she said, her voice quavering.

'You'll feel better after you've had a nap. Have one now. I'm going to run Robert into the garage to pick up your car. I put it in for a service.' He called Ellen in. 'Take Mrs Miller up to her room; she needs to rest.'

'Yes, sir.'

Ellen helped her into her nightgown. 'Is there anything I can do to make you comfortable?' she said, sounding slightly worried when tears trickled down Julia's cheek.

'Thank you, Ellen, I'll call you when I wake, and you can bring me a cup of tea.'

As soon as Ellen left, Julia began to cry in earnest. Everything was too much to cope with – her marriage, her father's death, falling in love with Martin – and having to give him up. And now she was having a baby and didn't know who'd fathered it. Her life was a mess, and there was nothing to look forward to.

She didn't hear the door open, just a soft, 'Mrs Miller? Ellen told me you were upset.'

'Oh, Agnes . . . nothing is going right in my life.'

Agnes took her in her arms, rocked her back and forth, then lay her down on the pillow and tucked her in. 'There, there, my dear. It's your body doing this to you. It has to adjust, you see. It'll soon settle down when the baby gets a bit bigger. Close your eyes and settle down, dear. I'll sit here with my knitting until you go to sleep. It's going to be a shawl to wrap the baby in. It will be a bonny baby, just you wait and see.'

Julia had very little choice but to wait and see. She gazed through her tears at the pretty fan-shaped pattern and gave a watery smile. 'It's pretty, and so sweet of you. Thank you so much

. . . I wish my father was here. He would have so much enjoyed being a grandfather.'

Of course there was something to look forward to, she thought as she drifted into sleep – her baby. If it were a boy she'd call him Benjamin after his grandfather. He would have liked that.

The winter was warm and mostly dry. Latham insisted that she eat a proper diet; oatmeal for breakfast; vegetable and chicken broths for lunch; steak and vegetables for dinner. And there was fruit, some of it out of season. Where Latham got it from she didn't know. He came home from London one day with a peach. Another day he handed her a small basket of perfect grapes.

Eating so much didn't seem to do her any harm. The only weight she gained was on her breasts, which were tender, and which grew even larger as her pregnancy progressed.

Ellen smoothed oil into her distended stomach every day. 'It will prevent stretch marks,' she said.

The nurse arrived in March. Fiona Robertson had an accent to match her name and wore an air of efficiency. If Julia had been regimented by Latham before, now it was doubly so.

With her body getting unwieldy, and the baby using her as a punching bag from the inside, she found it easier to do what she was told. Fiona Robertson had a routine. When the nurse told her to eat, Julia ate. Told to sleep, she slept immediately. They walked together for an hour every day, though Julia's was more of a waddle than a walk.

'Don't walk too fast and tire yourself out, now. Let's stop and rest.'

They sat on the garden seat, and where once Julie would have listened to the sounds of nature, now she had a talkative Scot.

'It's pretty here in the spring. Are those bluebells growing up near the copse?'

'No, they're anemones.'

'Fancy that. Up you get now. The exercise is good for you. Mind you don't slip on those loose stones.'

'It's gravel and I'm used to it. Please don't fuss, Fiona.'

A chiffchaff sang a song from a branch of catkins when they passed.

'Such a sweet song,' Fiona observed.

'Don't say another word, and look at that.' They watched entranced as a gaudy peacock butterfly emerged from its dull larva, then smiled at each other and headed back to the house for afternoon tea.

Julia had gradually gathered her infant's clothing together. Agnes Finnegan's shawl had become a complete layette, with sweet little bonnet, booties and mitts edged in crocheted blue shells. Latham had brought her a catalogue to choose clothing from, and came down from London every week with parcels to unwrap.

The nursery had been prepared and the latest Marmet baby carriage purchased, shining with chrome.

Her child was to be born in the little flat her father had occupied, which had now become the nursery wing. Fiona Robertson was already settled in there.

'I'll get a nanny for the child,' Latham said.

Dismayed, Julia frowned at him. 'I don't want a nanny. I intend to care for the baby myself.'

There was an argument. Julia was getting her own way more and more because Latham didn't want to upset her. He made a concession. 'At least agree to me asking Fiona Robertson to stay on for three months after the birth. It will give you time to recover from the birth.'

Because Julia quite liked the nurse, she couldn't hurt her feelings by saying she didn't want her, so she nodded.

'Don't blame me if the child grows up with a Scottish accent,' she warned Latham, and he laughed.

She was in her final month when Irene arrived on the doorstep. 'Good lord, darling; you're an absolute giant.'

Julia managed a laugh, despite knowing that she and Latham were still involved. 'Believe me, I feel like one.'

'Who's that fearsome Scottish creature who guards the entrance to your cave?'

'Nurse Fiona Robertson. Latham hired her to look after me.'

'Poor you . . . She looks terribly grim.'

'Actually, she's very nice, and good company. Not that I need much company, because the neighbours drop in now and again for a chat. How are you, Irene?'

'Actually, I think I'm in the same state as you're in . . . such a nuisance.'

When Julia's eyes widened Irene smiled and held out her hand where a platinum band decorated her finger. 'Don't worry, I'm safely handcuffed, darling. The man's name is Jacques Argette . . . pronounced Arjay. Latham was best man at the wedding; what a hoot.' She gave a little shiver. 'Jacques is an artist, and such a brute in bed. Just my type . . . very *avant-garde*. The parents are furious, of course. They'd stop my allowance if I weren't already of an age to have control of it. Daddy told me to get rid of the child and get a divorce. He's willing to pay Jacques off.'

'And will you?'

'I must admit I don't want to be saddled with a child . . .'

'You wouldn't—'

'Of course I wouldn't. I do have a sense of decency about some things. I can have it adopted, or farm it out.'

'Is your husband with you?'

'Good God . . . I hope not. He's frightfully unsuitable, and reeks of garlic. He says it's good for his libido. The parents are tearing their hair out, and have refused him a bed in the stately kennel. He married me because I can afford to keep him in paint and canvas. Actually, I think he's in love with Charles as well as with me. So amusing . . . Charles leads him on, of course. Rupert is quite put out about it.'

Julia no longer found herself shocked by Irene's outrageous statements, though she knew her friend well enough to suspect that her observations were based on truth. She'd heard that some men could be rather effeminate in nature. Rupert was one of them. But Charles? No, surely he was just amused by the notion.

'Why did you marry this Jacques?'

Irene shrugged. 'Because Latham finished with me when he learned he'd fathered a child on you. I wanted to make him jealous.'

'And was he?'

'No . . . He didn't care about how I felt. He never has. All he cares about is you and the coming baby. You know, Julia, while we're being truthful, I might just as well ask you why you married Latham, when you knew how much I cared for him.'

'My father pushed me into it when he was dying. He panicked and wanted me to be secure. Latham is a good man in many ways and I thought I'd learn to care for him.'

'But you didn't, did you?'

'Not as much as I hoped I would.' Irene's skin had a papery yellow look to it, and her hair was stringy. 'Have you been ill?'

'Do I look frightful?' She hung out her tongue and crossed her eyes trying to focus on it.

Laughter huffed from Julia. 'Actually, you do have a slightly yellow tinge. You should look after yourself, otherwise your baby will be sickly.'

'I had a bout of jaundice a few months ago. It was inconvenient, but now it's cleared up. The doctor has given me a blood tonic to take. It's frightfully constipating. I'm given to understand that Ellen is working for you now.'

'She is, but you've known that for some time, so why ask?'

'Oh, good, you won't mind if she does my hair for me while I'm here, will you? She always gets it exactly right and I'm going to dinner with the Oliver family tonight. It will be such a drag. She disapproves of me, you know . . . everyone does.'

'They don't, and I don't. You always make me laugh. Sometimes I wish I was more outgoing like you.'

'Good old Julia, you're always so sweet and nice. You don't know how much I envy you that. You'd better ring for Ellen because I can't stay much longer.'

'You can use the bathroom attached to my bedroom.' Julia rang the bell and gave instructions to Mrs Finnigan to pass on to Ellen.

'Oh, good. I'll have a rummage through your wardrobe to see if you've got something decent I can borrow while I'm here. How are you getting on with the maid?'

'Ellen is very good at her job, and she suits me perfectly. I apologize for stealing her away from you, Irene, but I heard she was looking for another position, anyway.'

'Don't fret about it. She was one of mummy's maids really. I only borrowed her now and again. I thought you hiring her was a master stroke, especially after that letter she sent. Now she'll have to keep her mouth shut about your little escapade.'

'What letter? What are you talking about?'

'Oops . . . forget I said anything. I expect Latham got to it first, anyway. Be careful of Ellen, Julia. She's a frightful liar. I bet she's told you all sorts of tales about me and my family.'

'Well, no . . . actually, Ellen's been extremely discreet. You're showing an inordinate amount of interest in her. Don't think of trying to win her back. I won't allow it.'

'I expect my mother gave the girl the standard royal lecture on loyalty to former employers before she left.' Rising to her feet, Irene stretched. 'Come upstairs and we'll have a good old chat while my hair's being done.'

'I will in a minute or two. I'm just going to see Fiona Robertson. She likes me to have a drink of orange juice about now. It's full of vitamins apparently, and good for the baby. Would you like one?'

'Only if it's got a measure of gin in it.'

Julia grinned. 'They say that gin is a mother's ruin.'

'Exactly.'

The juice gave Julia the urge to relieve herself. She used the downstairs cloakroom, then went up the stairs slowly, her hand on the banister. She stopped when the baby quivered, placing her palm against the movement. There were only three weeks left to go, and a flicker of excitement filled her. It seemed so near, yet so far.

Whispered voices came to her ears as she neared the top.

'I warn you, Ellen . . . say one word and you'll be in trouble.'

'Agnes Finnigan said that someone who worked for the old gentleman told Robert that Mr Howard had a severe angina attack just after the letter was delivered.'

Julia's eyes sharpened. The letter again – *what letter?*

'Just remember it's in your handwriting, Ellen.'

'Only because you made me write it, Miss.'

'Nobody will believe your word over mine. All you have to do is keep your mouth shut . . . now be quiet about it, will you. Confessing won't bring the old boy back, and how was I to know he had a weak heart. Look what you're doing girl . . . you've missed that bit.'

They'd been talking about her father!

Heart thumping, Julia turned and went downstairs, feeling slightly sick and trying to put two and two together. She gathered that a letter sent to her father – one that had informed him of her own foolishness – had caused the collapse that had put him in hospital. Irene had dictated it. Ellen had written it. Latham had possibly intercepted it. Now her father was dead.

She sat in the armchair and took a deep breath. She must stay calm, and until she found out the truth she must act as though she knew nothing.

The telephone rang. Latham, no doubt. He was checking up on her welfare more often, so her own home had begun to feel more and more like a prison.

She was tempted not to answer it, but if she didn't, Agnes would. 'Latham,' she said with a sigh.

'How did you know it was me?'

'The telephone has a more authoritative ring to it when it's you.'

'Stop it, Julia. Sarcasm doesn't suit you.'

'Then why does it feel so good?'

'Don't upset yourself; it's bad for the baby. How are you, my dear?'

'If only you knew how sick I am of hearing what's good for the baby and what isn't. I'm quite all right. I'm perfectly healthy, my baby is perfectly healthy, and I have a visitor.'

'It's *our* baby, Julia. Who is your visitor?'

'Mrs Argette.'

'Argette . . . Argette . . . Have I met her?'

As an answer it was a let-down. She didn't want to play his games, and impatience nearly choked her. However, she found great satisfaction in saying,

'Yes, of course you've met her, Latham,' and a bitter laugh squeezed out from inside herself. She sent it down the wire to him. 'It's Irene Curruthers, who married a French artist called Jacques and you were the best man . . . all of which you forgot to tell me about.'

'Probably because I didn't think it was important. He was one of Irene's whims to get her parents off her back. No wonder you're feeling fractious.'

'Because Irene's married a French artist? Why should I be upset by that?'

'It's obvious that you're spoiling for a fight and using any excuse.'

'You're trying to make me feel like a bitch. I'm perfectly calm.'

'No, you're not calm at all. I'll be home tomorrow evening and we'll talk things over rationally.'

'By all means. You must excuse me now, Latham; Irene came over so Ellen would do her hair, and now she's going through my wardrobe. It will be my jewellery box next.'

'Give her that green dress with the poppies on. I don't like it on you.'

Julia had worn it when she and Martin had become lovers. 'It's my favourite and I've only worn it twice. Besides, she'll need something with a bit more room in it to accommodate the baby she's carrying.'

There was a sudden silence from the end of the line. That was a better reaction to her goading. 'Are you still there, Latham?' she cooed.

'Irene's in the family way?' he spluttered.

'That's rather a quaint way of putting it, Latham. Irene is expecting a child in November. Goodness, didn't she tell you? Her memory seems to be as bad as yours.'

'I must go, Julia . . . I'll see you later and we'll talk.'

'Yes . . . I do rather think we need to talk.' She took a shot in the dark. 'Especially about the letter.'

'What letter?'

'The one my father received just before he had his collapse . . . the one concerning me. My, my, you do have a bad memory . . . I marvel that you're so successful at business.'

Voice guarded, he muttered, 'I don't know what you're talking about.'

Sick at heart that he could lie about something so important, she couldn't keep the accusation from her voice. 'Yes you do.'

'Have you been going through my desk drawers?'

'Not yet. What was in the letter?'

'Believe me, my love, you don't want to know. Stay out of my study, there's a good girl. There are files I don't want disturbed.'

'I do want to know, Latham. I've got a right to know.'

'I'll deal with it when I get home, and I won't hold anything back.'

She didn't believe him.

'How did you learn about the letter? Servants' gossip, I suppose. Now look, I don't want you to mention a word about this letter to anyone.'

'Why not?'

'Because I'm trying to find out who wrote it.'

She could have told him how she'd already found out, and she could tell *him* who'd written it. But something stopped her. She'd rather tell him that face to face, and when the timing was right.

Irene shouted from the top of the stairs, 'Yoo-hoo darling . . . what's keeping you. Where's my gin and orange?'

'I'll just be a jiffy, Irene,' she shouted back.

'You're not drinking gin are you?'

She allowed her edginess to show with an exaggerated sigh. 'Please don't take me for a fool, Latham. Goodbye, I'll see you tomorrow.' She hung up.

Fifteen

Tired of being kept in the dark, Julia burned with frustration and curiosity over the mentioned letter.

The issue itself made her feel tense, and angry, although she knew she might be reading more into it than there was, and could have questioned Ellen about it. But Latham had told her not to mention it to anybody. She supposed there was some sense in that, considering what she'd overheard.

Julia felt fatigued and heavy after Irene's visit. The strain of being nice to her unwelcome guest in the face of her hypocrisy had been an endurance feat. She'd been nearly at screaming point when Irene left, carrying two of Julia's outfits in a paper carrying bag.

Now the baby pressed against her bladder and its feet pushed against her diaphragm in a quivering stretch. It was hard to believe there was another human being inside her, small, warm, alive and perfect – an infant who would love her and be nurtured by her. Girl or boy, she didn't have a preference. Latham wanted a boy, and what Latham wanted he usually got.

She placed her hand against the knobbly bits. Elbow or knee, she wasn't sure which. 'I'm sorry, but there isn't any room left for you to do your stretching exercises in,' Julia told it, wincing.

She tried hard not to think about the letter, but nevertheless curiosity got the better of her, and her feet carried her into Latham's study. She closed the door behind her, feeling like an intruder. His modern taste had infiltrated through to his work-space. His files were in a cupboard and she threw the doors wide. Where to start?

But no, the letter wouldn't be in a file, since Latham had indicated that it was in a desk drawer – why else would he have asked her if she'd been through his desk?

The pale wooden desk had three drawers to one side, and a silver inkstand with crystal inkwells on top. There was an ashtray and lighter, and a box of Cuban cigars, which struck her as odd because she'd never seen Latham smoke. Perhaps they were for guests. The blotter was clean. A set of bookshelves housed leatherbound books. On a side table stood a silver tantalus, the crystal decanters wearing silver necklaces with brandy, whisky and gin etched on them. The study was white with a navy-blue carpet – rather nautical with a model of a clipper on a shelf.

There was a photograph of them taken on their wedding day in an enamelled frame and another of Latham standing between Irene and Charles on a patio covered in grapevines. Irene was looking up at him, openly adoring and Latham looked amused by it. It couldn't have been taken more than two years ago, but Irene looked as though she'd aged about ten since then. How cruel Latham had been in his treatment of her.

Julia opened the top drawer in the desk. Several writing pads resided there with packets of matching envelopes, erasers, pencils and boxes of pen nibs. He carried a black fountain pen with gold trim and his name etched on the clip – a gift she'd bought him for his birthday.

The middle drawer was stuck – or locked!

The bottom drawer held the type of oddments that such drawers collected: half a pair of cufflinks, a golf ball, a box of matches, a key! She snatched the key up, inserted it in the lock of the middle drawer and cried out in frustration. It didn't fit the drawer.

She wouldn't be beaten, since she could almost smell the letter now.

Going to the fireplace she picked up the poker and tried to insert the end into the gap between the drawer and the body of the desk. It wouldn't budge. No amount of shaking the drawer handle would dislodge the drawer. It was stubborn, like Latham.

She intended to be more stubborn. There had to be a key somewhere. Going to the cupboard she pulled out all his files and emptied them on the floor. Nothing! She looked in all the vases and possible hiding places.

What if the drawer was simply stuck? Taking a grip on the handle she put her foot against the desk and began to pull. Something moved! She pulled harder. There was the sound of screws splintering wood and the handle came off. Staggering backwards with it Julia tripped over the edge of a rug and fell flat on her back.

She lay there, looking up at the ceiling, then turned over on all fours and managed to get to her feet. What if she'd done some damage, hurt the baby?

Her hands went over her stomach. 'I'm so sorry, my little one,' she whispered. Nothing drastic happened in the time she took to recover.

She looked around her. The room was a mess and she didn't have the energy to put it to rights. Latham would be cross with her when he saw what she'd done. Let him be cross, she thought. She didn't care. It served him right for not showing her the letter that had caused her father to have that attack.

She closed the door behind her and went in search of Fiona. 'I fell,' she said, 'but it was on the carpet and I landed on my back. I didn't hurt myself.'

The nurse clicked her tongue. 'You're looking tired, Mrs Miller.'

'I've got a bit of a headache.'

'Because you missed your rest today, I expect. Lay down on the bed, my dear, and let me take a look at you.' As the nurse's capable hands felt around the shape of the baby she said knowledgeably, 'I think the head's engaged. I shouldn't be at all surprised if the baby didn't arrive a wee bit early.' A metal cone was pressed against Julia's stomach and Fiona's ear applied to the narrow end.

Fiona smiled to herself. 'The baby's heart is ticking quite nicely.' However, when she checked Julia's pulse, she frowned. 'My, what have you been up to? That's racing along, which is not good for the baby. You'd better get into bed and stay there until the doctor visits in the morning.'

Upset by the way she'd placed her baby in danger, Julia burst into tears. 'My husband will be furious with me when he gets home.'

'Nonsense, dear. He's a lovely wee man.'

'You don't know him. He used to beat me, and he has a mistress.'

'Your imagination is getting the better of you, dear.'

'No it's not. Ask Agnes. I only married Latham because my father wanted me too. I'm in love with somebody else.'

'Hush now, dear.'

'You don't believe me, do you?'

'I'm aware of certain situations in your household and sympathise with you. Some men are like that, and there's nothing women can do about it, except endure. I just don't want you to get upset. The baby will settle your man down, just you wait and see.'

Fiona was humouring her; Julia could hear it in her voice. 'Have you ever been married, Fiona?'

'No I haven't, Mrs Miller. I'm completely on my own. I was in love with someone once, a doctor. He married someone else.'

'I love a doctor too, but he's gone away. You will keep that a secret, won't you?'

'Of course. May I give you a word of advice, Mrs Miller? You must learn to be happy with what you have. Everything will feel better after the baby is born, I promise. Come on now, into bed with you.'

Julia was more than happy to go to bed. Entertaining Irene had exhausted her, and her emotions were drained by her argument with Latham. Sleep brought forgetfulness.

When she woke the lamp in the corner gave out a soft glow. Latham sat by her bedside reading a book, and she couldn't decide whether he looked cross or not. She felt a moment of pity for him because she couldn't bring herself to love him.

He must have sensed that she was awake because his glance went to her face and he smiled. 'Nurse Robertson rang and told me you'd had a fall. Are you all right?'

'Yes . . . I'm sorry if I caused you to worry . . . I couldn't wait until tomorrow. I didn't mean to break the desk. The handle came off in my hand, and I flew backwards and landed on the floor.'

Unexpectedly, the telling-off she expected didn't eventuate. Instead, one eyebrow rose and he grinned wryly at her. 'And you knocked all the files out of the cupboard as you flew past, I expect.'

She giggled. 'I was looking for the key.'

Because Latham was always unpredictable, when he reached out to touch her face she expected a slap and flinched away from him.

'What have I done to you?' he whispered.

If only he'd been gentler in the first place. She could never love him now – not now. Her heart belonged to another, and that would never change. But she was moved by this sudden glimpse of vulnerability in him and felt unhappy that he wanted so much of her that it obviously wasn't in her nature to give.

'The letter was in my safe . . . I did say I'd let you read it.'

'What does it say?'

'Are you sure you want to know, even though your father didn't want you to see it?'

She nodded.

He took it from his pocket and handed it to her. The colour drained from her face as she read it through. Yes, it was in Ellen's handwriting, and the girl couldn't spell. How spiteful Irene had been to do this. Even now, eighteen months after the event, she'd made it obvious to Ellen that she intended to carry on with the deceit if need be.

When he took the paper from her and shoved it in his pocket she said, 'This is a vile thing to do to my father, when he wouldn't have hurt a fly.'

'Obviously it's written by somebody at that party who was uneducated . . . and when I find out who sent it I'm going to tear them apart with my bare hands.'

Latham was capable of doing such a thing. But if Irene was to be believed he had already brought their association to an end. Irene was married and expecting a baby. What if Latham hurt her? 'Will you do something for me, Latham?'

'Of course.'

'Burn the letter and forget about it.'

'Burn it. It's the only evidence we've got?'

'Evidence of what, that I made an abject fool of myself? At the time I was carried away by a foolish idea, and although nothing came of it I bitterly regret the whole affair. My father is dead and I don't want you to take revenge on his behalf, since I was partly to blame . . . so will you please allow the matter to drop, and right now.'

His expression told her that the thought of dropping the issue was alien to his nature. She placed her hand over his and injected a little humour into the situation. 'Do this for me, please. No harm was done, and you rescued me from a fate worse than death.' Though she briefly wondered which fate would have been worse in fact.

When he took the letter from his pocket, screwed it up, placed it in the grate and put a match to it her respect for him went up a notch. Finally he'd listened to her point of view and had conceded to it.

'Thank you,' she said, watching the paper twist and curl in the flames to become dark flakes of ash that floated up into the chimney. 'Were there really three naked men there? I can't remember.'

'Only two . . . You made a derogatory remark about their manly appendages then turned on your side and went to sleep.'

'Did I?' Her eyes flew open and she laughed. 'I did no such thing . . . you're teasing me.' She paid him a small compliment. 'You were very kind the next day, you know.'

Smiling a little, Latham leaned forward and kissed her. It was a rare moment of shared intimacy that she enjoyed, for it was in his nature to exact a price for every favour. Odd that it was his mistress she was saving from his ire at this moment. Perhaps she would become as devious as him in time, but in the meantime, for her own sake she must try to become a better wife.

It took every effort in her to hide her reluctance, because for this deception she practised she'd pay a heavy price. Latham would expect her to be a perfect wife in every way from now on.

Fiona Robertson had been right, the baby arrived two weeks early.

Julia was seated on a seat in the garden admiring the roses when the first pain cramped. Placing her hands against the small of her back she smiled as it worked its way to the front. Her hands came round to cradle her stomach. 'All right, baby, it seems as though today is going to be your birthday. I believe you and I have some work to do before the day is out. Just stay put there until I get us back to the nurse.'

She walked slowly, her hands cradling her heavy stomach. She was in shouting distance of the house when the second pain came, much stronger. She doubled up. A gush of warm water flowed down her legs and filled her shoes.

Footsteps came running. Ellen said, 'I saw you from the window. Oh, my God . . . your skirt's all wet.'

The pain subsided and Julia drew in a deep breath. 'My water has broken. Help me into the house, please, Ellen, then you can go and find Fiona.'

There was a note of panic in Ellen's voice. 'She's gone off into the village to get some things she needed.'

'How long ago?'

'Twenty minutes.'

'Good . . . then she won't be very long.' The time between the two contractions had only been a few minutes, and from what Julia had read on the subject, they should be further apart at the beginning of labour.

Shuffling indoors she left a trail of droplets behind her. The next pain was strong in comparison to the two before, and there was pressure on her pelvis. She gasped and sank down on the nursing chair while the pain passed.

'Are you all right, Mrs Miller?'

'I think the baby's in a bit of a hurry. Help me change, please Ellen. There's a cotton nightgown that does up down the front in that drawer. I'll wear that for the time being.'

'Yes, Ma'am.'

There came the sound of the nurse's voice talking to Agnes Finnigan.

'There she is,' Ellen said with some relief, then shouted, 'Nurse Robertson . . . Mrs Miller is having the baby.'

Two sets of footsteps pattered across the floor. Fiona became all efficiency, and soon Julia was going through the preliminaries necessary to ensure the child's comfortable passage into the world. Agnes Finnigan hovered, wringing her hands.

She was sent packing by Fiona, who gave her a task to do.

Julia's labour pains stopped.

'The baby is having a rest and gathering strength. First babies usually take their time. Mrs Finnigan has telephoned your husband and he's on the way home. And the doctor will come as soon as he's needed.'

Fiona was a wonderfully calming woman, and Julia smiled. 'Thank you, Fiona.'

A warm cotton blanket was tucked around her. 'Now, my dear, I want you to get some rest. You were up early. It's only eleven o'clock so get a couple of hours sleep if you can. Don't worry if the sheets get a bit damp because there's a rubber sheet protecting the mattress. I'll be pottering around, and you'll just need to call me if you need me. Would you like some music to listen to? I believe there's a nice piano concerto on.'

Julia went to sleep to the deliciously light strains of Schumann's Piano Concerto.

She woke to the excitement of the Saint-Saëns Organ Concerto. She gazed at the clock. She'd slept for exactly four hours and was lying in a damp patch. A pain gathered force in her back, then it tore into her. She groaned.

Fiona joined her. She folded back the blanket and placed a cold hand on Julia's rippling stomach. She glanced at the clock. 'Tell me when the next pain comes, my dear.'

It wasn't long, about five minutes. The blanket was replaced.

'Time to call the doctor, I think, then I'll change the bedding. After that I'll tell your husband you're awake so he can spend a minute or two with you.'

Latham wore a worried look on his face. He took her hands in his. 'Julia, are you all right? I heard you groan.'

'You'll probably hear me groan a lot more. It's . . . painful.' Here it came again, a long drawn-out cramping pain. She tried to relax, to let the pain roll over her. Groaning helped, and because he'd made her groan with pain on occasions in the past when he'd been rough with her, she used the opportunity to get her own back by groaning louder than she needed too.

When she finished groaning Latham looked as though he'd rather be anywhere else but by her bedside, which gave her a great deal of satisfaction.

Fiona bustled back in. 'Time for some gas and air, I think. You should leave now, Mr Miller. The maternity ward is no place for husbands.'

'I'll be in my study if I'm needed.'

'Aye . . . but your wee contribution to this event has already been made, so I doubt if you will be needed just yet.'

Julia, who'd just inhaled the gas and air and felt as though she was floating on a cloud, chuckled, and even Latham managed a shamefaced grin at the nurse's saucy remark.

Julia's laughter quickly turned into another long drawn-out groan and she clutched at Latham's hand. Her fingernails dug into him, leaving several red indentations in his skin.

'I'll be all right, Latham. I promise. It won't be much longer.'

Latham lifted her hand in his and kissed it, whispering, 'I'll leave you to it then. I love you.' He left.

The nurse's glance followed him. 'Anyone can see that he adores you. He's a good man and you'll come to love him in time, I'm sure.'

And that was a problem to her. Life would be easier if he didn't love her, Julia thought, because she'd never be able to love him.

The baby put in an appearance an hour later, slithering into the doctor's hands with a loud and lusty fanfare.

'You have a handsome son,' he said.

Fiona Robertson smiled. 'He certainly has a good pair of lungs.'

Craning her neck to catch a glimpse of him, Julia was disappointed that she could only see a leg with a foot on the end, beyond the doctor's stooped shoulder. But it was such a sweet little leg and foot.

'Patience, Mrs Miller; I have yet to cut the cord.'

She remembered Martin's remark about her belly button and smiled. 'Make it a pretty one.'

'I take it you'd rather have a rose than a cauliflower, so I'll do my best.'

The nurse wrapped the child in a flannel rug and placed him into Julia's waiting arms. He was red from crying and his face was all crumpled. His hair was dark and spiky.

Julia fell instantly in love. 'There, there, my roaring little bull; I'm sorry it was so painful,' she said, and she kissed his wrinkled forehead.

The boy stopped bawling and his head moved at the sound of her voice.

'Here I am, my love.'

His eyes opened, and they were a deep blue like Martin's. 'You are so much like your father,' she whispered, and opened the top of her nightgown as he turned his head to nuzzle against her breast. His mouth closed around her nipple and he sucked it in, claiming it as his own. His eyes closed and he fell asleep.

'There's a clever wee lad, and bonny with it,' Fiona said.

There was a sense of wonder in Julia that she could have produced a son of such perfection. She couldn't stop looking at him, at his miniature nose, his feet and the translucent shell-like hands with their tiny nails.

'Everything seems to be all right down here, Nurse. Placenta is intact and has come away clean, and there are no stitches needed. A very easy birth indeed, Mrs Miller, and a handsome healthy boy as a result. Well done. Do you have a name picked out for him?'

'We've decided to call him Benjamin after my father, though we'll probably call him Ben . . . and Latham as a second name, after my husband.'

'A fine name indeed. I'll go and see Mr Miller, give him the news and share a glass of brandy and a cigar with him while Nurse Robertson cleans you up. We can do the paperwork. Mr Miller will be pleased to know that baby Ben has inherited his looks.'

Julia doubted that he had. Ben was made in the image of Martin Lee-Trafford. But she wasn't worried. Like the doctor, Latham would see only what he wanted to see.

Latham came through later, after the nurse had cleaned her up and made her comfortable. Ben had been cleaned, and oil applied to his skin. Although Fiona had wanted to put him in his crib, Julia wouldn't allow her to.

She twisted a spike of his hair around her finger, turning it into a curl. 'I'm not parting with him yet. He needs to get to know me.'

There was a touch of disapproval in Fiona's next words. 'You'll spoil him, cuddling him like that, Mrs Miller. Children need to be trained right from the beginning.'

'They need to know that they're loved right from the beginning, so they feel secure.'

There was a knock at the open door and Latham came in. He nodded to the nurse, who left the room, then sat on the edge of the bed and gazed at the baby. A smile softened his mouth and he pushed the shawl away from Ben's face with his finger. Julia held her breath. 'The doctor said he looks like me . . . yes, I can see a strong resemblance.'

She pointed out, 'Ben's eyes are blue.'

'I recall that my mother's eyes were blue,' he said, which saved Julia from having to lie about the colour of her own mother's eyes.

'May I hold him?' he said.

She giggled at that. 'Of course you may.'

She placed him in Latham's arms and he sat there stiffly, as though the boy was made of porcelain and any movement might shatter him.

'Relax a little, Latham. He won't break.'

Ben yawned, and giving a small yelp, he burrowed his nose into Latham's pullover.

Alarm appeared on Latham's face. 'Here . . . it's no good doing that, young man. Your mother sees to all that sort of thing.'

Ben's eyes opened and he gave a loud wail.

Latham grinned. 'I don't think he likes the look of me.'

'His reasoning isn't that far advanced, as yet. Besides, I doubt if he can see you clearly. The nurse said it might take several weeks before his eyes are able to focus. They go more on sound, touch and smell. If you handle him and talk gently to him he'll soon begin to recognize you.'

'Hello, Ben, my boy; I'm your father,' he whispered, and kissed his dark head. When Ben pursed his mouth his cheeks bulged and a frown creased his brow.

Latham exchanged a smile with her. 'I hope I'm better looking than that.'

'Not when you're cross. He's just a bit squashed from the birth. He will be quite handsome when he's recovered.'

The glance Latham bestowed on her was surprisingly prideful. 'He really does look a lot like me.'

She didn't allow her relief that Latham had accepted this little cuckoo in the nest to show.' It won't hurt to hope, I suppose. It's early days yet . . . He's more interested in learning how to feed, I think.'

Latham handed him back, then undid her nightgown and placed the boy's mouth against her nipple. Ben curled his tongue under her nipple and began to suck.

Pushing the flimsy cotton fabric over her other breast aside Latham gazed at her. He pulled her arm aside when she went to cover herself. 'Your breasts look lovely like that, so full and so swollen.' He gently kissed the unengaged nipple then covered it. He stood and gazed down at her. 'You look tired.'

'Giving birth is hard work, and I have reason to look tired . . . but Latham . . . I'm so happy I could burst from it. Ben's such an adorable baby and I just love him.'

'Do everything the nurse tells you then. She was right about not spoiling him; boys need discipline.'

She protested, 'Ben's a newborn baby; he needs love.'

'He will be loved, but I'm given to understand that babies thrive on a regular regime. To start with he can have his feeds at regular intervals, not when he feels like it.'

Perhaps she was being sensitive, but there seemed to be a faint threat contained in his words. Latham had told her he loved her on several occasions, yet he found it necessary to question and ill-treat her. To Latham, love meant possession. Holding her helpless infant close to her heart she was filled with dismay. She was too weak to defend Ben at the moment, should she need to. Yet she tried.

'What does Fiona Robertson know? She's not a nanny.'

'You could have had a trained nanny, Julia . . . It's not too late.'

She didn't want to argue with him, not now, but said anyway, 'I want to look after him myself . . . do everything for him.'

'And you will eventually. That's why the nurse is staying on, to make sure you know what you're doing. She's worked out a schedule for the next three months and I'd like you to follow it. By that time you will probably be ready to resume your place by my side. We'll spend more time in London, and take in a play every now and again.'

Fiona was a nice, well-meaning woman and Julia liked her, but how could someone who'd never been a mother teach *her* how to be one? Babies were individuals, and mothering them an instinct that was both emotional and protective, not something one learned to do from a book.

Already she could feel a connection forming between herself and Ben. It was a thin thread, and the more she handled her infant the stronger that would become. She didn't want him attaching himself to a woman who would be gone from his life in a few weeks.

But it seemed that there was no choice being offered to her. For her lying-in period the baby was brought to her at regular intervals to be fed. When Ben cried during the night she could detect the hunger and need in his cry, and her heart bled for him.

She felt out of sorts, but accepted the congratulations, cards and gifts from visitors, who were advised not to stay too long, and could only view the infant from afar, and when Fiona was in the kitchen and Julia had charge of him.

Irene arrived. She looked healthier than the previous time Julia had seen her. She gazed at Ben for a long time, her eyes calculating as they finally darted to Julia. She gave a small, knowing smile that sent a chill running through Julia. 'He looks more like you than he does Latham.'

'Nonsense, he's the image of Latham, everyone says so.' She felt the urge to prick back. 'He also looks like my father. You remember him, don't you? I've called my baby after him. A pity he didn't live long enough to see his grandchild.'

Her barb hit home because Irene looked away and mumbled, 'Of course I remember your father.'

'You can hold Ben if you'd like to.'

Irene shuddered. 'I wouldn't dream of it, darling. I know you think he's the gnat's buzz and all that, but to be frank, he smells of sour milk and so do you. It's rather unpleasant.'

'All babies smell like that.'

'Well, I'd rather not smell like it so I'll get a wet nurse to feed mine . . . and don't ask me to become his godmother.'

Now it was Julia's turn to shudder. 'I wouldn't dream of asking you.'

Irene's eyes flew open at her retort. 'For heaven's sake, why not, pray?'

'Since we're being frank, Irene, a godmother is responsible for a child's morals. I don't think you have many of your own, and you need to grow up.'

Irene laughed. 'You're certainly stretching your claws now, and you're no fun any more.'

'Life isn't all fun, and bringing up a child is a responsibility. You have to make the proper choices.'

Irene said a trifle wistfully, 'Oh, I don't blame you for thinking that way, and you're right about me being immoral. Actually, you're a much better person than I'll ever be . . . a pity you're so self-righteous with it.'

'Am I? I don't mean to be.'

Irene chuckled. 'Sincerely, Julia, you'd be the first person I'd approach if my child ever needed support. In fact you'd be the only person I would trust. However, that doesn't mean I think you're perfect, and you're being an absolute mother superior at the moment, as well as a ruddy prig.' She held out a package. 'Here, I bought Ben a gift . . . a teddy bear. It growls when you tip it forward. Listen.'

The package gave a muffled 'Maaaaaa' and Julia laughed. 'It sounds like a lamb being strangled.'

'I think it needs some air. I'd better go now before I contaminate your dear boy.'

Words, Julia thought. That's all it was, and she wouldn't allow herself to be fooled by them. She knew when she was being manipulated. 'Oh, do shut up with the conscience-pricking stuff, Irene. Thank you for the teddy bear.'

Irene grinned as she kissed her cheek. 'I brought your clothes back. I gave them to Ellen to wash.' Her eyes gleamed with malice. 'Now I shall go and find Latham, have a cup of coffee with him and chat about old times. He must be getting tired of playing the doted husband and father.'

Bitch, Julia thought.

Two days later Latham went back to London. 'The baby disturbs my sleep and makes me tired during the day,' he said by way of excuse.

Julia got out of bed as soon as the car drove off.

Fiona protested. 'Mrs Miller . . . it's only been ten days. The doctor advised three weeks. Look how weak you are; what will Mr Miller say when he finds out?'

'He won't find out if you don't tell him. Stop fussing. I haven't exercised my muscles so I'm bound to feel weak at first.'

She also felt strangely thin, as though she were made out of paper and was balanced on legs made of stalks. That wasn't going to stop her from reclaiming her child and exercising her rights as a mother though, and she had noted that Fiona took sleeping pills.

The very next time Ben cried in the night she lifted him from his crib and took him through to her bedroom. There she sat in the nursing chair in front of the window. Tucking a knitted rug around them both, she put him to her breast and hoped the nurse didn't wake while she sang softly to him. It was cruel to miss this feed out and keep him hungry in an effort to train him to sleep during the night.

Ben snuggled against her; his initial gulps frantic as he worked to take the edge from his hunger. She enjoyed her baby's mouth tugging at her breast – enjoyed his little sighs and mews of contentment, and most of all enjoyed their private moments of togetherness.

It was early morning and there was a full moon riding across the sky in her window. The landscape was painted in lumines-cent white – the grass and summer flowers were drenched in heavy dew, so it looked as though it was sprinkled with pearls. A faint mist diffused the light.

She caressed her baby's soft skin, marvelling at him. There seemed to be nobody but the pair of them alone in a world filled with moonlight.

As Ben's stomach distended with her milk his tension left him. She laid his floppy body against her shoulder and he deflated with a loud, rasping belch.

'I'll always love you,' she whispered to her son, because her parents had made sure she knew she was loved, and she wanted that security for Ben.

She'd said exactly the same thing to Martin. 'I'll always love you.' And she always would.

She carried a memory of Martin like a soft ache inside her. Although that ache was filled with the sadness of loss, she would rather carry it with her than not. And she had his son as part of her body and her heart. She whispered, 'Where are you now, Martin; are you well and happy?'

She would write him a note and tell him about the baby – send it to that lawyer to forward to Martin so he could celebrate her joy.

There was a quiet bark and something moved in the shadows. She narrowed her eyes in on a fox, which turned to stare at her through gleaming eyes when she gave a little gasp. It stood there unafraid and untamed – off to raid a chicken house somewhere, or to lay in wait for an early morning rabbit to emerge from its burrow to frisk about in the early morning dew.

Only the fox didn't take what it needed to survive. It killed and maimed for the pleasure of it. Suddenly, its ears pricked up and it turned predatory eyes towards the woods. It was gone in a moment, a streak of fire across the garden in the cool glow of the moonlight.

The child in her arms gave a soft murmur and showed signs of waking. Julia placed him on the other breast and allowed him to top himself up before taking him back to his crib to tuck him in.

'There, that should last you until six o'clock. Sweet dreams, my love,' she murmured, and kissed his soft, pink cheek.

Sixteen

Martin didn't know whether to laugh or cry when he read the letter from Julia, so he did both.

June 1923
Martin, dearest,

I know we decided it was better not to remain in touch, but I was desperate to share my news with you. I have given birth to a son. Benjamin Latham is so sweet, so greedy and so very basic and special that I'm convinced he's the most perfect specimen of an infant in the entire world.

I can almost hear you laugh at that. Yes, I do know all new mothers must think such thoughts of their firstborn, but in Ben's case it's the absolute truth!

He is named in honour of my father, and after my husband. Ben is so adorable, and I know you would love him.

Martin, please don't answer this letter as it will make life awkward, and I'm doing the best I can under the circumstances. I just needed to share this special moment with you . . . only you would know how much. I will not write again, my love, but will leave you in peace to get on with your life. Please be strong for both of us.

Wherever you are, I wish you every happiness and success. Know that I think of you often. Give my regards to Clarence and Billy Boy. I do hope they're behaving themselves and affording you pleasure as companions.

Much love always.
Julia.

A son! Martin had delivered several first sons over the past six months, and yes, they were all special to their mothers. So were the daughters. The women from these parts had nothing much to look forward to except a hand-to-mouth existence. Every penny was stretched to the limit, every rag had its use. Hems went up and down with each successive child and clothes were patched and darned. For the most part the locals were decent, hardworking, honest – and perpetually hungry.

He couldn't help but wonder how Julia would fare with her son living in an environment such as Colifield. But it wasn't his business to compare. Status was mostly an accident of birth. If he'd been born here he'd likely have gone down the pit at the age of fourteen. But having been raised in the same sort of environment as Julia, he'd been given a good education and encouraged to enter a profession that would not only bring him respect, but also had the potential to provide him with a comfortable living for life.

Martin loved his profession, which gave him a great deal of satisfaction now he knew his mind had healed. Ideally, he'd also like a wife and children, someone to go home to every night, someone to listen to his complaints and grumbles – to argue, and to laugh and cry with him. But if he couldn't have Julia, he'd remain single.

He slid the letter into his waistcoat pocket, knowing he would leave these grim surrounds when his contract was up. He would hand the job over to Mrs Seeble's youngest son, who was currently at medical school in Edinburgh. Her two other sons ran a law practice with their father.

Godfrey Seeble assisted Martin while the Tomlinsons took a well-earned break. The experience would afford him valuable training on the job. Godfrey, who had the calm and capable nature of his mother, had been quick to learn, and enthusiastic. For him it was truly a vocation.

Between them they'd made it through the month, and the practice was now about to revert to normal.

'It's a bit humbling to learn one can so easily be managed without,' Jack said with a wide smile. 'If I'd known I would have stayed away for another month.'

'You're just back in time for an outbreak of measles. I doubt that the Philips' youngest daughter will survive it. It's affected her lungs. The child was weak and sickly to begin with and she's got no strength to fight it off with.'

'Nature is selective sometimes. Have you warned her parents there's not much hope?'

Martin nodded. 'I've also informed the priest on their behalf. I'd like a second opinion on Adele Brown as soon as possible.'

'What am I looking for?'

'Ovarian cancer, which has spread into other areas of her reproductive system.'

'Left it too late, has she?'

'I'd say so. A total hysterectomy might prolong her life but I think the cancer is well established. She's a widow with four young children.'

'She has a sister, I recall. Will she take the children?'

'Apparently not. The sister has several children of her own and can't afford to take them in. They'll have to go to the orphanage.'

Jack sighed. 'If she's a catholic the local priest will see to that. They have some scheme that sends orphans to Canada. There are many organizations that have orphan migration schemes to Australia and New Zealand, including Barnardo's and the YMCA. The lads work on farms as cheap labour while the girls are trained in domestic skills.'

'You know, Jack, most of those children will be used as free labour, and many will be abused.'

'It can't be helped, and they could also be abused here. Some people take advantage of the weak. Organizations are doing what they think is best by relocating them and giving them a future to look forward to. It might not be an ideal one, but there's nothing left for them here except to live on the streets and break the law to support themselves. Do you have a viable alternative for the thousands of orphans created by the war and the Spanish influenza?'

'Unfortunately no.'

'You have a soft heart, Martin, but you must try to separate your emotions from your job. We can't take everyone's troubles on to our shoulders. We're qualified to heal our patients' physical ailments, and are just a small cog in the wheel. There are others more fitted to help the helpless, hopeless and homeless.'

Martin laughed. 'And some of them happen to be working in this practice.'

'Ah, you noticed, did you?' Jack said with a faint smile. 'The difference is that our emotions don't bleed as much as yours do. You have a nurturing soul, Martin. You should get yourself a wife and some children to care for.'

'There's only one woman for me, and she happens to be married.'

'That will break a few maidens' hearts around here. Is that why you came here?'

'Partly. For her sake I made a clean break. I thought it would be such a busy area that I wouldn't have time to think of her.'

'And?'

'I find her impossible to forget. But she wasn't the only reason I came here. Hugh said you'd be a good teacher, and you are. I've learned a lot, especially from you and your wife's attitude towards those in your care. Your patients trust you. I can't hope to emulate that, but I'm grateful.'

'You're more than competent at your job, Martin, and have rightly earned a great deal of respect . . . and you never know what's around the corner. You might find a good woman yet.'

Martin left Colifield a year later, the train transporting him rapidly away from the grey smoky air. There was a touch of regret in him at leaving, mostly because of the friendships he'd left behind, but he was looking forward to the future with some enthusiasm.

The further south he went the greener the land became. He'd forgotten the power of the colour green, a soothing balm for the eyes. And he'd forgotten the sight of the rich gold undulation of wheat in a summer breeze, the redness of poppies, the purple blue of harebells and the crowded, but cheerful spills of golden rod in the hedges.

Clarence and Billy Boy were travelling in a large wire-fronted crate in the goods van. Godfrey Seeble had moved into the flat he'd just vacated, and had offered to look after them, but Martin couldn't bear the thought of leaving them behind.

'I promise you that this is the last time you'll have to go on such a long journey,' he told them when they reached London.

They seemed surprisingly calm as he exchanged a damp wad of a Newcastle newspaper in their prison for the more sedate London Times. He rubbed their chins and left them in the care of a kindly keeper in the station luggage office along with his suitcase, while he bought himself a small Morris tourer that hadn't seen many miles.

He paid the keeper a florin for the care of his cats and loaded them into the back seat. He would have liked to let them out for some exercise before he motored down to Hampshire, but he didn't dare in case they took fright and fled.

He spoke soothingly to them when they began to fret. 'It won't be much longer, I promise. You'll like Bournemouth. It will be quite genteel after Colifield, and there's a conservatory which you can have the free run of until you get used to the place.'

After half an hour on the road the cats resigned themselves to another journey in captivity, and they fell asleep, waking every so often to plaintively voice their complaints.

It was a warm August evening and the sun was beginning to dip below the horizon when he entered his childhood home.

Overseen by his lawyer, his goods had been taken out of storage, checked against the inventory, and delivered earlier. The house had been cleaned ready for his arrival and he could no longer smell his childhood in it.

There were letters on the sideboard. Eagerly he picked them up and shuffled through them. One was from his lawyer. It contained a short welcome home message, and a long account for the recent business done on Martin's behalf. The basics had been bought and were in the larder, the note said. There was a letter from the medical board and a bill for the gas that the tenant should have paid. It was a small one, so he wouldn't bother to chase them up for it. The final letter wasn't in Julia's handwriting. But why should he expect a letter from her when she'd said she wouldn't write again

'What did you expect after all this time?' he said, and didn't have an answer. He hoped she was happy with her baby to love as he opened the letter. It was from a handyman-come-gardener offering his expertise. The place would certainly need one before too long. He threw the letters back on the sideboard to read at his leisure.

He filled a dirt tray for the cats, opened a tin of sardines and gave them a saucer of milk, and another with water to wash everything down with. He set them free in the conservatory. They cautiously emerged from the cage and sniffed their way around. Billy Boy got to the food first and hooked a sardine out of the dish. Clarence followed suit. When the food was gone they began to clean themselves. They could sleep in the travelling crate until they got their bearings, and Martin left them to it.

He went through to the two front rooms running along one side of the hall. They had an adjoining door. One would be his consulting room, the other the waiting room. He'd have the front room partitioned off to make space for a reception area, and the patients could use the downstairs cloakroom if they needed to.

He was tired after all that travelling. He made himself a jam sandwich and washed it down with a cup of tea before he went upstairs. He pushed open the window and the room was filled with warm air sprinkled with the tangy smell of the sea. Fully clothed, he fell on to the unmade bed. The sea gave a soft hush as it ran up on to the sand, soothing him.

A ship was anchored off shore and a woman waded ashore. Her evening gown of gold lamé shed the water as she emerged and he noticed that she wore a fox fur around her neck. Its mouth was open, showing a pink tongue and sharp white teeth, as though it had died taking its last breath. He reached out and touched its gleaming eye, then jerked as its teeth closed around his hand.

His father appeared. 'She's nothing to you, son.'

'She's my mother.'

'Not any more.'

'She's my mother,' he insisted.

'If she'd loved you she would have written.'

He woke with a start to broad daylight, the words falling from his tongue. 'Perhaps she has written, and my father kept the letters from me.'

And he remembered the boxes he hadn't opened, and the documents files he hadn't got around to sorting out.

But although he searched through them he found nothing.

It was Julia's twenty-third birthday and they were in Surrey. Latham had thrown her a party in the garden. The French doors were opened to give access to the patio and the garden was a riot of summer colours.

Agnes Finnigan had made her a birthday cake. Robert was dispensing drinks and keeping an eye on Ellen, who trotted around serving the guests with snacks and wine. She sent Robert the occasional smile. Julia smiled, having noticed before that the pair were interested in each other, and she was watching the romance blossom with interest.

Latham was showing off Ben. Her son was getting a bit fractious. Latham nodded to Fiona Robertson, who had stayed on as nanny despite Julia's protests.

'We'll put him on a bottle,' he'd said. 'I need you in London from time to time to act as hostess.'

'But I want to feed him myself.'

'For God's sake, Julia, he's over a year old. You've fed him for long enough and have begun to make a fetish of it. Nurse Robertson said a feeding bottle is just as good, and more reliable.'

As usual, Julia had been overruled. Latham plied her with the best clothes and jewellery money could buy and she became the perfect sparkling hostess. She hated being in London with him, hated her role, that only required her to look elegant, smile and agree with everything Latham said – when she wanted to be with her son. In private her life was hell, unless she did exactly what she was told – but there was still a spark of rebellion in her that wouldn't be subdued.

Irene wasn't at the party. She now lived in France. Latham had taken up with her again; Julia could smell Irene's perfume on his clothes. Julia pretended she didn't know what was going on, and only mentioned her now and again.

'She's given birth to a girl,' Latham had told her when she'd asked him if he'd heard.

'What's her name?'

'Lisette.'

The next time Latham was going to France she bought Lisette a sweet little doll dressed in a pink velvet dress and bonnet, with ribbons and lace. 'Can you remember the father's name for the card,' she asked Latham, simply out of devilment, and his eyes narrowed and she thought he was going to lash out at her.

'Jacques,' he said shortly.

She wrote on the card, *To Jacques and Irene, congratulations on the birth of your daughter Lisette. Best wishes from Latham and Julia Miller.*

That had been six months ago. She'd been tempted to take Ben and leave Latham, but she had nowhere else to go and he controlled all the money. Besides which, he would hunt her down, and he'd find her and take her back. He might even separate her from Ben. Then her life wouldn't be worth living.

She'd wondered how much longer they would all keep up the charade. Why couldn't he just be satisfied with one woman – preferably Irene, who loved him?

The past year had been difficult. No matter how hard she tried to be the wife he wanted her to be, Latham had gone back to his old habits.

Now he rapped a spoon against a glass and the guests gathered around. He beckoned to her and slid a sapphire and diamond ring on her finger.

'To the mother of my son, my beloved wife . . .'

She could sell her jewels.

'who is more precious to me . . .'

. . . and her mother's silver fox fur coat as well.

than life itself.'

. . . and her father's car . . .

'Would you please raise your glasses . . .' His fingers tightened against her already bruised skin. '. . . to my beautiful wife, Julia.'

'To Julia!'

The gasp she gave when he pinched her was lost in the cheers, and she managed to pull a smile to her face as she made the required response. 'Thank you, darling, how very sweet. You're much too kind and generous.'

He took her face in his hands and kissed her mouth until she felt like gagging. Releasing her he gazed into her eyes, his hooded and bland, as always. 'Nothing is too good for my Julia,' he said.

He'd kill her if she left him, and she'd never see her son again. As it was, Ben was beginning to turn more and more to Fiona for the meagre amount of mothering he got! It must be easier to look after a child when the deepest of emotions were not involved, she thought.

A week later they were back in Surrey and as soon as they walked through the door, the first place she went was the nursery.

She was feeling happy. Not only was she going to see her son, but Latham had told her he was going to France for a couple of weeks. Charles Curruthers would come for him in the aeroplane.

Ben was in his cot, but awake. He scrambled upright, gave her a big smile that sent her heart into a roll and held out his arms and shrieked, 'Mummy!'

She inhaled his baby boy smell as she kissed the soft folds of his neck, making him giggle. 'Ben, my dove! I've missed you so much. You've grown a thousand teeth since I last saw you, and look how tall you're getting.' Scooping him from his cot she hugged him tight.

Fiona had disapproval written all over her face as she bustled through. 'Mrs Miller, I've been trying to get him off to sleep all morning, and look how excited you've made him.'

Julia knew it was about time she asserted her own authority where Ben was concerned. It was ridiculous to expect her to take instructions from an employee. 'What for, when he sleeps all night. He's not going to want to sleep if he's not tired, is he?'

'You don't understand. He has to have regular hours of sleep—'

'I do understand that, Fiona, but he needs to sleep when he's tired, and nature takes care of that. I'm his mother. I love him, and I'll cuddle him any time I wish. Now, if that upsets your routine I'm sorry, but you'll just have to put up with it. In fact, I want to know exactly what your routine is. Is that understood?'

'Yes, Mrs Miller.' Fiona went off tight-lipped, and began to fold nappies.

Julia knew Fiona took her job seriously, and she would complain to Latham, but she didn't really care.

Sure enough, she was summonsed to Latham's study. She sighed. 'Are you going to take me to task for my disagreement with Fiona Robertson?'

'I am. The woman is employed for her expertise.'

'Then what's my role in the bringing up of my son?'

He sighed. 'Julia . . . I'm doing my best to understand you, but most women would be pleased to have help with such good qualifications. Who else would look after him while we're in London?'

'If we took him with us I'd be able to look after him myself.'

He said mildly, 'My dear. I'm sure you wouldn't enjoy dealing with his nappies and bottles. Think of what it would do to those long nails of yours. Now stop all this nonsense; I don't need it when I'm on the eve of my departure to the continent.'

'Why are you going to France?'

'I have business there.'

'Irene, I presume . . . doesn't her husband mind?'

'I don't know what you're talking about.'

Her heart began to pick up speed. 'What if I said: If you go to France I won't be here when you come back?'

A nerve flickered in his jaw. 'Are you saying that?'

'Yes.'

He laughed. 'I'll drag you through the courts and get custody of my son. Your name would be mud.'

'I haven't done anything wrong.'

Opening the top drawer in his desk he took out a piece of paper and threw it on the desk. The colour drained from her face so fast that she experienced a moment of dizziness. 'But you burned that . . . I saw you?'

'You saw me burn a receipt that was in my pocket. You see, Julia, I keep every little scrap that I think I might find a use for. Now, if you're going to leave me, pack your suitcase and get out.'

Thanks to Latham she had nowhere else to go – no money at her disposal and no friends.

He gazed at her. 'Well, are you going or not?'

'You know I've got nowhere else to go if I do. But I want you to know that I despise you.'

'I don't care if you hate me. You're mine, and you'll remain mine until I decide otherwise.' He rose from his chair and came round the desk. When she turned to run he grabbed her by the hair and began to slap her face. Her head jerked from side to side and she screamed.

The door opened and Ellen's frightened face appeared. It disappeared just as quickly.

When she kicked Latham in the shin he grunted and punched her in the diaphragm. She doubled up, gasping, and with blood pouring from a cut lip. He straightened her up and pushed her. Staggering backwards she fell into the fire grate with a scream and banged her head.

Through rapidly closing eyes she saw Latham pick up the brass poker and advance on her. He'd never been quite so savage before.

The door crashed open and Robert came in. He twisted the poker from his employer's hand and threw it aside. 'What are you trying to do, kill her this time?'

Latham gazed at her, the glazed look on his face beginning to clear. 'It was an accident.'

Robert lifted her into the chair. 'Let me look at you, Mrs Miller. That's a nasty cut you've got there. He took a folded handkerchief from his pocket and pressed it against her scalp to staunch the flow.'

'Is she all right?' Latham said.

Robert gazed up at him. 'No she's not all right. You've gone too far this time, and the gash in her head needs stitching. You'll need to send for the doctor.'

Latham picked up the phone and was put through to the doctor. He said, 'My wife's had an accident. She tripped over a rug and fell into the fireplace. She's managed to cut her head and it needs stitching.'

He turned to Ellen who was fluttering in the doorway, her eyes wide and frightened. 'You, girl . . . Go and tell that Robertson woman to come and see to my wife's injuries. You can look after my son in the meantime. And if word of this *accident* gets around, you'll be dismissed.'

Ashen-faced, Ellen's glance darted to the rug not far from Julia's foot, where the letter that had caused the fracas in the first place lay. 'Yes, sir.'

'That goes for you as well, Robert.'

If Latham could use sleight of hand, she could use sleight of foot, Julia thought fuzzily. Stretching out she scraped the paper under the rug with her foot.

Robert curled his lip at Latham's words, but he said nothing, though he saw her action. He didn't seem to be afraid of Latham, but he was a much younger man.

Latham touched her bloodied hair with the tip of his finger. 'I'm sorry, Julia, but you shouldn't have provoked me. I'll never do it again, I promise.' He flipped back the rug, picked the letter up and smiled at her. 'I'll never allow you to leave me, you know – not ever. After all, I hold the winning card.'

She would like to leave him, but she would never leave her son. Latham knew that.

Her senses spun when she shook her head.

Seventeen

Nothing was allowed to change Latham's schedule. Two days later the Bristol took off from the meadow with Charles Curruthers at the controls. Julia's heart lightened.

She was still hurting. Her eyes were blackened and swollen so badly that Ben had cried out in fright when he first set eyes on her.

Fiona had gently hugged her. 'I'm so sorry. I'll put some witch hazel on those bruises. Your husband has told me that you mustn't have visitors until you're better.'

'I'm sorry if he's appointed you my jailor, Fiona.'

'He hasn't done that . . . but my job will be in jeopardy if I disobey his orders.'

As soon as the drone of the aircraft faded away she called Robert in. 'Thank you for coming to my aid, Robert.'

'It was my pleasure, Mrs Miller. I might as well tell you now, I'm going to leave your husband's employ . . . and I'm taking Ellen with me.'

'Oh . . . I'm sorry. Have you told my husband?'

'Not yet. If you don't mind me saying so, Mrs Miller, you shouldn't have to put up with his treatment. You should leave him.'

'I can't, Robert. If I do he'll keep my son, and I'll never see him again.'

'Go while he's in France. Find somewhere to hide.'

'I haven't got anywhere to go. Latham controls everything, and he'd move heaven and earth to find us. All I've got of my own is my father's car, my mother's fur coat and her jewellery. Besides, he has evidence that could condemn me in any court in the land.'

'The letter that Ellen wrote . . . that you tried to hide under the rug?'

Surprised, she gazed at him. 'You know about it?'

'Ellen told me. She wrote it under duress, and regrets that she ever set eyes on Irene Curruthers.'

'Tell her that I know the truth and will stand by her. I don't consider her responsible for the letter. That's what started the argument with Latham in the first place, and why I tried to hide it. He's using it to keep me with him. I thought he'd burned it in front of my eyes, but it turned out to be a receipt he had in his pocket.'

Robert nodded. 'He's a devious so-and-so. But he's been generous to me in the past, with bonuses for my loyalty. Unfortunately, he has no loyalty towards his staff. He's used me up. He promised me the management of your father's factory, then decided against it.'

'Where will you go?'

He shrugged. 'I haven't worked it out yet, but I've heard of a pub that's going to be available. It's in Southampton and is managed by a relative. I'm thinking of applying for the licence.'

'Well, I hope you get it. I won't say anything to Latham.'

'I'd appreciate that. At least my soul is still intact over this. You know, Mrs Miller, if you need to sell anything I have a cousin who has a pawn shop. And I'd give you a fair price for the Morris. I've also got this notebook,' and he placed a red mottled book in her hands. 'It contains the names and addresses of women your husband has been involved with on a casual basis. Three of them are married to powerful men who could easily bring him down. I'll be around for the next few weeks, so think about it.'

'How would I get away without the car?'

'I could drive you to the station if need be.'

'Not while he has that letter in the safe, Robert.'

'He wouldn't have left it in the safe; he'll have it with him in his briefcase.'

Revenge rose in her like bitter gorge. This argument wasn't over yet. She would ring him, tell him who wrote the letter, tell him that Ben wasn't his, and then tell him to go to hell! Since Irene had caused this with her mischief, let her bear the brunt of his anger for once.

It didn't go quite as she'd planned.

'Latham, it's Julia; we didn't finish our conversation. That letter . . . I know who was responsible for it.'

There was a short silence at the end of the line, then a guarded, 'I'm listening.'

'It was instigated by Irene, who bullied a servant into writing it. It was done out of pure spite because you married me.'

'I'll look into it.'

'I asked you before, and I'll ask you again. Let the matter drop.'

'And if I don't?'

'Did I tell you I have a diary with names, addresses and dates in?' She reeled off a couple of women's names to refresh his memory.

He roared with laughter and called her bluff. 'So, the kitten is turning into a lioness. I didn't think you had it in you, Julia, my pretty. Go on then, sharpen your claws and do your damnedest. See how far you get. Chances are that somebody will step out of the shadows and wring your beautiful little neck. And it might even be me, so watch your back, my lovely. Why don't you stop being a shrew and just do the job I married you for . . . adopt the role of a doting wife, a perfect hostess, and a breeder of children for me?'

'Who is it?' a woman whispered.

There was a background noise, the sound of a baby crying. Latham didn't bother to muffle the sound. 'Mind your own business. This is a private conversation, so get out and take Lisette with you. And don't go too far, I want to talk to you. Before you go, where's Charles?'

'In the back room, sleeping it off.'

'Wake him up . . . give him some coffee.'

'Give him some yourself.' A door slammed.

If Latham didn't care about his indiscretions, then neither would Julia. Her caution fled before the wave of anger she experienced. She'd got this far and she might as well be hung for a sheep as well as a lamb.

'Oh, by the way, Ben's not your son,' she said. 'I had a love affair shortly after we were married.'

Too late to heed the warning to bite her tongue, the words were out.

'Don't try and pull that one on me, Julia. I know he's my son. He's too much like me to be fathered by anyone else.' He lowered his voice. 'Look, Julia, I'll come home in a day or two. We'll sort this out, I promise. I'll give you the letter and you can give me that address book you have. It will be a fair swap.'

Her conscience began to prick. 'You won't hurt Irene, will you? She didn't look very well the last time I saw her.'

'Don't fret about Irene, she can take care of herself. And don't do anything stupid before I get home.'

'Promise you won't take Ben.'

'Of course I won't take Ben. I was angry when I said that, that's all. I love you,' he whispered, and hung up.

Julia didn't trust him. She called the staff together and said, 'You all know what's been going on. I've decided to leave my husband. He told me he'll be home in a day or two. Fiona, would you pack what I'll need for Ben.'

'I'm having nothing to do with this,' she whispered. 'I was employed by Mr Miller to look after his child. You can't take him anywhere without his father's permission. If you do he'll report me to the nursing agency. It will be a black mark on my record, and I'll never be employed again.'

Latham was good at putting pressure on people.

'I'm his mother. I don't need my husband's permission.'

'Where did you intend to go, dear?' Agnes said worriedly.

'I don't know.' Julia burst into tears.

'There you are then,' Fiona said. 'You can't sleep on the street, you know, and if any of us help you to abscond with the child we could be charged with kidnapping.'

Julia hadn't thought of that – she hadn't thought of anything but herself. She felt totally useless – incapable of doing anything, even pack a suitcase.

Fiona put an arm around her shoulders. 'There, there, dear . . . you're overwrought, and haven't got over your fall yet.'

'Fiona, you know damned well that it wasn't a fall, but a push.'

'In such cases it's better not to refer to the cause. The doctor said you were mildly concussed, and that can make you confused.'

'The only one who seems to be confused here, is you.'

'Let me take you upstairs so you can have a nice rest. I'll give you a sleeping pill.'

And Julia went, meekly, because she couldn't think of anything else to do.

Latham had finished with Irene. She no longer attracted him, and had a dried-up yellow look to her. In deference to Julia, he'd only hit Irene once, a quick jab to the stomach. It was punishment for lying to him about the letter. She was curled up on the bed, holding her stomach and gazing at him through reproachful eyes.

'We're through,' he said.

She gave a wry smile. 'You don't mean it, Latham. You'll be back, you always are.'

She was wrong. 'Not this time. I'm going home to Julia and my son. I love her, I always have. I'm going to spend the rest of my life making them happy.'

She gave a spiteful laugh. 'It's too late for that. Julia hates you, and I don't blame her.'

Irene's brat gazed at him from her cot, making him feel guilty. He didn't like the child much. Lisette reminded Latham of his mother with her thin, worried face and skinny limbs. He'd never seen her smile, and the child usually stank of urine, and worse.

'It's about time you changed her napkin,' he said. Irene had proved to be as lousy a mother as she'd told him she'd be.

The man whose name the child bore had long gone, clearing out Irene's bank account to support himself while he studied in Paris. He would never amount to anything as an artist.

'Here, spend this on the child, not on dope,' and he threw a wad of money on to the table. He left Irene on her bed, where she'd fallen, and went through to the other room.

'Charles, wake up. I need you.' Taking him by the scruff of the neck Latham shook him awake. 'What have you taken?'

'A bit of this and that. Leave me alone,' he mumbled, and spluttered when Latham threw a jug of cold water in his face.

Latham dropped a couple of pills on to his tongue. 'Swallow these.'

Charles did as he was told. 'What was it?'

'A stimulant made from the fruit of a coffee tree, and it will wake you up fast.'

'I didn't want to wake up yet . . . I was quite enjoying the innocence of being asleep.'

'I need you to fly me back home . . . it's urgent. Julia is leaving me.'

Charles gave a lazy laugh that infuriated Latham. 'It serves you right. I wonder if I'll be in with a chance. I think your lovely little Julia rather fancies me.'

Did this upper crust little ninny take nothing seriously? 'Over my dead body,' he snarled.

The pills did wake Charles up. By the time they got to the airfield his heart was pounding, the caffeine roaring through his veins like an express train. He started the engine and they headed out over the channel into a faint mist. They'd been in the air for fifteen minutes when the engine began to splutter and cough.

'What is it, what's happening?' Latham shouted out.

Charles laughed. 'You're not going to believe this, Latham, but in our haste to leave I forgot to fuel her up.'

'Then return to France and do it.'

'We won't make it . . . Enjoy the dive, old thing; it will end with a truly heart-stopping moment, I promise.'

The engine cut out completely, and the nose went down. Through the clouds Latham saw a steamer on a sea that resembled ruffled blue taffeta. The ship was as small as a matchbox.

As they began to spiral like an injured moth he wondered if Julia would mourn him.

Behind him, Charles was laughing like a maniac.

'Shit!' Latham said in panic, and realized he was no longer in control of his fate. He screamed all the way down.

Julia was roused from her nap by Ellen. 'I'm sorry to wake you, Mrs Miller, but there's two policemen at the door. They said it's urgent.'

Thank goodness she hadn't taken Fiona's sleeping pill. Her first thought was that they'd come to take Ben from her. 'Did they say what they wanted?'

Ellen shuffled from one foot to the other. 'It's about Mr Miller. He's been involved in an accident, they said.'

'I see . . . Tell them I'll be down in a few minutes, and ask Agnes to take some refreshment through.'

Pulling on a pair of brown slacks and a long-sleeved cream blouse to hide the bruises on her arms, Julia gazed at herself in the mirror. She was a mess, but there was nothing she could do about her face. She tied a pale-green chiffon scarf over the bandage on her head.

Latham had suffered an accident, Ellen had said, and Julia grimaced – there was some poetic justice in the thought.

Both men stood as she went in to the sitting room. They were wearing uncomfortable-looking blue uniform tunics with a row of shining buttons down the front that stopped at a broad-buckled belt. Two domed helmets stood side by side on the table. Both pairs of eyes widened when they saw her injuries, and they appeared awkward and ill-at-ease. One of them wore stripes. She smiled encouragingly at him. 'Sergeant . . . ?'

He eased his collar with his finger and coughed. 'Sergeant Smithers, and this is Constable Woollard.'

'Please be seated, gentlemen. I'm sorry to have kept you waiting. I do hope you'll excuse my appearance. Silly of me, but I tripped over a rug and fell into the fireplace. The doctor had to put stitches in my head.'

One of the men nodded, as though he'd heard it all before.

Agnes came in with the tea tray. 'Will you have some tea?' Julia said brightly, aware she was using avoidance tactics.

'No thank you, ma'am,' they both said together, and as Agnes turned to leave the sergeant said, 'Perhaps it would be better if your housekeeper stayed.'

'Yes of course, if you would please, Agnes. Take a seat.' She turned back to the policemen. 'Now, I believe you want to talk to me about my husband . . . an accident my maid said. Is it serious? But yes, it must be serious if you've come to tell me about it.'

'Perhaps you'd better sit down too, Mrs Miller. I'm afraid your husband was killed in the accident.'

Her knees began to tremble and she sat with a thump, staring at him. 'How could that happen? Latham was here two days ago.'

'On the day you had your accident?'

'Yes . . . he called the doctor for me. Are you sure it was him? He's in France, you know, and we talked on the telephone only this morning. He was perfectly healthy then, and said he'd be home in a couple of days.'

'There was identification in the wallets of both the men.'

'But how did it happen? Latham was a careful and experienced driver.'

'He wasn't in a car. He was in an aeroplane and it nose-dived into the sea and disintegrated. Two bodies were retrieved by a steamer. One of them was your husband, the other is a young gentleman called Charles Curruthers. We've informed his family of the tragedy.'

Julia put a hand across her mouth to stop herself from crying out. She mumbled, 'Oh, my God, Charles as well? What a dreadful thing to have happened.'

Agnes put a comforting arm around her and patted her bruised shoulder. She tried not to wince when the housekeeper said, 'There, there, my dear. He'll be at peace, now.'

'Where's my husband's body? In London?'

'In the morgue. It will be released to a funeral director after formal identification . . . not a task for a lady to undertake in this instance, I'd suggest.'

'I can't go to London looking like this, and I still have mild concussion. The doctor wants me to rest.'

'Robert might have a solution,' Agnes offered. 'Mr Miller set great store by him.'

Although Julia had disliked her husband to the point of leaving him, she wouldn't have wished him dead. On top of everything else it all seemed too much. She began to weep.

The policemen rose and picked up their helmets, eager to make their escape. 'I'm sorry we've been the bearer of such bad news. You'll need to go to London to make arrangements for the body. I shouldn't leave it too long if I were you. Best to get these things done quickly.'

'Thank you, you've been very kind,' she snuffled.

After the police had departed Agnes told the rest of the staff the news. They all looked at one another. Fiona burst into tears.

Ben cried because Fiona did. For once, Fiona didn't protest when Julia picked him up and cuddled him on her lap. 'Everything will be all right, darling,' she soothed.

The shock the news had brought with it was beginning to abate, and Julia knew she must be strong and make arrangements for his burial.

Julia contacted the same undertaker who'd buried her father, and tentative arrangements were made for the funeral. Robert turned out to be invaluable. He rang the staff at the London house, then informed Latham's managers and business acquaintances of Latham's demise. He arranged for one of the managers to identify his body.

'I don't know anything about Latham's businesses,' she confessed.

'Don't you worry, Mrs Miller . . . I do.'

'How well?'

'As well as Latham knew them.'

Julia made her first business decision. 'I know you have intentions to leave, Robert, but would you consider putting it off and
being my advisor . . . at least, for the time it takes to sort everything out. By that time I should know where I'm going.'

He nodded and held out his hand.

'Now . . . I'd better phone his lawyer.'

Latham had left each of his staff an appropriate amount of money.
The bulk of his estate would be divided between Julia and Ben.
There was also a legacy for Irene and her daughter, in the form
of an allowance.

Julia hugged her guilt to herself. It had been vindictive of her
to tell Latham that he wasn't Ben's father, but thank goodness he
hadn't believed her!

She buried Latham a week later, in the same cemetery that
contained her parents. Her fading bruises were hidden under a dark
veil. She expected Irene to put in an appearance, but she didn't.
For Latham she arranged for a deep-yellow rose to be planted.

Afterwards she said to Robert, 'Gold doesn't always glisten,
does it? Sometimes it's an illusion. I guess Latham knows that by
now.' They headed for the car.

The London staff had arranged refreshments. There were many
mourners all offering their condolences. Robert stood by her side
the whole time. She kept up the charade of a grieving wife for
Latham, if only for her own sake. There were moments when she
felt dizzy with the relief of knowing that she'd never again be
subjected to a beating such as the final one Latham had delivered
to her.

The next day she attended Charles' funeral in Surrey. She could
hardly believe that the golden-haired, bright and beautiful Charles,
who'd been such an outrageous and funny companion on the
rare moments she'd met him, was gone. Irene didn't attend her
brother's funeral either.

The Curruthers were barely civil to her, so she took the hint
and didn't ask after their daughter, or go back to the hall.

A week later, after the stitches had been removed from her
head, Robert took her up to London for a business meeting with
Latham's lawyer and clerk.

'Hello, Mr Adams. How are you?' she said to the clerk.

He smiled at her. 'I've brought a summary of Mr Miller's holdings for your reference.'

'Thank you, Mr Adams.'

'Have you decided what you are going to do with the factories. Not knowing is unsettling for the customers.'

'I have decided,' she told them. 'I don't have the skills to run Latham's business enterprises, and neither do I want to. I want everything to be sold . . . the factories, the London house and the big car.'

The lawyer smiled. 'I was hoping you'd come to that conclusion. Selling up shouldn't be hard, and we'll hold out for the best price. I'm already getting discreet enquiries about the dispersal of the estate. The proceeds will make you a very wealthy woman, Mrs Miller.'

'I'm already a wealthy woman, it seems. Latham left us generously provided for, with a large amount of money held in an account in my name, which I can use immediately. There is also the legacy from my father's estate, which is invested, I believe. However, the bulk of the money that sales of the business bring in will be placed in trust. It will support a charity in Latham's name . . . a temporary care home in the country for children under school age, whose mothers are too ill to look after them. The property in Surrey can be used for the purpose.'

The lawyer raised an eyebrow. 'Your home in Surrey? There will be a board of trustees appointed, I hope.'

'Yes, of course. It's in an ideal location. The air is healthy and there's plenty of room. I'm going to ask Fiona Robertson to accept the position of matron, and I imagine Mrs Finnigan will be happy to stay on in charge of the cooking and housekeeping, though they'd both need some extra help. My husband thought very highly of them both. We should be able to cater for about forty needy children.'

'Where would you get these needy children from?'

'They'd be referred by the church, or doctors. Word will soon get round.'

'And where will you go?'

'I'll live in the guest flat for the time being, raise my child and help out where I can. I'm not entirely useless. I can do some of the paperwork, type letters and try and raise money.'

Robert, who accompanied her to the meeting, chuckled. 'It should work, as long as you remember that Fiona will be in charge.'

Julia gave a bit of a shamefaced grin. 'She won't be in charge of my child, and that will make a big difference. With several children in her care her regimental skills will be useful.'

Not hearing from Irene had begun to bother her, because the strength of Irene's feelings towards Latham had been strong. Now she asked the lawyer, 'Have you been in touch with Mrs Argette? I expected to see her at the funeral of her brother.'

'I sent her a letter, but have received no reply, and nobody answered the telephone.'

'So she doesn't know she's a beneficiary under Latham's will?'

'If she read my letter, she'd know. I asked her to come to London so we could discuss the situation. You know, Mrs Miller, I'd advise you to challenge that particular legacy. The woman concerned was notorious—'

'Don't go on, please. I know what the situation was between Mrs Argette and my husband, and I wouldn't dream of challenging Latham's will in this matter.' She looked him straight in the eyes. 'Is that understood?'

'Yes, Mrs Miller, you're a gracious and generous woman, and you make me feel ashamed of myself.'

Julia doubted it.

When she broke the news of her plans to the staff. Fiona was overjoyed to be offered the position of matron. 'To be honest, I thought you'd dispense with my services, Mrs Miller.'

'You astonish me, Fiona. Your competence for the position is beyond criticism, and to be quite honest, I never even considered asking anyone else, because I know you're an honest, straightforward person who possesses a great deal of common sense,' and she grinned as she added, 'Even if we didn't always see eye to eye.'

'Like the time you sneaked in and took Ben from his cot for a feed, and I let you get away with it.'

'Only because you knew you wouldn't be able to stop me. I'll be hiring an architect to advise us on how and where to convert the bedrooms. Fiona, if you like you can plan how many beds, sheets and things we'll need.'

'I'm sure the church committee will keep us supplied with

knitted baby blankets, baby clothes, socks and matinee jackets,'
Agnes Finnigan said happily. 'It will be a good cause for them.
And we'll have to have a patron . . . that will be you, Mrs
Miller.'

With such a lot to do Julia didn't have time to blink. She fell
into bed every night and slept deeply, waking refreshed. Looking
after Ben was a delight, though Fiona hovered over her like a
bird waiting to pounce on a worm.

One night there was the sound of a car, and the dogs set up a
frenzy of barking. Julia gazed at the clock. It was two a.m., and
somebody was leaning on the doorbell.

She pushed the window open. 'Who is it?'

'It's me, my angel . . . Irene. Come down and pay the cab,
would you? I've run out of money.'

'At this time of night?'

'What has the time of night got to do with anything? Just do
it, else I'll sleep on your doorstep.'

Pulling on her dressing gown, Julia went down. The cab cost
a small fortune, since Irene had come down from Southampton.

'Here, take Lisette will you. ' A large-eyed child was placed in
her arms. She had the look of Latham, and seemed lethargic as
she gazed around her.

Robert came down. 'I heard the dogs.'

'It's me, Robert. You can go back to bed.'

'Mrs Argette . . . How are you?'

'How do I look?'

'If I may be frank . . . like hell.'

'You needn't have been that frank, but I must admit I do I
feel like hell.' She staggered a little and passed a hand over her
brow.

Robert helped her into the sitting room. 'Is there anything I
can do?'

'Take Lisette to Fiona and ask her to see to the child. She'll
need a bottle.'

'They took my daughter away from me,' Irene said after Robert
had gone. 'After Latham left I knew he was through with me.
He was going home to you. Then I got a phone call from my
father. He accused me of being responsible for leading Charles

astray and causing his death. That's how I learned that Latham was dead too . . . until the lawyer's letter came. He advised me to give up the claim to the legacy. I wouldn't of course, because Lisette was entitled to something. God knows . . . She was such a nuisance and nobody wanted her. Not my husband, not Latham . . . not even me.'

'I went on a bender, and took some other stuff when the booze ran out. I clean forgot about poor Lisette, and she doesn't cry much. She doesn't do anything much . . . not even smile. But then, I wouldn't smile if I had me for a mother, either.'

'Hush, Irene, stop punishing yourself.'

In her usual manner Irene tried to make light of the situation. 'I haven't finished. I'm having a moment of dramatic desperation and it's your duty to listen to me. The cleaning lady took her to the convent, and got me to the hospital. They pumped my stomach out.' She shuddered and tried to make light of it. 'An absolutely ghastly experience, darling,' and she burst into tears. 'I left the hospital and stole Lisette from the orphanage. I just walked into the garden and took her from out of her cot. I could have been anyone, and nobody tried to stop me.'

'How did you get here?'

'I thumbed a lift on a donkey and cart to some port where I managed to bribe the fishermen. They dropped me off in Southampton, but I must have lost my purse in the boat, because it was gone from my bag. I didn't have much money on me, and I had nowhere else in the world to go. You won't turn me away, will you?'

Julia put her arms around Irene. 'Of course not, I'll look after you.'

'I'm so bloody tired. If anything happens to me, you will look after her, won't you?'

'Of course.'

'Really look after her, I mean. I want you to legally adopt her as your own, and give her a good life. You'll be a better mother to her than I could ever be.'

Irene's wild talk was beginning to scare Julia. 'Nothing will happen to you. We'll look after you until you get better, then we'll talk again.'

'Only I won't get well, I'll only get worse. There's something wrong with my liver. Cancer, the hospital said. I want you to adopt her while I'm still alive, so I won't have to bother to come back and haunt you.'

Poor Irene. 'What about your parents, won't they—'

'They refuse to acknowledge either of us. If my mother knew I was here she'd probably burn your house down with me in it. I can't say I blame her where I'm concerned, but poor little Lisette has nobody. I was tempted to leave her in France, but couldn't bear the thought of her becoming a French nun. I bet they wear ugly black knickers that come down to their ankles and smell of mothballs.'

Julia chuckled. She couldn't help herself. Even in the face of her terminal illness, Irene's wit could make her laugh. She didn't feel sorry for herself, though she was emaciated to the point of being a bag of bones.

'I'll give you Latham's room, which is next to mine.'

'Ah, yes . . . I remember it well. How exceedingly civilized of you. And to think I once called you a frightful prig.'

'I do believe I can be one at times. All Latham's things have been cleared out of it. In the morning I'll ask the doctor to call on you, and we'll talk again.'

There was a knock at the door and Agnes came in with a tray. 'I thought you might both like a mug of cocoa to help you get back to sleep.'

'Thank you, Agnes, that's kind of you. I'm sorry you were disturbed. Now you're up, do you think you could make up the bed in the room next to mine? Mrs Argette can wear one of my nightdresses. She will be staying with us for a while.'

'Yes, Mrs Miller.'

'Not for long though,' Irene thought to add.

Before she went upstairs, Julia went through to the flat. Lisette was settled down to sleep in Ben's pram.

Fiona had an attitude of mild outrage hovering about her. 'The child was filthy and she's much too thin for a child of her age. I gave her a good wash, and she gulped down her bottle as if she hadn't been given a good feed in days, the poor wee mite. I think she has lice in her hair, too, but I'll tackle those tomorrow before Master Benjamin catches them. The child settled down easily enough. I'm surprised that woman had the cheek to come here, I really am? You shouldn't have taken her in.'

'Hush, Fiona, be charitable. Mrs Argette was a friend of both my husband and myself. She's terminally ill, and came here because she had nowhere else to go. She's desperately in need of my help. Would you deny her that?'

'Under the circumstances, no.'

'Then try and forget anything you've heard about her past. She has asked me to adopt Lisette, and I'm inclined to do so.'

'Aye, well, that would be a kind thing for you to do . . . though she's not a very pretty child. Not like Ben.'

Julia gazed down at the solemn-looking waif and tears filled her eyes. 'She doesn't have to be pretty, she just has to be herself, and be loved.' Julia stooped and kissed the girl's pale cheek and whispered, 'I love you, my little Lisette, and I know Ben will. That will do for a start.'

'Watch out for those lice, they can jump a long way,' Fiona said gruffly.

'Who fathered Ben?' Irene said when Julia went upstairs to bed. 'I know it wasn't Latham.'

'Mind your own business.'

'You're not going to let me die without satisfying my curiosity, are you?'

'I suppose not, and she grinned. 'Actually, it was someone you never met . . . Martin Lee-Trafford.'

'That doctor your father hired to manage the factory? But I thought . . . and Latham told me . . .' Irene began to laugh.

'Shut up and go to sleep,' Julia said, and closed the door between them.

A month later Irene died. Julia sent a note to her parents and arranged a funeral, as Irene had requested. There was to be no service, just a few words spoken around the grave site.

Irene's headstone read, *Irene Argette, wife of Jacques and beloved mother of Lisette.*

'I'd hate to embarrass the other Curruthers in the district, either living or dead,' Irene had remarked about her request that her maiden name be left off.

Julia and her household were the only mourners at the graveside, but beyond the churchyard wall was the Rolls Royce belonging to the Curruthers family.

It was early October. The nights were drawing in. The glorious autumn drift of sycamore and maple leaves was being mashed underfoot and the trees that had once shaded the earth were now uncovering large glimpses of sky. Irene's grave would soon be covered in a thick layer of decaying foliage.

Julia went to clear the dead flowers away from Irene's grave ten days later. She was going to plant daffodil bulbs to bloom in spring.

It was a fine, mild day and she took the children with her in the twin pram she'd bought. They were seated at either end, one dressed in pink, the other in blue. Lisette faced her. Good food had added a soft pink bloom to her cheeks.

Julia smiled at the girl.

For a moment the child stared back at her through Latham's eyes, then her eyes lightened and she decided it was time she smiled.

Julia was transfixed by the event. 'Fiona was wrong . . . You *are* beautiful . . . You're the most beautiful girl in the world when you smile.'

'Mam mam,' Lisette whispered hesitantly.

'That's right, my love. I'm your mamma, and I love you.' She brought the pram to a halt and kissed Lisette.

'Me'swell,' Ben said, and began to giggle when she blew a raspberry against his soft neck.

Ben loved having Lisette for company. 'Yes, you wretch,' and Martin came into her mind. Ben was growing more like him every day. Perhaps she should contact him, she thought, then hesitated. He hadn't answered her last letter, and she now had two children. Perhaps she should just let sleeping dogs lie.

Engrossed in her thoughts she wheeled the pram past Irene's grave and had to retrace her steps. No wonder she'd gone past, and she gazed down at it. A marble fender and a low wrought-iron fence had been erected, the space neatly filled in with gravel.

Her parents had tried to confine Irene's natural exuberance in life, and hadn't succeeded. She'd been a free spirit. Now they were doing it in death. At least it showed they cared a little, she supposed.

But it was neat – too neat a bed for Irene.

Taking out her trowel Julia stepped over the fence, carefully pushed the gravel aside and planted her bulbs. When she'd finished she smoothed the gravel back over it.

The daffodils would push their spears through the earth and their muted clamour would blaze their brazen beauty for Irene in the spring, and for every spring to follow.

Eighteen

Turning the letter over in his hand Martin stared at the return address. 'J.R. Singleton,' he said to the cats. 'Are either of you acquainted with him?'

Clarence gave him a superior look. Billy Boy meowed.

The telephone rang.

'Dr Lee-Trafford's surgery.'

A rather nervous voice said in a whisper, 'I'm Jane Singleton.'

'How odd . . . I've just received a letter from a J.R. Singleton posted from Edinburgh. Is that you?'

'Yes it is. Have you read it?'

'Not yet.'

'Then I'd better ring you back in half an hour.'

'I'll be seeing patients then. Look . . . to save time perhaps you'd like to tell me what this is about, Mrs Singleton. If it's the partnership you're a little late. The position has been filled by a doctor who lives locally.' And one who he knew was sound, since he'd gone through medical school with him.

'It's nothing to do with the partnership, Martin. I know that this might come as a shock, but I'm your mother.'

His mother! The breath nearly left his body and he put his hand on the back of the chair to steady himself. 'My mother?'

'Can we talk?'

'I only have ten minutes before surgery,' which sounded somewhat curt and unwelcoming even to his own ears. 'I'm sorry, I didn't mean it how it sounded.'

'I know how difficult this must be for you, as it is for me. I need to see you, Martin, to explain.'

'There's nothing to explain.'

'Yes, there is.'

'Where are you?' he said.

'In Edinburgh, but I'm going to London in April to visit my daughter and grandson.'

Her daughter? He stated the obvious. 'Then I have a sister?

Good Lord!' and he laughed. 'That's wonderful. Are there any more surprises . . . *Mother.*'

Her voice wobbled with tears. 'None that I can think of. Your sister's name is Avis.'

His own tears weren't far away. 'You're crying.'

'I thought you might not want anything to do with me.'

'On the contrary, I made a rather belated attempt at trying to find you myself. I even wrote a letter, but it was returned. You know that my father is dead?'

'Yes.'

The clock on the mantelpiece chimed the hour and at the same time the doorbell rang. 'Look, Mother, I really must go since my partner is coming in. Will you give me your number so I can call you back? This afternoon I expect, about four. And yes, we must make arrangements to see each other. I can easily get up to London in April.'

He wrote down the number she gave him, then said, 'By the way, how did you know I was still living here . . . at home?'

'I didn't know for sure . . . but thought it was worth trying. Then I was convinced that you wouldn't be there, because I went down to Bournemouth about three years ago and the place was boarded up. The old woman who lives next door told me your father was dead, and she thought you'd been killed in the war.'

'I was one of the lucky ones who survived it, but I spent some time in hospital.'

'Poor you, are you fully recovered?'

'Perfectly. So why did you look for me if you thought I was dead?'

'My husband knew someone who made enquiries on my behalf. They wouldn't tell me much, just that you were alive, and had been awarded a medal and bar for bravery. I was overjoyed to learn that you were still alive, and knew I wouldn't rest until I found you.

'Anyway, my dear, I called your father's lawyer, but he was having a week off. So I told the secretary who answered that I was from the police department and needed to contact you urgently. She gave me your details. Up till then I had no idea you were a doctor.'

The doorbell rang again – this time for longer. He must get

a receptionist, he thought, and some domestic help. The paper-work was mountainous and his sink would soon be full of dirty dishes.

'It was lovely to talk to you, Martin. I'll expect to hear from you later, then.'

'You will . . . I promise.' He dropped the receiver back in its rest and headed for the door at a run.

His fellow practitioner, Andrew Pethan, came in followed by a trickle of patients – followed by a small flood. By noon they'd mopped up a couple of latecomers.

Martin hadn't expected, when he'd hung his shingle on the door, that business was going to be quite so brisk. He made a pile of sandwiches and some tea for lunch and they discussed the situation.

'Bournemouth's population is growing,' Andrew said.

'And several of your patients have followed you here; I hadn't considered that.'

'Will you do the rounds this afternoon, while I catch up on the paperwork and get the banking ready? We desperately need a receptionist, and certainly can afford one now,' and he suddenly wished Mrs Seeble was available. 'I'll put an ad in the paper.'

'Advertise for a receptionist with nursing experience,' Andrew advised. 'There are plenty of sensible and mature women with experience looking for work. In the meantime, I'm sure my wife wouldn't mind helping out for a short time while the children are at school, even if it's to sort the files out.'

Within a fortnight they had a competent woman of middle years who'd been a member of the Queen Alexandra Imperial Military Nursing Service. Her name was Olivia Stark, but she was to be called Nurse Stark. There no nonsense about her. She was efficiency itself, and soon had the practice organized. The men sighed with relief, and the cats slunk off to Martin's private quarters and stayed there. A separate advertisement found Martin a cleaner for three afternoons a week, selected by Nurse Stark.

With that settled Martin made plans to meet his mother in London and gained Nurse Stark's permission for a day off in advance. She noted it on the large calendar that she'd hung on the wall.

'Doctor Pethan wants a day off in February, so you can cover his patients then.'

It was a cool day in early April when Martin took the train up. The landscape was taking on a tender green mantle and the showers of rain hit the train windows, and the quivering drops chased each other down the glass.

He'd assembled a special gift for his mother, copies made of the photographs taken of him during his childhood. He'd placed them in an album for her, so she'd have a sense of him growing up. He bought a gift for his sister, Avis, and a teddy bear for his nephew. Suddenly he had his health and career back. And he'd discovered his family. There was order in his life again, and with it came a warm feeling of hope, as though his life had just begun.

He admitted to himself that there was one big gap in it. The thought of Julia hit him so strongly that he could almost sense her presence and smell her perfume. Emeraude, by Coty, he recalled. He *could* smell it! The woman in the opposite seat was wearing it. But she wasn't Julia.

His mother was waiting for him at Waterloo station. He recognized her straight away, even though she'd aged. He grinned at the thought. He'd certainly aged too, but inside he could feel the bewildered little boy she'd left behind.

His mother was still slim and elegant. She wore a grey three-quarter coat with a fur collar and a little hat with a flamboyant bunch of cherries on that matched the colour of her shoes. She was as beautiful as the mother of his memory. A little way behind her was a younger woman – his sister, Avis Singleton, with his nephew Timothy held in her arms. She was small and dainty and had tawny-brown eyes and a wide smile.

His mother's glance went anxiously over the crowd of alighting passengers and settled on him. Her smile came like a mouse tentatively moving from the safety of its hole. Her mouth formed his name and her eyes filled with tears. He strode forward and drew the trio into his arms. His mother's tears fell.

Avis kissed his cheek and whispered, 'Ever since mother told me about you I've wanted to meet you. She was so very scared that you'd reject her. You won't, will you?'

'If I was going to do that I wouldn't be here.' He found his mother a handkerchief to dry her tears on and handed it to her, making light of them. 'Here, mop them up before you drown me. Allow me take a look at your son, Avis.'

Baby Timothy had inherited the blue eyes of his grandmother, from where his own had also been inherited.

'I detect a strong resemblance in him to you,' Avis said.

'Do I detect the trace of an American accent?'

'Canadian. I was born and grew up in Montreal. We moved to Edinburgh when I was fifteen. Now I'm married I live in London.'

'Then it won't be too far to visit once I'm settled in.'

'That would be nice.'

'It will be. Lord . . . I had no idea I had a sister, and a beautiful one at that.'

She laughed. 'I think I'll like having you as a brother,' she said and she kissed his cheek.

Martin was only there for the day, so he took the baby from her. 'Here . . . allow me to carry him.'

The child fitted comfortably into his arms, and he gazed down at his nephew and offered him a smile. 'Hello, Timmy.'

The child smiled back at him.

Julia had just seen Robert and Ellen off. Married quietly the day before in the village church, only the staff who had known them had attended. The pair were now on their way to Southampton, where Robert had managed to take over a public house as licensee.

'I'll drive you up to London, since I've got to see the lawyer and sign some papers. We'll go up the night before.'

'I prefer to do the driving,' Robert had said with a smile.

'Then allow me to book you into a hotel as a special thank you for being such a help.' And there had been dinner, champagne and the honeymoon suite as an extra surprise.

The station was full of hissing engines and the echoing, raucous voices of porters. The platforms were crowded.

'I'll miss you . . . good luck,' Julia said, hugging them both.

'I reckon I'll make a good barmaid,' Ellen said just before they'd boarded their train, and Julia had given a faint smile, remembering

Martin coming to dinner with her father and saying more or less the same thing about her. She'd been cool and he'd laughed and he'd kissed her rather unexpectedly.

'Thank you for everything, Mrs Miller,' Ellen called out.

As the train disappeared Julia's stomach chose that moment to growl, reminding her it was past noon.

She went into the station café and had lingered over an unappetizing ham and cheese sandwich, and a pot of tea that was the colour and consistency of varnish. There was a paper somebody had left behind. The headlines read: Fascists win the election in Italy.

Not that the result of the Italian election had much to do with her, and neither had the election in her own country the year before. She was a woman, and therefore not deemed sensible enough to vote until she reached the age of thirty.

'Damned cheek,' she murmured, and softly snorted. A lot men knew about women!

The second page revealed a small news item about the official opening of her children's home, which was already full of needy babies and toddlers, and had a waiting list. She thought that she might buy a cottage in the village for herself. The comfortable flat could then be used for the key staff, while accommodation in the attic rooms was freed up.

The news item read:

> Mrs Julia Miller, opening the Latham Miller Memorial home for children. Mr Miller, a noted industrialist, perished when the private aeroplane he was a passenger in crashed into the English Channel during a flight from France. Mrs Miller opened the home in memory of her husband, and has been appointed patron. A board of trustees has been appointed, headed by William Hedgewick of the law firm Hedgewick and Williams, who manages the legal business of the Miller enterprises.

And couldn't be prised off such a lucrative enterprise. Much to Julia's disgust she'd not been allowed to serve on the board because she was a woman. Another injustice, considering it was her money they were handling, though admittedly, Latham had earned it with their help in the first place. At least she'd reserved the right to appoint somebody on the board who would act on her behalf. Jeepers! Latham would have a fit if he knew how she was spending it, and she didn't give a rat's grunt.

Guests at the opening were Lord and Lady Curruthers. Mrs Miller is pictured with two unfortunate children who are in need of care. In her address she thanked her sponsors, Jellico Linens, who made a generous donation of sheets, towels and baby napkins, and Millikins, who have pledged a two years' supply of dried milk powder.

Actually, she was pictured with Ben and Lisette, who were sitting astride the grey dappled rocking horse, giggling, while she hung on to them. The Curruthers family was in a separate picture, looking aloof and regal. And although Julia was grateful for the milk powder, the maid she'd hired to come in and do the laundry was a farm girl, and she'd persuaded her father to keep them supplied with fresh milk and eggs. The meadow had been turned into a vegetable plot.

Julia had many feelers out for sponsorship, including most of her father's friends. She was shameless about using his name and reminding them of his former friendship with them.

She looked up from the article. A few minutes earlier, two smartly dressed women had been talking together not far from the window. The younger one carried a child in a blue cape, bonnet, leggings and booties.

When the figure of a man strode towards them and wrapped his arms around them so they stood in a huddle, Julia had wished she'd had someone to meet. Despite her busy life she felt lonely.

Now the man took the infant from the younger woman and kissed him. The child looked like Martin.

They began to walk in her direction and she froze. It *was* Martin! 'Oh, my God!' she breathed. Biting down on her tongue to stop herself from crying out she felt the tears begin to gather and congeal like a cold slab of lard in her stomach. Martin had married, and was now a father. His wife was petite and pretty. Jealousy filled her.

But she mustn't think like that, *she mustn't!* She loved Martin to pieces, and wanted him to be happy. He'd been through a lot, and it would be uncharitable of her to think any less of him for seeking a secure home life. If that meant him being happy with someone else, so be it.

He looked well. His eyes sparkled with the happiness he felt at seeing his family. She longed to speak to him.

'Martin . . . my love,' she whispered.

He couldn't have possibly heard her yet he glanced her way. She held her breath when he seemed to gaze into her eyes. But the windows were partially steamed up, and she lifted the newspaper to shield her face.

She caught a glimpse of the baby as he turned away, the quick flash of dark-blue eyes, the wisp of a dark curl escaping from the bonnet. The boy bore a strong resemblance to Ben, the son Martin didn't know about.

Her heart cracked open like an eggshell when they turned and walked off towards the entrance where the taxi rank was situated, laughing and chatting familiarly together. Martin turned, looking back for a moment, then he was gone.

When they went out of sight Julia felt empty, though her heart was pumping in a most agonizing fashion, as if the joy of seeing him was being wrung out of her by the thought that this might be the last time she did.

But she had Martin's child to love, she thought. And she had Latham and Irene's daughter, as well. It was her responsibility to bring them up to feel loved and wanted, so they'd become responsible adults – more responsible than the majority of their parents, perhaps.

Yes, Irene, I know I'm being prissy again, she thought, and choked back a laugh.

On top of that, none of her small family would ever have to go without – not like some of the poor little waifs coming into her home. She was blessed indeed.

Shaken by the near encounter, Julia waited until ten minutes had passed, then left the dingy, sooty-smelling surrounds of the station on foot.

Her car was still at the hotel garage. One of the staff brought it round while she paid her bill, and she made her way out of London and headed for Kent, thinking of Martin.

A small smile played around her mouth – she was glad he'd looked so happy.

'Stay that way always, my love,' she said.

It had been wonderful seeing his mother. They talked honestly.

'I wrote to you every birthday,' she said. 'My letters were never returned so I hoped you'd read them. Then your father sent them back to me all at once in a little parcel. They hadn't been opened.'

A rather cruel gesture on his father's part, Martin thought, but he didn't intend to take sides now. He'd learned that dwelling negatively on the past could be a painful process, and a useless pastime as well. 'I'd rather we moved forward than looked back.'

A surprised expression touched her mother's face. 'Yes, I suppose you would, and so would I. I don't blame him, you know. Your father found it hard to express emotion and bottled things up. I fell in love with somebody else. If you ever come to Scotland you'll meet my husband. He's an accountant. I know what I did was wrong, but I didn't dream that your father would be so . . . well, that he would have denied me so completely. He took you from my arms, and I never saw you again.'

'It was selfish of him, but he was a good father to me. You don't have to make excuses for your actions. And although he wasn't about to compare his and Julia's situation with hers, he said, 'I fell in love with a married woman myself . . . I still love her . . . but we chose to not see each other again.

'Was it the right choice, Martin?'

'It doesn't feel like it . . . It feels as though a large part of me is missing.'

She'd placed a small parcel of letters in his hands then, tied in a blue ribbon. 'These are for you.'

They were the letters that his father had returned to her – the ones she'd written to him. They were still sealed. He could almost feel the dampness of her tears absorbed by the paper at the time of writing. He knew what they'd contain – years of pain for what had been lost, and just being human. It was a hard punishment, he thought, as he placed the letters inside his attaché case.

He still felt the fragility of that parting inside him, like a wound that wouldn't heal. He couldn't cope with her pain yet – not yet – perhaps not ever.

It was enough that she'd survived to tell him what he already knew – that being apart from somebody didn't mean that the bond of love they'd established in the past was broken.

It was odd, but he was reminded of Julia everywhere he went: in the tilt of a woman's head, a quick burst of her laughter, the glimpse of a stranger walking on the beach or sitting in a restaurant. This morning he thought he saw Julia sitting in the station cafeteria, and the image had been strong. But the window had steamed up and it had just been someone reading a paper.

Yet, when he arrived back at the station to catch the evening train later in the day, he went to the place. Buying a cup of lukewarm tea and a bun he sat at the same table and ate it. Not that he'd expected the woman to still be sitting here.

After a while a young serving girl began to busy herself cleaning the tables. 'We close in a couple of minutes, sir.'

'I'm sorry if I've held you up. It's all right . . . I'm off to catch my train now.'

'Don't forget your paper, sir,' she called out.

'It's not mine . . . but if you don't want it, I'll take it to read on the train.' It might contain a cryptic crossword to keep him occupied.

'Thank you,' he said when she handed it to him, and he tucked it under his arm.

Someone had started the crossword and abandoned it. Two hours later Martin conceded to the superior brain of the crossword compiler.

Returning to the first page he read the Italian election post-mortem. He found that the thought of a fascist government under Benito Mussolini, especially with such a huge majority, was a slightly disturbing concept. He turned to page two.

The picture of Julia hit him with such force that the breath left his body, and he forgot to replace it for several seconds. His hands trembled and his knees felt weak.

Running his finger over the image of her dear face, he read the article. Latham Miller was dead. She'd converted her home into one for needy children. How typical of her way of thinking.

As for the two children on the rocking horse, they were the healthiest, happiest orphans he'd ever seen – and he'd seen plenty of waifs and strays in Colifield.

Doubt set in. Why hadn't she written to inform him of Latham Miller's death?

Was it because he hadn't answered her last letter, because she'd asked him to be strong for them both, knowing he would be? He tore out the article and placed it in his briefcase.

Julia was now an extremely wealthy woman, and that was an obstacle in itself, he realized.

The cats greeted him when he arrived home. He let them into the back garden for a pee, then took them on to his lap and made a fuss of them. 'It's cold out there, isn't it, chaps?'

Was this how he'd end up – a lonely old man like his father with only the cats for company?

'Is it hell! Julia is worth fighting for, and damn her money. She was welcome to it.' Flicking through his address book he found the number of the Millers' home in Surrey, and hoped it hadn't changed.

Nineteen

Fiona Robertson answered the phone.

'Could I speak to Mrs Miller please?'

'At this time of night?'

'Yes, at this time of night. Tell her that it's Doctor Lee-Trafford. Tell her I love her and I miss her.'

A grin spread across Fiona's face for Julia had confided in her about her love for this man. 'Ah yes, I believe I've heard of you. Wouldn't you feel more comfortable telling Mrs Miller all that yourself. I'll see if I can find her.'

'Who is it?' Julia whispered.

'Someone called Doctor Lee-Trafford,' Fiona whispered back.

Julia's heart began to pound. Frantically she shook her head, then she nodded just as frantically. 'Oh, goodness,' and she patted her hair into place! 'Do I look all right?'

'Can you wait a moment, Doctor? She just wants to put some lipstick on and comb her hair.'

Fiona grinned and listened some more, then said, 'The doctor thought he saw you at Waterloo station this morning.'

Julia snatched the phone from her. 'Hello, Martin. I saw you too.'

'Why didn't you come and talk to me?' After such a long time of not hearing his voice she wanted to drown in the depths of it.

'You were with two women, and a child who looked very much like you. Your wife and child, and your mother-in-law? I didn't want to embarrass you.'

'You wouldn't have. The baby is my nephew, Timothy. The older woman is my mother, and the younger one my half-sister Avis. It was a reunion with my mother, and the first time for meeting my family.'

She felt as though she was dropping rapidly through the air and her stomach had been left behind. She applied imaginary brakes and began to float. A smile of delight spread across her face and she was sure it was beaming out like the lamp in a lighthouse. He wasn't married. 'Can you forgive me? I thought you'd married. I've been trying hard not to hate her all day, because, my darling, I wanted so much for you to be happy.'

Fiona got up and left the room.

'It's so lovely to hear your voice. How have you been?'

'Missing you. Why didn't you get in touch before?'

'I didn't know that Latham had died. I saw an item in the paper, just today. Why didn't you let me know?'

'I thought everyone knew. It was all over the newspapers.'

'Not in Colifield where I was working.'

'Where are you now . . . still in London?'

'I've set up my shingle in Bournemouth.'

'Tell me you still love me.'

'I'll always love you, Julia mine. I told you that right at the beginning.'

'But things have changed since then, and we need to talk. You might as well know the worst. I've given most of Latham's money to support charities.'

'Good,' he said. 'That solves a problem.'

'What problem was that?'

'I didn't want you consider me to be a fortune hunter.'

Laughter trickled from her. 'I haven't left myself completely penniless. I've decided to come down to Bournemouth. I'll bring the children with me.'

'Children?'

'I have two. One is my son, Ben, and I've adopted Irene Curruthers' daughter.'

'Oh? I can't remember ever meeting her.'

'Irene was Latham's mistress and a friend of mine, of sorts – but only when it suited her. She died from liver cancer. Towards the end nobody wanted to know Irene, or her little girl, not even her parents. Lisette was such a sad child who needed to be loved. Irene asked me to adopt her. She's such a quiet, sweet little poppet. I looked after Irene until she died, and she was very brave until the end.'

Julia wondered if she was taking Martin too much for granted after all this time, since she'd learned from Latham that men didn't necessarily tell the truth, but what they thought you wanted to hear.

'Will you mind that I have two children to care for? You see, Martin . . . I must put their welfare before my own?'

'Of course you must. You know, I'll love you more than ever for that.'

'Before you decide, I also have two dogs that used to be Latham's. He loved them, and I can't have them destroyed. They're nice dogs, loyal, and well behaved as long as they get a good walk every day. I can't leave them here.'

'Of course you can't,' and she heard laughter in his voice.

'They go to the gate when they hear a car, in case it's Latham coming home, and it's heartrending to watch them, because they don't understand that he won't be coming, even after all this time. They do need a new master they can attach themselves to. Do you mind dogs?'

'I love dogs, and we have a beach to walk them on in the evening . . . though I don't know what Clarence and Billy Boy will say about it.'

'Oh, cats are very adaptable and will soon get a couple of dogs under their control.'

He laughed. 'You're doing one of your famous chats about nothing. Where shall we keep your orphaned elephants? I don't think my garden is big enough for any more waifs and strays.'

'Stop teasing me, Martin Lee-Trafford. I just wanted to warn you of what you'll be getting into. No elephants.' She picked up the dancing lady he'd given her on the first Christmas they'd met and smiled at it. She'd found it amongst her father's things in the attic, still intact. Martin had told her it had reminded him of her.

'Have I established my credentials yet?' he said quietly.

'You seem to have all the qualities I expected you to have, and more.' She laughed then. 'I might as well tell you now that Latham fathered Lisette. If you look at the clipping in the paper you will see that she looks a little like him. The other child is Ben.'

Had he noticed the resemblance? She heard the rustle of paper, then he said, 'The children are not much alike.'

'No . . . they're not. It's an awful lot for you to take on, but will you marry me then, Martin? All of us, really.'

He laughed. 'I'm supposed to ask *you* that.'

'Then ask me.'

'I love you, Julia. Will you become my wife?'

She decided not to tell him about Ben yet – she'd surprise him. 'I most certainly will, and I'm definitely coming to Bournemouth to see you.'

'When?'

'I don't know . . . I'll have to work out some travel arrangements. I want to leave my father's car for use at the children's home, so I'll have to come by train. Besides, I couldn't have my menagerie leaping about in the car when I'm trying to drive. Perhaps Fiona might be able to take a day off and help me . . . though she's already stretched. We didn't expect the home to fill up so fast.'

It would be enough time to arrange for her boxes to be sent down to Bournemouth, and for the staff to be informed of her impending marriage. The flat could be handed over for the use of Fiona and Agnes now. They were the senior staff, after all, so they deserved the best accommodation, and she was sure that Fiona would be pleased to see the back of her, though they had become good friends since Latham's death.

'I'll come and get you in the car,' Martin said. 'You can't manage by yourself with two children, two dogs, and the luggage. Will two weeks be enough time to sort yourself out?'

'Goodness, everything is coming in twos. It sounds as though we're setting up a Noah's Ark.'

Two weeks later a car drew up outside the house. The dogs wagged their tails, looked hopefully at Martin, then sniffed his ankles and followed him into the porch when he made a fuss of them. The pair began to compete for his attention.

Julia answered the door and shooed the dogs back into the garden with: 'Off you go, you can meet him later.'

Drawing him inside she took him through to a comfortable flat attached to the main house.

'I'll show you around the children's home later,' she told him.

'I'm impressed by what I've seen so far.'

'That's good, because I'm going to ask you to accept a seat on the board of trustees, on my behalf, and you might as well know what you're being a trustee of. But now, meet Lisette Miller and Master Benjamin Miller, otherwise known as Lisette and Ben.'

The girl scuttled off and stood behind Julia's legs for safety, holding tightly to her skirt at the sight of a stranger in their midst. Julia picked her up and kissed her. 'He won't hurt you, sweetheart, I promise. Take a seat on the couch, Martin.'

The boy trotted on sturdy legs to where Martin sat. Martin sucked in a breath as he looked at him. Nothing had prepared him for this.

'Hello, Ben, my boy,' he managed to get out.

'How do-de-do,' Ben said and held out a chubby, and rather grubby hand.

A pair of eyes as blue as his own looked into his as he shook the little hand. The boy had dark curly hair and a smile a mile wide. He'd inherited that from his mother, plus her dimple.

'Surprise!' Julia said softly, when he gazed at her with a grin on his face and an enquiry in his eyes.

He shook his head. 'I'll be damned . . . didn't Latham suspect?'

'No . . . He was convinced Ben was his. For a while I felt guilty about Ben, but Latham was constantly unfaithful, you know, and he treated me so badly. I was the perfect daughter to my father, and that was because I reminded him of my mother, and I loved him and wanted to please him.'

'Your father loved you, dearly.'

'I know. But Latham expected me to be the perfect wife, you see. I couldn't be because I didn't love him. Most of the time I didn't like him . . . sometimes I despised him. God knows, I did try. I was a paper doll to both of them, an ideal. You're the only person I know who ever allowed me to be myself. You treated me as an individual and thought my opinion mattered.'

'You'll never be a paper doll to me. I should have taken you away earlier.'

'You had your own problems to deal with, my love. Just before Latham's death I told him Ben was the result of an affair and that I was going to leave him. He didn't believe it, and was coming home to try and save our marriage when he died. Irene told me that he'd finished with her that morning. And he didn't want the responsibility of Lisette, though he was supporting her.'

'You went through all that by yourself. Poor Julia.'

'The staff supported me wonderfully, and I didn't have time to grieve, not with Irene to look after, as well. She needed me, and was very demanding, and the children needed me . . . and turning this house into a memorial for Latham was the best way I could think of to get rid of his money and build a memorial as well.'

'It was a wonderful way. I'm proud of you.'

'It's unhealthy to have as much money as he had accumulated. I felt like cashing it all in and making a grand bonfire out of it on Guy Fawkes Night. I won't pretend I know how, but the money just keeps growing in the bank vaults like mushrooms. No matter how fast I spend it, it just keeps multiplying. I don't understand a damn thing about money, even though I pretend that I do.'

Martin laughed.

'Then I remembered there were lots of children like Lisette, who needed a home and good food while their mothers recover from illness, and for those who lose their mothers we try and find homes for them.'

'Dearest Julia. I can't tell you how much I adore you.'

She beamed a smile at him. 'I'm so glad, because I'm sure we'll be perfect for one another.'

Ben scrambled on to the sofa next to Martin and subjected him to an intense and thorough examination. He patted Martin's head, touched his cheek, and grinned when Martin wiggled the end of his nose. It had been a while since there had been a man in Ben's life. He must have liked what he saw because his arms slid round Martin's neck and he squeezed him tight. He turned and smiled at her, saying firmly, 'Dada.'

Not to be outdone, Lisette demanded to be put down. Standing in front of Martin she banged her palm on his knee for attention.

'Hello, my lovely.'

Lisette giggled, then coming over shy, returned to the safety of Julia's lap.

'Well, they seem to approve of you, so that's one hurdle over with.'

The children lost interest in the adults and headed for the toy box.

Martin stood and held out his arms to her and she rose from her chair and slid into them. He smelled so familiar, and she felt she belonged there in his arms. His mouth touched against hers in the longest of kisses.

He gazed down at her afterwards, through eyes full of love. 'I've imagined this so often.'

'So have I,' and she laughed. 'Kiss me again, then I must finish packing. We'll leave after lunch, or in the morning, whichever suits you.'

'Today would suit me better. I have a busy practice to run.'

They set off, Julia occupying the back seat with the two children and the terrier. All three of her companions fell asleep within half an hour, while the Labrador kept Martin company in the front seat, and panted against his thigh and offered him affectionate sighs and the occasional lick. Martin wished it were Julia.

Julia was wishing the same thing. Leaning forward she planted a kiss at the corner of his mouth then softly whispered against his ear, 'I love you, Martin.'

Outside, the sunlight shone through the showers, the air was filled with a silvery light and a rainbow arced across the sky.